PRAISE F

"Highly flammable ... .ce of the year. Cayne's debut erotic romance was impossible to put down."

—MsRomanticReads Romance & Erotica Book Reviews on *Under His Command*

"A Romantic BDSM story, Kristine Cayne's erotica debut hits all the right spots and set them on fire."

—Provocative Pages on *Under His Command*

"UNDER HIS COMMAND is an edgy, sassy, and oh-so-sexy novel! In other words, erotica at its sizzling best. Another 5-star achievement from talented author Kristine Cayne!"

—Laura Taylor, 6-Time Romantic Times Award Winner, 2-Time Maggie Award Winner, & RWA RITA Finalist

"This baby gives new meaning to the word HOT! Insanely creative, toe curling and to top that, an amazing story as well! If this is Kristine's first erotic romance, imagine what she'll think of next!"

—Jackie Munoz on *Under His Command*

"Stock up on ice cubes because this is definitely one sizzling debut.... As rich as a white chocolate cheesecake, Cayne's entrance into the suspense genre is invigorating, explosive and simply intoxicating...."

—RT Book Reviews, 4½ stars, Top Pick! on *Deadly Obsession*

"This is a read that will have you staying up late to not only enjoy Alyssa and Remi's out of this world chemistry, but so see what lengths some will go to in order to preserve what they feel is right."

—Night Owl Reviews, 4.5 Stars, Top Pick! on *Deadly Addiction*

"...Cayne creates an entertaining tale, packed with distinctive characters and a suspenseful storyline."

—RT Book Reviews on *Deadly Addiction*

ALSO BY KRISTINE CAYNE

Six-Alarm Sexy Series

Aftershocks (Prequel)
Under His Command (Book One)
Everything Bared (Book Two) – coming summer 2013

Deadly Vices Series

Deadly Obsession (Book One)
Deadly Addiction (Book Two)
Deadly Betrayal (Book Three) – coming fall 2013

Other Works

Guns 'N' Tulips
Un-Valentine's Day

SIX-ALARM SEXY

VOLUME ONE

AFTERSHOCKS
&
UNDER HIS COMMAND

Jaimie likes it hot. Are you ready to play?
Kristine Cayne
04-2015

KRISTINE CAYNE

Copyright © 2012 Kristine Cayne
Excerpt from *Deadly Obsession* copyright © 2012 Kristine Cayne
Excerpt from *Revenge* copyright © 2012 Dana Delamar

All rights reserved.

ISBN (print): 0984903496
ISBN-13 (print): 978-0-9849034-9-8
ISBN (ebook): 098919700X
ISBN-13 (ebook): 978-0-9891970-0-7

Book cover design by Judi Fennell, 2013
www.formatting4U.com

Cover image licensed from The Killion Group, 2012
thekilliongroupinc.com

Publisher's Note: This is a work of fiction. Names, characters, places, and incidents either are the product of the author's imagination or are used fictitiously, and any resemblance to actual persons, living or dead, business establishments, events, or locales is entirely coincidental.

Without limiting the rights under copyright reserved above, no part of this publication may be reproduced, stored in or introduced into a retrieval system, or transmitted, in any form or by any means (electronic mechanical, photocopying, recording or otherwise), without the prior written permission of the copyright owner.

The scanning, uploading, and distribution of this book via the Internet or via any other means without the permission of the copyright owner is illegal and punishable by law. Please purchase only authorized electronic editions. Your support of the author's rights is appreciated.

ACKNOWLEDGMENTS

I'd like to thank all the wonderful people who encouraged me to write this new erotic romance series that I'd been considering for some time. I've always admired the strength and courage it takes to be a firefighter, but I also wanted to acknowledge the hardships that come with such a dangerous profession. I believe the Six-Alarm Sexy series does just that.

To my wonderful husband for your constant support even when I'm far less than a perfect wife because my fingers are glued to the keyboard and my eyes to the computer screen. And to my fabulously talented boys, for showing me that ability has nothing to do with age.

To Dana Delamar for having such enthusiasm for this project and for keeping me focused on weekly deliverables. I hope someday, we'll be writing one of these together!

To Kyle Moore, Public Information Office for the City of Seattle Fire Department, for your patience in answering my numerous questions. Your answers helped make my firefighters and the rescue scenes realistic and exciting.

To the brave men and women of the SFD's Technical Rescue Team. The world is a safer place because of you. Colin, as promised, your namesake appears in Aftershocks and he will appear in later books in this series as well. Stay safe.

To Jackie, Michelle, and Arianne for being fabulous beta readers. Your insights and suggestions made this a stronger book. I can't thank you enough!

Last but definitely not least, to all my readers for taking a chance on a new author. I hope you'll enjoy this venture into the steamier side of romance. Never fear, my stories will always have an HEA.

PART I

AFTERSHOCKS

PREQUEL TO THE
SIX-ALARM SEXY SERIES

CHAPTER 1

Seattle, Washington State, July 2014

Resentment burned in Erica Caldwell's chest as she knelt and wiped a tear off her daughter's cheek. Chloe's big blue eyes rimmed with long black lashes—the mirror image of her father's—pleaded with Erica to make everything better.

"I'm sorry, sweetie. I know you were looking forward to staying with Daddy tonight. But he had to… work."

She almost choked on those last words. Jamie kept letting Chloe down, the same way he'd always let her down. The man couldn't ever do anything as planned or on time. He was always cancelling, postponing, or forgetting. Just like he'd forgotten to sign their divorce papers. Again.

"But Daddy said we'd watch The Little Mermaid and eat ice cream sundaes in the living room," Chloe whined.

Pulling her daughter close, Erica smoothed her hand through Chloe's brown curls. "We can watch the movie together." Work was piling up and she'd been counting on the free evening to catch up. But Chloe came first. She always would.

A smile lit Chloe's face and she clapped her small hands. "And can we eat ice cream sundaes in the living room, too?"

Erica couldn't help cringing at the thought, but seeing the hopeful look on her daughter's tear-stained face, she caved. "Just this once."

"I love you, Mommy," Chloe said, flinging herself at her mother.

Erica's heart melted as her daughter's warm pudgy arms circled her neck. There was nothing in the world like a child's hug. "I love you too, sweetie." Straightening, she helped Chloe snap up her pink Hello Kitty raincoat, then slipped the small matching backpack over her shoulders.

After popping open her umbrella, they headed out of the daycare, hand in hand. "We have to run over to the courthouse before we go home. I forgot some important papers on my desk." When Erica stepped off the curb to cross the street, her sneaker landed in a puddle, splashing the hem of her pants. Good thing she'd taken a moment to change out of her heels before racing over to pick Chloe up. Her new Vera Wang pumps would have been ruined.

Back on the sidewalk, Chloe pulled her hand free to hop up the steps and into the courthouse lobby. After waving to Mr. Simmons, the security guard, she placed her backpack on the conveyer belt. Chloe had once told Erica he reminded her of a skinny Santa, and given his round face and ever-shiny bald head, Erica had to admit her daughter had a point.

"Now, don't you be working too late tonight, Miss Caldwell," he teased Chloe as he motioned for her to walk through the metal detector.

Chloe laughed as she skipped through it. "Oh we won't, Mr. Simmons. Mommy said I could have an ice cream sundae for dinner."

Simmons turned an arched brow on Erica. Heat rushed to her cheeks. "That's not what I said," she muttered, hurrying after her daughter and away from Simmons. By tomorrow lunchtime, every employee in the courthouse would think she was the worst mom in the county. The way Simmons could go on, he'd probably have child services coming to interview her about her parenting skills. *And it was all Jamie's fault.*

Ushering Chloe into the elevator, she jabbed the fourth floor button. When the doors didn't close fast enough, she punched it again. Chloe stared at her, a puzzled expression on her pretty face. An expression that looked exactly like the one Jamie frequently gave her. A headache began pounding at her temples. And that was Jamie's fault too. Sure, it was irrational, but she didn't care. Right now, she needed to vent. Fumbling in her purse, she pulled out her cell phone and as soon as the elevator doors opened on her floor, she pressed the call button.

Chloe started skipping down the hall. Since the building was empty except for a few stragglers, Erica didn't bother telling her to stop. "Don't go too far, sweetheart. Stay where I can see you."

As if he'd been waiting, Jamie answered immediately. "Rickie, is everything okay?"

The nickname arced through her like an electric shock. "Stop calling me that! You know I hate it."

"You used to like it."

"Well, now I don't," she shot back.

Hearing his weary sigh, she bit her lip to keep from apologizing. She didn't need to try to please him anymore.

"Did you get to the daycare before it closed?" he asked.

Considering he'd barely given her four minutes' notice that he couldn't pick up their daughter, it was a darn good thing the daycare was just across the street from the courthouse. She'd had to race through the halls and jaywalk across the street and still she'd arrived just as the clock struck six. The daycare charged ten dollars for every minute past closing, and the charge doubled every five minutes. He might have money to burn, but she certainly didn't.

She gritted her teeth and took advantage of the fact that her daughter was out of hearing range. "Chloe's upset."

"I'll make it up to her."

"Don't bother."

"What's that supposed to mean?"

"Jamie, life with you is a roller coaster. She's only four years old and already you're making promises you don't keep. It's too confusing for Chloe." And for her. Half the time she didn't know whether to hate him or love him, so as much as the failure of their marriage rankled her, she'd settled on leaving him.

"I'm sorry, Rickie. I just couldn't make it tonight."

"Uh-huh. And why is that? You traded shifts with Hollywood, and there's no big hockey, football, baseball, or basketball game on tonight." She paused and when he didn't comment, she knew. The bastard had a date. He hadn't even waited for their divorce to be final before going back to his old ways.

Pain stabbed her chest and she had to lean against the wall to catch her breath. After all this time, he shouldn't have the power to hurt her like this anymore. She wasn't like her mother—she could survive without a man. After her father had died, Erica had been shunted from one relative to another, while her mother floundered, unable to care for herself, much less her young daughter. Orphaned at seventeen, Erica had had to dig herself out of the hole her mother had made of both their lives.

Until Jamie's humanitarian mission to Indonesia, Erica had thought she'd been achieving her goal of self-sufficiency. But the emptiness she'd felt after he'd left, the loss that had filled her, said differently. Just like her mother, Erica had allowed herself to become reliant on a man. But no more. She'd used the time he was gone to make changes, to grow and strengthen herself. And good thing too, given how they'd ended up. Not only had she survived without Jamie since their separation, she'd built a happy and secure life for herself and her daughter.

After all that, hadn't she earned her get-out-of-jail free card?

"Which fire bunny is it? I bet it's Belinda. That witch was always trying to get into your bunker pants even when we were still together," Erica spat into the phone.

She shouldn't care. It really didn't matter who he was dating anymore. But no matter how much she tried to convince herself otherwise, she did care. She did want to know. When he didn't respond, she pushed like a sick masochist desperate for pain. "Well?"

"I'm having dinner with Dani."

Oh God. "You're going on a date with a member of your team?" The earth seemed to shift under her feet. "How long has this been going on?"

"Rickie—"

"Forget it." She cut him off. Some things she was better off not knowing. Their relationship was over, and she really didn't want to hear that he'd been cheating on her. She needed a clean break from him—the sooner the better. "Just sign the damn papers."

Silence filled the line.

Pushing off the wall, she looked around. While she'd been caught up in the conversation with Jamie, she'd let Chloe wander off. Her office lay just around the corner, thirty yards away. Chloe loved the whiteboard. She'd probably raced ahead to draw a nice picture for her. Hurrying down the hall, she covered the mouthpiece and called, "Chloe? Sweetie?"

"I can't sign them," Jamie said, his voice thick with something she couldn't identify.

Was he having second thoughts? When a spark of hope made her traitorous heart flutter, she swore silently. Jamie was bad for her.

They were bad for each other. "Why not?"

"I lost them."

"I thought you'd only forgotten to sign them. How could you lose them again?" She'd already had to go through the trouble of getting new certified copies and delivering them to him once. "Enough with the games, Jamie. You don't want me and I don't want you. Find the papers and sign them."

The floor shifted again, rippling before her eyes, and this time, she knew it wasn't just due to her emotional state.

Earthquake.

She had to find Chloe. Now.

Swaying, she staggered around the corner and shouted for her daughter. "Chloe!"

No answer.

"Where are you, Chloe? Answer me! This isn't funny."

All she heard was the groaning of the old building. No one was in the hall, so Chloe had to be in her office. Hopefully, she'd remembered Jamie's earthquake training: drop, cover, and hold on. Erica propelled herself into her office. The room was empty. Her lungs seized and her stomach bottomed out. Where was her daughter?

ഗ 🚒 ର

Jamie Caldwell shot to his feet as a wave seemed to warp the floor of the firehouse kitchen. With one hand, he braced the big pot of spaghetti sauce simmering on the stove. His other hand gripped the phone. "Rickie! Erica! What's going on?"

No answer. No sound. Nothing.

He checked the screen. Great. The call had dropped. The tremor ended and he blew in relief, glad it was just a small shake-up. Before enrolling Chloe in the daycare across the street from the courthouse, he'd made sure it was up to the most recent earthquake codes. Erica and Chloe were safe there. He couldn't say as much for the old courthouse where Erica worked. Following the big Nisqually quake, the building had been seismically retrofitted, but two years ago, they'd discovered weak spots in several of the carbon-fiber wraps used to reinforce support columns throughout the courthouse.

While the city and county governments agreed that the retrofitting needed to be redone, in a move typical of Seattle's political squabbling, the project had been put on hold until they could decide which department would pay for the work. He'd told Erica he didn't want her working there, told her it wasn't safe. Lot of good it had done. She'd dug her heels in. In fact, he was pretty sure that was the exact reason she'd accepted the position of administrative specialist with the King County Prosecutor's Family Support Division.

Quickly he dialed Rickie's number. They weren't at the courthouse, but he needed to know they were okay. Her voice had sounded more than a little anxious when she'd called for their daughter.

Instead of a ringtone, he got a fast busy signal. The circuits were no doubt overloaded with people calling to check on their loved ones. People like him. Damn. He'd keep trying until he got through.

He dropped back into his chair and his gaze landed on the papers he'd been staring at for the last hour. The divorce papers. He'd lied to Rickie to stall for time. Once he signed on the dotted line, his marriage would be over forever. And he wasn't sure he wanted that. Wasn't sure at all.

Flipping through the pages, he stopped at the one outlining his visitation rights. In an utterly unsurprising move, Erica was suing for full custody of Chloe. She'd graciously consented to him seeing his daughter for one weekend a month and one day a week according to his work schedule. At that rate, by the time his daughter was in elementary school, she wouldn't even remember she had a father.

Damn the woman.

"Hey, LJ! Did you feel the quake?" He looked up when he heard Dani's excited voice. The team, Battalion 5's Platoon A, had started calling him LJ, short for Lord James, when he'd let slip that he'd been named after his ancestor James Caldwell, the fourth son of Viscount Kensworth.

A sharp bark announced the arrival of Coco, Dani's chocolate Labrador Retriever and the reason for Dani's nickname, K9. The search-and-rescue dog nudged Jamie with her muzzle until he rubbed her ears.

"Did that little tremor scare you?" he asked the dog.

Dani reached into the cupboard and pulled out a box. "Coco's a bit jumpy. Thought I'd give her a treat."

At the word "treat," Coco skidded across the linoleum to get her chew stick. After filling a bowl with water and placing it on the floor, Dani turned to Jamie. "I just read the report. It was a 4.0, epicentered in the south Puget Sound, about six miles deep."

"The Seattle fault's been really active. I hope we're not in for the 'big one.'" He chuckled, making air quotes. "Any damage reports?"

"None so far." She pulled out a chair and sat at the table across from him. "What're those?"

"Divorce papers."

"Ah. I see."

He turned the papers over and leaned back in his chair. "What exactly do you see, K9?"

At the harshness in his tone, she held up her hands and stood. "Nothing at all. Forget I said anything."

Jamie rubbed the back of his neck and looked at his friend. They'd been working together for three years, and he'd put his life in her hands more than once. It wasn't fair for him to transfer his anger to her.

Anger and fear.

Yeah, he had to admit it. He was scared shitless. If the divorce went through, he wouldn't just be losing his wife—he'd be losing his daughter too. "Sorry. You didn't deserve that. I'm just a little tense. Rickie and I were arguing when the quake happened. The call dropped and I haven't been able to get through since."

"You're worried."

"Yeah, it's still no excuse."

"I'm a big girl, LJ. I can take it." She laughed, and he returned her smile. It must have been a damn sucky smile, because she immediately sobered. "You don't want the divorce."

"It's not that clear-cut."

"Why not? You love Erica."

"What makes you say that?"

She tapped his hand. "You've been separated for almost a year, and you're still wearing your wedding ring. I'd say the answer's pretty obvious."

He couldn't help the snort that rumbled up from his chest. "Loving her has never been the problem."

She checked her watch. "Hollywood isn't here yet, so we've got some time. Want to talk about it?"

"I should just sign the damn papers and get it over with." He shrugged and checked on the spaghetti sauce he was cooking for the evening clutch meal. When Hollywood, Platoon C's lieutenant, had agreed to fill in for the second half of Jamie's shift, Jamie hadn't even bothered to ask him to take on his kitchen duties. The man's cooking was so god-awful, Hollywood was likely to give the whole team food poisoning.

"But you don't want to sign them."

"I love Erica and Chloe. But…" He hesitated, unsure he should be spilling the gory innards of his marriage into his friend's lap.

She prompted him. "But…?"

He took out a clean spoon from the utensil drawer and sampled the sauce. After adding a touch more salt, he stirred the simmering mixture and returned to his seat. Seeing the expectant look on Dani's face, he sighed. She wasn't going to let this go. "We don't get along. Two more opposite people don't exist."

"Erica is who she is. Why's it bothering you now?"

"Things have changed in the last few years. She's changed."

"How so?"

"When Chloe was born, she became the center of Erica's world, and I…" He shook his head and trailed off. Even thinking the words made him sound—and feel—like an ass.

"And you were jealous."

"Yes, dammit. But not of Chloe."

"I don't understand."

"At first, I'd take care of Chloe while Erica was resting. I loved giving her a bottle. Bath time was our favorite. I'd bundle her up in a warm towel and rock her until she fell asleep. When she got a little older, I'd read her a bedtime story, whenever I was home." He rose from his chair and got a bottle of water out of the fridge. He held it up and when Dani nodded, he tossed it to her and grabbed another for himself.

"Sounds nice."

"It was." He returned to his seat and opened his bottle, taking a long drink. "Remember when we went to Indonesia on that humanitarian mission?"

"How could I forget? I thought we'd never make it back."

"Yeah, we were gone long enough for Erica to realize she didn't need me. When I got back, she'd taken over and there was no place for me in her life or Chloe's."

Dani's eyes rounded, and she set her bottle on the table. "Christ, Jamie. All this time and you never said a word. Did you at least tell Erica it bothered you?"

"We argued about it, but what could I really say without sounding like a whiny ungrateful bastard? Chloe was happy and healthy, and

Erica was taking great care of her."

"But you missed it."

"Hell yeah."

Coco finished her treat and laid her head on Dani's lap. Absently, Dani scratched her ears while frowning at Jamie. "Isn't Chloe staying with you on your days off?"

"That was the original agreement, which only lasted a couple months. In her infinite wisdom, Erica decided it was too disruptive for Chloe to be pulled out of daycare during the week."

"But you could bring her there in the morning and pick her up in the afternoon. You'd still get time with her."

He shook his head. Erica had immediately shot down that idea.

"You're shitting me." Dani stared at him, disbelief clear on her face. "When do you see her?"

"Once a week, on a day Erica decides, I get to pick Chloe up at the daycare at closing time and bring her back the next morning. Once a month, I get a weekend. She stays with me for forty-eight hours."

"Exactly?"

"Not a minute more, not a minute less."

She frowned at him. "When did you become such a doormat?"

"Excuse me?"

"I don't get it. At work, you're the man in charge. But you're letting her push you around. She decides what's what, and you just nod your head."

Put that way, he sounded like a wuss. He shifted in his seat and the creak of the wood sounded ridiculously loud. "It's not like that. I thought it would make her happy if I went along with things."

"Congratulations. Now you're both miserable. Even I, the queen of failed relationships, can see that you need to man up and tell her what you want. Otherwise, accept that your marriage is over, sign the papers, and move on."

"I know."

"But you haven't made up your mind yet."

He grinned. "I told her I lost the papers. Twice."

"Now that's not too hard to believe." She tossed her bottle cap at him. "You need to stop playing games, LJ. Seriously, get your head out of your ass before you lose your family."

That was why he'd cancelled on Rickie. He had some serious decision-making to do and until he made up his mind, he couldn't see her. It would just confuse him more. They'd end up arguing and he'd be caught in a sort of turned-on frustrated state. He needed some alone time to decide what he was going to do—sign or don't sign—and the Caldwell family cabin, secluded as it was in the Cascade Mountains, was just the spot to do some serious thinking.

He probably shouldn't have lied to her about his plans, shouldn't have implied that his dinner with Dani was a date. But he hadn't been able to resist one last attempt to spark some jealousy in her. He'd sparked something all right—anger. He just wished he'd been there. Erica was exceptionally beautiful when her brown eyes burned with indignation. He smiled, recalling some of their more memorable fights and the make-up sex that had followed.

From that first night, she'd grabbed him by the balls, turning his world upside down. Hollywood, his best friend, had dragged him to a party a friend of his cousin's was giving. The party was big and wild. He'd been about to leave when he spotted the beautiful blonde across the room. After confirming that she wasn't a fire bunny, he approached her with every intention of trying to charm her into a great one-night stand.

And boy did he succeed. She was fun and fascinating, and even before the night was over, he knew he wanted more.

But the next morning, he'd woken up to find her side of the bed cold and empty. They hadn't exchanged phone numbers or last names, so he'd had no way of contacting Rickie. Determined to see her again, he'd bullied Hollywood into trying to track her down through his cousin, but that had gone nowhere. In the end, he'd nursed his crushed heart with a ballgame and a six-pack.

When she'd knocked on his door a month later to tell him he was going to be a father, he'd been stunned by the news, but happy that whether she wanted it or not, Rickie was going to be in his life.

Dani rapped her knuckles on the table and Coco barked, drawing him out of his reverie. "It's been my experience that these things aren't usually one-sided. My dad was pretty hands-off when I was little, and I see my brother doing the same thing with his own kids. His wife does everything, and believe me, she isn't at all happy about it."

His shoulders stiffened. "Are you saying I intentionally let Rickie take over?" Ridiculous.

"Didn't you?"

A film of sweat formed on his brow. "No. Of course not."

"You never went home late so you wouldn't have to deal with the morning routine? You never told Erica you were out on a call just so you could go to a sports bar after work to have breakfast and catch a ball game with the guys? Come on, Jamie. I know you did."

Coco's sudden growl put them both on guard. "What's wrong, girl?" Dani asked as she tried to calm the dog. But Coco wasn't having it, and her growls turned to barks and whimpers.

Jamie gulped down the rest of his water, glad for the distraction. He should have known better than to talk about this with Dani. The woman loved to psychoanalyze the guys on the team and push their buttons. Sometimes she did it just for fun, though this time, she seemed to really believe what she was saying. But she was wrong. He wouldn't have let Rickie push him out of Chloe's life, even subconsciously. What kind of man would let that happen?

Before he could answer his own question, a violent quake shook the stationhouse. Cupboards banged open, dishes crashed to the ground, and the pot of spaghetti flew off the stove. The tangy scent of tomatoes filled the air as the hot sauce splashed across the floor, splattering the fridge, the walls, and the dog. Coco yelped and scampered out of the way.

Dani blanched. "This is no aftershock," she said, as the tremor went on and on.

The firehouse had recently been retrofitted to the highest standards and would survive all but a massive earthquake. That didn't mean they couldn't be hit by flying objects though. In the distance, Jamie heard his team members shouting and prayed no one was hurt.

He scrambled around the table, almost falling when the floor seemed to buckle. Grabbing Dani's hand, he pulled her under the sturdy table with him. Coco slid in between them and Dani wrapped her arms around the dog. They'd be safe here.

But where were Rickie and Chloe? He yanked his cell phone out of his shirt pocket and speed-dialed Erica's number again. When he got another fast busy, he swore and hung up. With a quake this intense, there was going to be some serious damage, and his unit, the Seattle Fire Department's Technical Rescue Team, would certainly be called on to help extricate survivors from collapsed buildings. It could be hours before he had time to call again. At least by now, Rickie and Chloe would be home in the house he'd had built for them. A house that could and would withstand anything.

Or so he prayed.

CHAPTER 2

Adrenaline surging through her system, Erica hung onto the doorjamb as the quake rocked the old courthouse. The building swayed and groaned, windows rattled and shattered as the earth continued to tremble. Cracks raced across the ceiling and plaster dust showered down, covering everything in a thin white film. She'd lived in Seattle all her life but had never experienced a quake as powerful as this one.

And her daughter was all alone.

Erica thrust herself through the open door to her office and back into the hall. Her arms outstretched on either side, she bounced from one wall to the other like a Ping-Pong ball. But at least she was moving in the right direction. Crashes and bangs drew her down the corridor to where most of the offices were located, as well as the large lunchroom. Dear God. Had Chloe gone to check out the offerings in the vending machines?

When she reached the older part of the building and saw the full extent of the damage, Erica's heart shuddered like the courthouse itself. This entire section of the floor looked like a war zone. "Chloe!" she called, her chest contracting so tightly her voice came out a mere squeak. She filled her lungs with the dust-choked air and tried again. "Chloe, where are you?"

Tears burned her eyes and a sob constricted her throat. Chloe was by herself. Alone. Her little girl needed her. And she needed her little girl. Needed to know she was safe.

The shaking finally stopped.

"Thank God." Blinking to clear her vision, Erica picked her way around fallen walls, ceiling tiles, and light fixtures, avoiding bits of sharp metal and live wires that sizzled like rattlesnakes. "Chloe! Can you hear me? Don't move. Don't touch anything. Mommy's coming." She could only pray that Chloe was somewhere safe and not trapped under all the rubble. Or worse.

Where should she start looking? What should she do?

Jamie. Jamie would know. Patting the pockets of her pants, she blew out in relief when her fingers closed around the familiar rectangular shape. Thank goodness she hadn't lost it in the quake. Yanking it out, she quickly dialed Jamie's cell number and waited for the call to connect. Instead she got a fast busy signal. Her fingers trembled as she hung up and tried 911. Still no luck.

Tucking the phone back into her pocket, she straightened her shoulders. Okay. She was going to have to do this on her own, like she did everything. Over the continued groaning of the building and the shrieks of security and car alarms coming in through the broken windows, she called out. "Chloe! If you can hear me, shout. Help me find you." She paused and listened, straining to identify each sound. When there was no reply, she moved further into the wreckage and called again. Bending down, she looked for places Jamie had told her were called voids, those empty areas that already existed or were created by falling debris where a person could be sheltered.

Ahead, an office wall had fallen against another, creating a tunnel. Maybe Chloe was there. Crouching, Erica inched forward, calling out, listening for any sign of movement. A loud crack overhead startled her and she scooted back, falling on her butt. The wall crashed down, missing her by half a foot. Heart pounding, Erica froze. Had she not moved in time, she'd have been crushed. What if something had fallen on Chloe? Oh God. What if her daughter was dead?

Heavy footsteps and shouting from the direction of her office reached her. Pushing to her feet, she called back. "Over here!"

Moments later, Mr. Simmons' bald head appeared around the corner. His hand went to his chest. "Mrs. Caldwell, thank God. When I got to your office and couldn't find you, I almost had a heart attack." He scanned the area. "Where's your daughter?"

Erica raised her hands, a lump in her throat strangling her. "Somewhere," she croaked. "She raced ahead of me…. We were apart when the quake hit."

He swallowed visibly, his eyes fixed on the rubble that had been the common area. "We'll call in help. But you need to come with me. We're evacuating the building."

Was the man crazy? "I can't leave my daughter!"

"We'll call the firemen. They'll find her."

Not regular firemen, but maybe Jamie. She hadn't been able to reach him by phone but surely the courthouse security had some sort of direct line? "Call my husband. He's with the technical rescue team."

"Okay, but—"

"Shh." She cut him off with an upraised hand. A sound.

She heard it again. "Mommy!"

Chloe. She was alive. Before her mind even had time to assimilate the word, her feet were on the move. She climbed over the debris, tearing her pants and scratching her legs and hands, desperate to reach her daughter. "I'm coming, Chloe. Mommy's coming."

Simmons grabbed her around the waist, pulling her to a halt. "Mrs. Caldwell, stop. It isn't safe. The building is unstable."

"Let go of me!" She twisted out of his hold and threw herself out of his reach. Her foot crashed through a downed wall, tripping her. Her arms pinwheeling wildly, she scrambled to right herself. Backing away from Simmons, she moved toward where she'd heard Chloe. "I'm not leaving my child."

The floor vibrated and chunks of plaster fell from the ceiling. When a piece bounced off her head, she stumbled and rammed into a wall. *Damn! Would this earthquake never end?* She had to find her daughter and get them both out of the courthouse before it crumbled to the ground.

"Mrs. Caldwell, please."

Something snapped and a large crack snaked across the ceiling. Dust filled the room as more drywall and several light fixtures shook loose. A boom rent the air and the building trembled. With Chloe's screams echoing in her head, Erica looked up and saw the crack widening. *The ceiling was caving in.* Her mouth went dry and her heart pounded in her ears. Was this the end? Was she never going to see her daughter again? Jamie? She'd made so many mistakes, had so many regrets.

Something—the wall?—landed on her back, knocking her facedown onto the crushed remnants of someone's desk. Instinctively she wrapped her arms around her head and prayed for the chance to make things right for her family.

☙ 🚒 ❧

The firehouse bells blared in his ears as Jamie crawled out from under the table and offered his hand to Dani. The usually spotless kitchen was a mess, but cleanup would have to wait. An announcement came over the speakers: "Structural collapse rescue, Ladder 27, Rescue 21, and Aid Unit 44 needed at 3rd and James. Multiple victims."

He scooped up the box of Coco's treats he'd almost crushed with his boot and set it on the table. "Better bring these. Looks like it's going to be a long night."

Dani nodded, her face pale, as she tried to soothe the trembling dog. Rising, she took Coco by the collar with one hand and the box with the other. "Let's go."

Racing through the lounge, they grabbed their radios from the battery charging station and made their way to the south apparatus room. Jamie pulled up short when he spotted Hollywood lounging against Ladder 27 in his turnout gear. Jamie could almost see the adrenaline coursing through the man's veins. "Glad you made it. We could use an extra pair of hands."

"I guess you're still in charge?"

He clapped Hollywood on the back. "Yep. I'm bumping you down to driver, Lieutenant." He turned to address the other team members. "Gabe, you're driving Rescue 21."

Once everyone had their turnout gear on, they jumped into their vehicles. Jamie sat in the passenger seat of Ladder 27 while Hollywood got behind the wheel. Dani and Coco took their places in the back compartment. As Hollywood turned on the siren and pulled onto 4th Avenue heading northwest, Jamie twisted around and looked at his younger brother, Drew, behind them in Rescue 21. *Christ*, he wished the kid weren't here. It would be so much easier to focus if he knew Drew were safe at home. As if reading his thoughts, Drew waved, face grim. Since he was in Battalion 5's Platoon B, they didn't usually work the same shifts. Wasn't it a kick in the ass that they were during the worst disaster to hit Seattle since the Nisqually earthquake? Fate was a bitch.

Jamie forced himself to focus. Drew was a member of the technical rescue team because he was qualified to be, more than qualified actually. He would be okay. Facing forward, Jamie got his first look at the chaos that had overtaken his city. Cars parked along the streets were buried beneath piles of bricks and chunks of cement. Broken glass covered the sidewalks, which hadn't fared much better.

Ahead, an oil tanker lay on its side, blocking the width of the road. Worse, smoke rose from the engine and flames licked around the edges of the hood. Hollywood slammed the brakes. "Shit! If that thing blows, it'll take down the neighborhood."

The driver had climbed out and stood in the entrance to a restaurant, watching his truck burn. "We get stuck in that mess, we won't be helping anyone tonight," Jamie said, punching the talk button on the Motorola digital radio attached to his turnout coat, and reported the incident.

"Engine 10 is already en route. ETA two minutes," the dispatcher answered.

"Can you get us around it?" Jamie asked Hollywood as he watched the flames reaching higher. From what he could see, there wasn't enough open space between the parked cars and the tanker for them to pass.

His expression tight, Hollywood nodded. "Shut the windows."

Metal screeched against metal as Ladder 27 pushed through the narrow opening, sending a shudder through Jamie's body. Hollywood cursed as the driver's side mirror caught on the downed truck's bumper and ripped off. Jamie twisted in his seat to watch the progression of his team. The acrid scent of burning paint filled the cabin as the flames grew.

Finally, they made it past the tanker. Rescue 21 and Aid 44 easily drove through the space Hollywood had made for them. When he once again looked down the road, Engine 10 was weaving through the traffic toward them.

Jamie relaxed. His team could concentrate on getting to their destination. And if anyone could get them there in record time, it was Hollywood. Besides being a valuable member of the technical rescue team, the guy had been the best driver in the SFD before becoming lieutenant of Battalion 5's Platoon D.

As he checked the Computer Aided Dispatch View reports on the MDC, the Mobile Data Computer, Jamie's heart almost stopped. How could he not have realized sooner?

Hollywood shot him a look through narrowed eyes. "What's wrong?"

"We're going to 3rd and James," he said, sounding like he'd

inhaled a mouthful of dirt.

"That's the King County Courthouse...." Hollywood's voice trailed off as he glanced at Jamie. "Oh fuck."

Oh fuck was right. Rickie couldn't possibly still be at work, could she? No. She and Chloe were at home. Probably scared shitless, but safe. Having left his bunker jacket undone, he fished his cell phone from his shirt pocket and speed-dialed the house. Four rings later, the answering machine picked up. Swearing profusely, he left a message and hung up. Immediately he dialed Rickie's cell phone. No fast busy this time. The phone rang and he held his breath. *Come on, Rickie. Pick up.*

The ringing stopped, but he didn't hear anyone answer.

"Rickie!" he shouted into the phone. When he heard no response, he checked his phone's display. Dammit. The call had died. He tried again and got a fast busy. What the hell did that mean? Had Rickie answered or had it been something weird with the network? She had to be okay. *They* had to be okay. Rickie and Chloe were his whole world.

His radio beeped, startling him. He pressed the talk button. "Caldwell."

"Everything okay, Jamie?" Drew asked, his voice gruff.

His throat tightened at the concern in his brother's tone. Maybe it wasn't so bad that they were on the same team tonight after all. He cleared his throat. "I don't know, kid. I can't reach Rickie."

"It's pretty late. She's probably at home. Did you try there?"

"Yeah. Voicemail."

There was a brief silence and then, mercy of mercies, Drew signed off. Cold fear had already taken root in Jamie's gut, and he didn't need any more of his brother's well-intentioned questions to help it along.

At the corner of 4th and Holgate, the truck came to a complete standstill. Jamie's gaze flew to Hollywood. The intersection was a massive knot, as cars from all directions tried to drive around the multi-vehicle pileup at its center. It would take hours to clear everyone out of the intersection. Wasn't his problem, but getting around it was. "We don't have time for this."

"I know, man," Hollywood said. His expression one of intense concentration, he took a sharp left onto Holgate, swerving around the maze of stopped cars. He rode the truck up onto the sidewalk and blew the horn repeatedly.

Gripping the dash, Jamie closed his eyes and prayed. Prayed for Rickie and Chloe. And prayed that his team made it to the courthouse in one piece.

The crackle of static from his radio filled the cabin before he heard the dispatcher's voice. "Ladder 27."

He pressed the talk button. "Caldwell here."

"A security guard from the courthouse is on the line. I'm patching him through."

A hole burning in his gut, Jamie grabbed the two-way and held it up to his ear. "Roger."

"Hello?" A man's shaky voice came over the radio. "This is John Simmons, head of security at the King County Courthouse. We've got a situation here. How long before you guys arrive?"

Jamie tried to reassure the man. "We're only a few blocks away. Tell me what you've got."

He heard Simmons blow out a breath. "Those damn faulty support columns are buckling. The ceiling on the fourth floor has already caved."

Rickie's floor. His hand crushing the two-way, Jamie wheezed out, "Have you evacuated?"

"Everyone's out except for the security staff and five others."

"Tell me about the five."

"Mr. Perez is trapped in the elevator on the seventh floor outside Interpreter Services. The door to Judge Tennison's office on the third floor west is stuck. Also on the third floor, Mrs. Anders is caught behind some live wires. We're trying to cut the power so we can get her out."

When the man stopped talking, Jamie prodded him. "What about the other two?"

"Woman and child. When the ceiling collapsed, the woman was buried."

His stomach clenched as his unease grew. *No. It couldn't be.* "And the child?"

"She called for her mother before the collapse. Since then, nothing."

He didn't want to hear it, but he had to know. Clearing his throat, he forced a calm, professional tone into his voice. Even though he was dying inside. "What's the woman's name?"

"Caldwell. Said her husband was on the Technical Rescue Team. Said to call him. Can you contact him?"

The words hit him like a sucker punch to the gut. White stars filled his vision and he had to take several deep breaths to regain his equilibrium. "You just did, man," he choked out.

"Mr. Caldwell? Shit, I'm so sorry."

"What floor is my wife on? What's on her? Is she conscious?" And, oh Christ, where was his daughter? Was Chloe even still alive?

"Fourth floor, center. Down the hall from her office."

Dani's small hand squeezed his shoulder. "We'll find them, Jamie," she said gently.

"Damn straight." His gaze slid to Hollywood. "Can you get us there PDQ? Or do I have to get out and hotfoot it?"

"Hang tight!" Hollywood shouted as he pulled a sharp right on to South King Street, gunning past CenturyLink Field. "At least the Sounders aren't playing tonight," he muttered.

The situation would have been pretty near catastrophic with an additional sixty thousand people milling about.

His mind shredded, Jamie stared numbly at the narrow traffic-snarled roads of downtown Seattle. He and his crew were Rickie and Chloe's best chance of surviving this nightmare. They just had to get there before the entire building collapsed, or it was game over.

CHAPTER 3

When Ladder 27 was still a half-block from the courthouse, going north on a south-running one-way, Jamie leaned over and slammed his palm firmly against the horn as Hollywood attempted to weave through the clogged street. People scattered and more than one bird was flipped his way. Tough shit. They were *alive*, whereas his little girl—

Nope. Not going there. Think positive, that's what he had to do. His platoon was the best, and he had to believe that they'd get Rickie and Chloe out safely. Anything else was self-defeating.

But despite Hollywood's best efforts, they were barely moving. Adrenaline spiked in his system and Jamie felt as though he were going to burst out of his skin. Instead, he shoved open the door and jumped out of the truck. Multiple what-the-fuck shouts from his team rang out. Yeah, it was stupid. With all the weight and awkwardness of the turnout gear, he could have twisted an ankle, but shit. His skin was crawling with the need for action, the need to do *something*, no matter how boneheaded.

Sucking in a breath to get himself under control before facing perhaps the worst situation of his life, he beat feet up the road, past City Hall Park to the 3rd Avenue entrance to the courthouse. As Jamie pushed through the rotating door, panting and sweating, a middle-aged bald man who seemed vaguely familiar came up to him. His uniform indicated he was one of the security guards. "Simmons?" Jamie asked.

The man nodded. "You Caldwell?"

Jamie inclined his head. "Any change since we spoke?"

Simmons motioned to the lobby's darkened overhead lights. "We managed to cut the power and get Mrs. Anders out of the building."

At least that was something. "Anything else I should know about? Leaks? Water? Gas?"

"None that we're aware of."

Not too reassuring given how long it had taken them to find the power main. He swallowed before voicing his next question. "My wife? My daughter?"

Simmons' eyes fell to the floor and a great pressure around Jamie's chest forced him to push his shoulders back to inhale. Damn. He hadn't expected anything different, but he had hoped. "You got guys to take my team to the vics?" His stomach revolted at the word he'd never thought he'd use to refer to his wife and daughter.

Nodding, the old guard said, "Ten plus me."

The ladder truck and Rescue 21 pulled up to the curb with Aid 44 right behind them. As the team assembled, Jamie began giving orders. "Drew, you and Gabe, take the disabled elevator on the seventh floor. Hollywood, take the care of the vic on the second floor. Evan and Colin, grab some of the security team and make sure all the floors are clear. Dani, you and Coco are with me on the fourth floor."

"Hold up a minute." Hollywood stepped close to Jamie and said in a low voice, "You sure you should be leading this?"

Suppressing the urge to ignore his best friend, he shifted his weight back on his heels to keep his feet still. Hollywood wasn't saying anything the captain wouldn't have said if he weren't tied up with the chaotic aftermath of the quake. "I can handle this."

"You know the protocol. You're too close."

Jamie crossed his arms and glared at his soon to be ex-friend. "Fuck protocol."

Hollywood held up his hands. "Fine. But if you change your mind…"

"I won't."

Jamie turned and gave the signal to his team. They secured SCBAs on their backs and hooked faceplates on their heads, but didn't close them. Then they grabbed ropes, pulleys, saws, and anything else they might need based on Simmons' description of the various situations. With Jamie in the lead, they all tromped through the lobby, their boots slapping the floor tiles, and met up with the security team.

"This way, sir," Simmons said, leading the way to the central stairwell. To stay in shape, Jamie and the team often trained in full gear, so going up four flights would be no problem for him and Dani.

But in the dim glow of the emergency lighting, Simmons' flushed face, slick with sweat, told a different story. Shit. Now was so not the time for the old man to rupture an artery or pop a valve. "Everything okay, Simmons?" he asked. "We can go the rest of the way on our own."

Simmons shook his head, and turning the corner, began plodding up the final set of stairs. "It'll be faster if I show you where Mrs. Caldwell is."

With Coco along, Jamie didn't need anyone's help to find his wife, but he understood and even respected the old guy's need to be useful. To a point.

Stepping out of the stairwell onto the fourth floor, Jamie quickly oriented himself. They'd come out on the opposite side from where the elevators were located, closer to the central part of the building than to Rickie's office on the eastern side.

"Were the offices damaged?" he asked the guard.

"Some, but nothing like this area."

Jamie had thought as much. Why hadn't Rickie and Chloe been in her office? "How much farther?"

"It's a little hard to see, but I believe she was"—Simmons moved a few yards ahead and crouched, looking under a plank—"here...." He let the sentence hang, and a bewildered look came over his face.

Worry punched Jamie in the gut. But the old man's confusion wasn't unusual when everything was reduced to a pile of rubble, all visual reference points gone. It did mean they had to spend precious minutes locating Rickie.

Jamie shouted her name, then waited for a response before calling Chloe's. Nothing. Dani removed Coco's leash and let her loose. As the dog maneuvered almost daintily around the dangerous debris, she sniffed and yipped. And Jamie's speeding heart shifted down a gear. He'd seen Dani and Coco in action many times. Their track record was impeccable.

When Coco's barks intensified, Dani shouted, "She's on to something."

Jamie rushed to them, careful not to fall or, worse, impale himself on the minefield of broken metal, wood, and glass. He knelt next to Coco while Dani ruffled the dog's fur and murmured, "Good girl."

Instead of seeing Rickie or Chloe, he saw a filing cabinet and a fallen wall behind it. Coco wasn't a cadaver dog, so if she'd stopped here, it was because she smelled someone. Someone *alive*.

"Rickie, Chloe!" he called.

When there was no response, he forced himself to put his training into practice and quickly assessed whether the cabinet was supporting the fallen wall. If so, moving it would bring the whole mess down on his wife or daughter—whoever was trapped underneath. After confirming that it was safe to move the cabinet, he lifted it away from the wall very carefully so as not to further destabilize the mound of rubble.

Dani shined her flashlight into the darkness of the void. As Rickie turned her beautiful face toward him, blinking at the light, his heart slammed against his chest like a crazed fly against a bright bulb. Her skin was pale and she had contusions on her face and arms. The rest he'd have to examine once they got her out. The important thing was that they'd found her—alive, but quite clearly trapped.

Lying on her stomach with the wall on her back, she inched a hand out to him. "Jamie," she whispered. "I knew you'd come." A tear slid down her cheek.

Love for Rickie welled in his heart until he thought he'd drown in it. He gripped her fingers and squeezed gently. "Always," he said, his voice gruff.

"Chloe?"

Christ. The hope in her voice pierced his heart. He ran his thumb along her wrist. "We'll find her. Stay still while I get you out of here." With that, he turned to Dani and nodded. She rose and set off with Coco to continue the search.

He laid his equipment and SCBA on the ground before searching the debris for materials to build a crib under the wall. All he needed was to clear a few inches so he could pull Rickie out. He'd lift the wall, angling it along the length of her body.

After finding a heavy chunk of cement to use as a fulcrum, a section of two-inch wide metal pipe, and several pieces of wood he could use for cribbing, he returned to Rickie. Kneeling beside her, he explained what he was going to do. Normally, leveraging and cribbing was done with several people, but he couldn't bring himself to call Dani back. As it was, it was killing him not to be searching for Chloe with her.

Standing at Rickie's head, he cleared out the loose debris and positioned the fulcrum, centering it on the wall. He placed the wood blocks on either side, ready to be pushed into place. The structure wouldn't be as stable as if he put the blocks on the edges of the wall, but this was the best he could do on his own. "I'm going to lift the wall and put the first layer of cribbing in place. Don't move."

He pushed down on the metal pole and, as the wall began to rise, he kicked one of the blocks into place, then the other. Slowly he released the lever until the wall rested on the blocks. A few more layers and he could pull her out. "It's going great, Rickie. We're almost there."

The second layer of blocks went into place easily. The third and final layer would be more difficult to do alone. He wiped the sweat from his forehead with the back of his hand, then bent to position the final set of blocks. Coco's loud bark pierced the relative silence. The hairs on his arms rose at the fear evident in her ensuing growls. He grabbed his flashlight and whipped it around in time to see Coco dashing away from the common area. He pressed the button on his two-way. "Dani, what's wrong with Coco?"

"Last time she did this, the quake hit. Take cover, LJ!"

Fuck! He threw himself on the ground so he could see Rickie. "Cover your head, honey. Something's happening."

Eyes unbelievably round and white in her dirty face, she asked, "An aftershock?"

"Maybe."

The floor began to shake. She swallowed and sucked in a sob. "I'm really scared, Jamie."

The crack in her voice made his heart break. It went against everything he'd ever been taught, but he inched himself forward until he was half under the wall. He rested his head next to hers and held her hands. "We'll get through this." And if they didn't, at least they'd die in each other's arms.

When the aftershock ended, Jamie stayed where he was but very carefully pressed the button on his two-way. "Team, report."

Dani came on first. "Looks like Coco's a good quake alert, LJ. I rewarded her with a treat, and now we're going back to the search."

Hollywood's deep chuckle filled the line. "Next time give us a little more warning, will ya? We're okay here too, LJ."

They waited and the line remained quiet. Fuck. Where was Drew? Working with elevators was always dangerous. Add in an earthquake and it was a recipe for disaster. "Drew? Drew? Come in," he said into the two-way, forcing his voice to remain calm, professional. The last thing he wanted was for the captain or Hollywood to pull him off the mission because his family was involved. Shit. That's exactly *why* he needed to stay.

After endless seconds, he heard the familiar cocky tone of Drew's voice. "Had a bit of a ride when the elevator dropped two floors, but we're okay now."

Blood rushed in his ears as Jamie's chest seemed to collapse in on itself. *Christ. A runaway elevator.* He dropped his forehead against the ground so Rickie couldn't read his reaction. So many people he loved were in this building, their lives and welfare his responsibility. Maybe Hollywood had a point after all.

"Rickie and I are okay, too," he said, once he'd gotten his racing pulse under control.

"Chloe?" Drew asked.

Dani answered. "Nothing yet."

Silence filled the air as everyone absorbed that statement.

Jamie clicked off his two-way and turned his head in the tight enclosure to kiss Rickie's tear-drenched cheeks. "Don't give up," he said firmly.

Her lips trembling, she nodded.

Carefully, he slid himself out from under the wall. The sooner he finished with Rickie, the sooner he could go find his baby girl.

ಜ 🚒 ಐ

Feeling punch-drunk, Erica lifted her head as much as she could to watch Jamie at work. He'd jerry-rigged some sort of contraption he called a crib to lift the wall. Seeing him looking so competent calmed her, gave her a sense of security. How he managed to push up the wall with the metal pipe and position the blocks under it at the same time she had no idea. His sheer strength amazed her. Maybe they would get out of this after all.

"Almost done, Rickie. I'll have you out in a couple more minutes."

Thank God. She hated that Jamie was stuck getting her free when they should both be looking for Chloe. But maybe she could help move things along.

She kept watch and when he pushed down on the lever to lift up the wall, she rose on her elbows and tried to wiggle her way out.

"No!" Jamie shouted. "Don't move!"

Why not? She was doing it. She was getting herself out. Pushing to her knees, she hit the wall with her back and lost her balance. She thrust her body forward and her arms clipped one of the cribbing blocks Jamie had set up. Oh, jeez.

The blocks on one side—the side she'd hit—tumbled. She screamed as the wall crashed down onto her arm. Through her tears, she saw that Jamie had somehow managed to jam the tumbled blocks under the wall. His quick action had probably kept her arm from being severed. She tried to speak, tried to tell him she was sorry, but no words would form. If he didn't hate her before, he'd hate her now.

"Rickie, are you okay? Talk to me," he said.

"My…" She cleared her throat and tried again. "My arm…" She couldn't speak as a sob of frustration shook her body.

"Your arm is pinned," he finished for her. "Why the *fuck* did you move?"

"I—I wanted to help."

"Are you sure that's it?"

With her free hand, she brushed strands of hair out of her eyes. She got that he was upset, but still. "Of course I'm sure."

"You know what I think," he said as he picked up a block of cement and moved to the side of the wall parallel to her body. She couldn't see him now. But she could hear him just fine. "I think you need to trust me for once in your life. I've been rescuing people for twelve years. I know what I'm doing here."

"I do trust you, Jamie."

"No you don't. Not with this and not with Chloe." He grunted and the wall lifted off her arm. "Can you move your arm? Pull it in next to your body. Slowly."

She followed his instructions. The fit was tight, but she managed to wiggle her arm free. It throbbed but she could move her wrist and fingers. "I got it."

"Good. Stay clear. I'm lowering the wall."

Except for a few inches of dim light ahead of her, she was back to where she'd been when Jamie had found her—trapped in near darkness. "What are you going to do now?"

"We're at square one again. Sit tight." Frustration deepened his voice. Come to think of it, she'd heard that tone more and more over the years. When she'd first met him, Jamie had been so light and carefree. He'd always had a joke to make her smile. She'd been so infatuated with him. Couldn't believe that such a hunk found her attractive. But after Chloe, things had changed. Only he hadn't. Except now, she couldn't remember why his sunny disposition had bothered her so much. She loved his smile. And she missed it.

Jamie cleared his throat. "What were you and Chloe doing here anyways? I was sure you were at home by the time the real quake hit."

She dropped her head onto her uninjured arm and gritted her teeth. Now she remembered. He was amazingly self-centered. "Jamie, you gave me four minutes' notice. Do you honestly think I had time to pack up all my things before picking Chloe up from the daycare? I barely made it before closing as it was."

"Sorry."

"You're sorry we got caught in the quake, but you're not sorry you copped out at the last minute. I'm the one who had to dry our daughter's tears when she learned you weren't coming. We're an inconvenience to you, Jamie. Admit it. Once and for all, just admit that you"—her voice cracked but she pushed the words out—"never wanted us."

"God, babe. That's so not true. I wanted you and Chloe from day one."

She laughed, the sound bitter. "If I hadn't shown up pregnant, we would never have been together. You'd have been perfectly happy with it being a one-night stand. Too bad I wasn't one of your fire bunnies."

"Rickie, I was twenty-eight when we met. I was ready to settle down and have a family. The last thing I wanted was another bunny."

"And see how well that turned out."

"Cover your head," he said before the wall lifted a couple inches.

Jamie slipped another block into place and with each inch closer to freedom, the pressure in her chest eased. "You might not be the best husband, but you're darn good at rescuing people. Thank you."

He cursed and she heard him suck in a deep breath. From his reaction, you'd think she'd insulted him.

"Look, when this is all over, let's go to Disneyland. Chloe will love that."

What the heck? "What are you talking about?"

"We just need a chance to reconnect. To be a family again."

"This is exactly the problem with our relationship, Jamie. You're Peter Pan. Will you ever grow up? We're in the middle of a divorce, and our daughter could be *dead*. I don't want to hear about Disneyland!"

As was usual for him, he didn't say a word. Whenever they argued, he clammed up. Did they mean so little to him that he couldn't even be bothered to fight? The wall rose again and Jamie pushed another block under it on each side of the lever.

His continued silence was getting to her. Why hadn't he disagreed with her comment about Chloe? Since this all began, he'd been a steady stream of reassurances.

Jamie crouched down and gripped her under her armpits. She kept her gaze on his face as he pulled her free, searching—and not finding. When she was kneeling in front of him, she forced herself to put into words the thought that was cutting a hole in her heart. "You think she's dead."

His eyes met hers. They gleamed in the soft glow of the emergency lights. He didn't speak, but his silence told her everything. Everything she'd hoped never to hear. A shudder tore through her. Her teeth started to chatter and great sobs wracked her body. Jamie pulled her against his warm chest and wrapped his strong arms around her, his face buried in her hair.

"She's not dead," he murmured. "I'd know if she were. I'd feel it in my heart."

She wished she could believe him—she needed to believe him. Her heart burned, torn in two. They'd had so little time together, so little time with their daughter. And now it was too late. With that last thought, she slumped against him. She'd have fallen if he hadn't been holding her so tightly.

Through her cries, she heard his radio crackle and Dani say the three sweetest syllables: "I've found her."

CHAPTER 4

Jamie leaned back and ducked his head, turning slightly away from Rickie before speaking into the two-way. "Is she...?" His voice broke and he clamped his mouth shut.

"I can't get to her. I'm sending Coco in with a headset. If she's conscious, maybe we can talk to her. Let her know we're coming," Dani said.

He swallowed and forced himself to keep his hopes in check. "Keep me posted. Rickie's free now. I'll be there in a couple minutes."

Rickie pulled on the sleeve of his turnout coat. "How is Chloe? What did Dani say?"

"She's located her but can't reach her yet. Let's get you outside and then I'll go help Dani."

A cloud descended over her features. Her eyes shot sparks and her hands went to her hips. As usual, his beautiful wife was preparing a mutiny. He held up a hand to stop her, but she wasn't having any of it.

"Jamie Caldwell, you're crazy if you think I'm leaving without my daughter."

Christ he missed her, missed the gentleness of her touch, the softness of her skin. His body tightened at the memories. Shit. This was not the time and place to indulge his fantasies.

Just one touch.

Giving in, he stretched out his hand to stroke her face, but she swatted it aside and flinched when her injured arm collided with his wrist. He dropped his hand and shook his head. What had he been thinking? That everything was forgiven and forgotten because he'd pulled her out from under a wall? Well, yeah. "Babe, listen. You're just going to get in the way."

She leaned forward, her features hard. "I'm. Not. Leaving."

"You can trust me with this. I'll get Chloe out of here even if I die trying."

Her breasts lifted as she blew out a sigh. "There you go again with this trust thing. What is your problem?"

"I know you don't trust me, and a part of me doesn't blame you." He sat her down on the cement block and opened the small first aid kit he'd brought up.

When he swiped the antiseptic over the cut on her wrist, she winced and rubbed her forehead. "Am I hurting you?"

"Not physically." He frowned and she waved her words away with a flick of her hand. "Why do you think I don't trust you?"

He ripped open the packaging of a bandage with a little more force than necessary. The gauze fell to the ground. Cursing, he got another and forced himself to slow down. "Because you never have." When she opened her mouth to speak, he put his fingers against her lips before continuing, his voice rough with pent-up frustration. "After I got back from Indonesia, you stopped trusting me. You wouldn't let me give my daughter a bath. When I tried to feed her, you'd take away the spoon. Later, you wouldn't even let me read her a bedtime story. And now"—he slapped a piece of medical tape over the gauze—"you barely ever let me see her."

"That's not it. We just have a different routine now."

"Now that you're on your own," he finished, stepping back.

She pulled her sleeve over the bandage and kept her eyes lowered. "Yes."

Anger filled his chest. "There isn't room for me in your lives. You've made sure of that."

She dragged her gaze up to his face. "I didn't know you felt this way." She paused and brought a finger to her chin. "Why didn't you ever say anything about it? Oh right." Her voice hardened and she poked her raised finger into his chest. "Because you were never around long enough."

Jamie grabbed her hand. When she tried to pull it away, he brought it to his lips and kissed her fingers. Rickie was so strong and independent, but the two traits he loved most about her were the very ones keeping them apart. She was right. He hadn't resisted her efforts to neatly package their lives, to make him somewhat extraneous. He hadn't had the heart. He'd watched the worst happen too many times. Watched his fellow firefighters die, and watched their too-dependent wives fall apart and lose themselves, destroying their families. Just like Rickie's mother had.

"If something happens to me, you and Chloe will be fine." Business as usual. He took comfort in that. But what if you don't die, dickhead? You've given up your life, your family, for something that might never happen.

As the words bounced around his head, Rickie pounded her free fist on his chest. Tears spilled from her eyes. "Shut up!" she cried. "Just shut up!"

He knew what this was really about—him dying on the job. He let go of the hand he'd been kissing and gripped her arms. "Calm down, Rickie."

"I don't want to calm down," she sobbed as her fists continued to rain down on him. She wasn't hitting hard enough to hurt him physically, but his heart was breaking.

He pulled her tightly against him, capturing her hands between them. "Shh," he murmured. "Everything will be all right."

He continued to rub comforting circles on her back, but with each passing minute, he believed his reassurances less and less. And that's when he heard the most wonderful sound in the world—his little girl's voice. "Daddy? Daddy? Are you there?"

His heart thrashing in his chest, he let go of Rickie and stood before he pressed the talk button. His throat constricted and he had to push past the tightness. "Chloe, baby. It's Daddy. Are you hurt?"

"I-I'm scared," she hiccupped, her voice raw from crying.

Rickie listened, her face ashen.

"I know, baby. We're coming to get you. It won't be long now. Are you hurt? Daddy needs to know."

"I have a booboo on my legs. Like Bugsy."

Bugsy? With the mic muted, he asked Rickie, "What's Bugsy and what happened to its legs?"

"Her pet guinea pig. She named it after the one in *Bedtime Stories*."

"I didn't know she had a guinea pig."

"That's because she didn't have it for long. She and her friend Nancy were playing with it. A big book fell on it and its leg was crushed. I took it to the vet, but there was nothing to do."

Okay, this was not good news. His daughter's legs were trapped. He could only hope they weren't crushed as well.

Forcing a light tone into his voice, he clicked the two-way back on. "Baby, did something fall on your legs?"

"Uh-huh."

"Can you tell me what it is?"

"No. Mommy's going to be mad."

He narrowed his eyes at Rickie. "I promise you, Chloe. Mommy will *not* be mad. Go on. Tell me."

"Mommy told me to stay with her, but I wanted to see what was in the candy machine."

Oh Christ. "Did the vending machine fall on you, baby?"

Rickie gasped and clutched his wrist, her nails digging into his skin.

"Yes," Chloe wailed.

His stomach burned like he'd swallowed battery acid. Chloe should have never even been here. She should have been at home with him watching *The Little Mermaid*. Instead, she was lying under a goddamn five-hundred-pound vending machine, and he couldn't even get to her.

Beads of sweat dripped down his spine and the sides of his face. His turnout coat was meant to keep fire away, but it wasn't much use when the flames were inside him. "Can you move your legs or your toes, Chloe?"

"Where's Mommy? I want Mommy," she choked through her sobs.

Rickie grabbed his arm and pulled herself up so she could speak into the two-way. "I'm right here, sweetheart. Mommy's right here."

"I'm sorry, Mommy."

"Shh. It's okay. We'll get you out."

Rickie's chest pressed against Jamie's arm as she took a deep shuddering breath, her eyes piercing his. He wrapped his arm around her waist and mouthed, "I promise."

When she laid her head on his shoulder, Jamie took back control of the two-way. He had to know how serious the situation was. "Do your legs hurt, Chloe?"

"They used to. Now I don't feel them."

Biting on his knuckles to keep from roaring, he prayed Dani was already working on getting through the debris. "We're coming to get you. Don't worry. You're going to be fine."

"Okay, Daddy." She sniffled some more and over the air he heard Coco yip. Good. The dog would keep her company and keep her from worrying.

A huge weight took residence on his shoulders as he released the talk button, cutting the connection to Chloe. Rickie stepped out of his embrace and shoved him hard, her eyes glassy with tears. "This is all your fault, James Caldwell. You're the reason our baby's life is in danger. If she didn't need you, I'd kick your ass."

He ducked his head. "You don't think I want to kick my own ass?" For all they knew, his baby's legs could be broken, or worse—she could be paralyzed. At the thought, his chest tightened and his eyes burned. *Christ almighty.* If there was ever a time for prayer, this was it.

The sensation of Rickie's soft palm on his cheek undid him. "Jamie. Hey, I'm sorry. I didn't mean that."

His breath hitched and his shoulders shook with the effort to keep his emotions in check. He was in charge. He was the leader. He had to be strong, or he'd never earn Rickie's trust back. "Yes, you did. And you're right. If I could, I'd change places with her right now."

Stepping closer, she hugged him. "I know you would. I never doubted your love for Chloe."

No. She just doubted his love for *her*. But that was a problem for another day. He cradled her face in his hands and peered deep into her eyes. "I will get our daughter back. If nothing else, trust that."

Looking contrite, she nodded numbly and watched as he collected his equipment.

When he was done, he took her hand. "Come on, let's go rescue our daughter."

৪০ 🚂 ৫৩

Strength and determination radiated from Jamie as he led her through what remained of the common area. Dust clogged the air and darkness surrounded them except for the narrow beam from Jamie's flashlight.

In a way, Erica was relieved that the man she'd met and fallen in love with was back. Nothing would keep him from saving Chloe. But this man also terrified her. They were getting a divorce. As soon as Jamie signed the papers, it was a done deal. This wasn't the time for her to waffle. This wasn't the time for her heart to whisper about possible mistakes. Because she wasn't making a mistake. She loved Jamie, every inch of him, with every inch of herself. He was the only one for her. No other man would ever take his place. She knew that like she knew her own name. But she and Jamie were oil and water. They'd never mix together. Not the way they needed to.

"Dani," Jamie called out, startling Erica. She'd been so focused on him, she hadn't even noticed the beams of light a few yards away.

The beams turned and landed on her and Jamie like the king and queen at a prom dance. She shook her head at her own tunnel vision. What was wrong with her? God, she hoped it was just nerves.

"Good to see you safe, Erica," Hollywood said.

"Yeah, glad you're okay." Dani said the words, but her eyes went from their locked hands to Jamie's face. Jamie just stared back.

Hollywood coughed. "Right. K9, normally I'd advise you to go in with the diamond chain saw, even though it weighs almost as much as you do." He paused while she snorted. "But since we don't have power, you'll have to make do with the cordless cutting edge saw. Take the pick axe and bolt cutters, as well as this pry bar. You'll need it to lever the vending machine."

"Thanks," she said, hooking the items into her belt.

"Why is Dani going in?" Erica asked. Surely one of the bigger men would be better suited for the task. "How's she going to get the machine off my little girl?"

Jamie set his equipment down. He looked like he was about to answer, but Dani cut him off, her eyes narrowing on Erica. "Because where Chloe is located is virtually impenetrable for anyone bigger than Coco. As it is, I'm going to have to cut through quite a lot of obstacles just to get to her. And these guys"—she waved her hand around—"would get stuck. And then we'd have another problem on our hands. As for getting the machine off her, I have the same training they have. I will bring your daughter out."

All right then. This obviously wasn't the first time Dani's abilities had been questioned. "Thank you," Erica said.

Dani nodded then grabbed a strap and wound her arms through it so it rested under her breasts.

Erica followed the strap to its end. Her breath caught when she saw the long bright orange board with black tie straps. "Oh God," she cried, pressing her hand to her mouth. "What's that for?"

"It's a spine board," Dani explained without looking at her.

Hearing her gasp, Jamie's arm snaked around Erica's waist and yanked her to his side. "It's just a precaution, honey. If Chloe can crawl, Dani will let her come out on her own."

"And if she can't?"

"If she can't, Dani will pull her out."

She rested her head on Jamie's arm and together they watched her husband's date wind her way through a mountain of wood, plaster, concrete, and metal to save their only child. What a damn nightmare.

Hollywood came to stand beside them. "Don't worry, Erica. Dani's the best."

Jamie pressed his two-way. "Status."

Erica leaned in close so she could hear.

"Hit a sheet of drywall. No way around. I'm using my blade to cut through," Dani said between breaths. "Should be done in a minute."

Soon after, they heard a bang and a crack followed by a "Hot dog!" After a grunt, Dani continued. "Okay, LJ. I'm on the move." They heard more noise as she tossed smaller objects out of her way.

"Careful, Dani," Jamie warned. "We don't want this pile of crap coming down on you."

"I always am, LJ. You know that." Dani laughed and the sound made Erica grit her teeth. She could just imagine what else the woman was always careful about. She pushed away from Jamie's side, sick at the thought that the woman her husband was sleeping with was saving her daughter's life. Unfortunately, when she stepped back she tripped and fell smack against Hollywood. An arm as hard as iron snapped around her waist, pulling her firmly against the man's granite-like chest.

His low laugh rumbled against her back as he leaned down and whispered, "Anytime you want to make him jealous, let me know. But this probably isn't the best time."

She shrugged out of his hold and turned her head to give him a piece of her mind. Hollywood grinned widely, his gaze flicking to Jamie. And oh, boy! If making him jealous had been her goal, she'd have succeeded. Jamie's eyes burned with possessiveness and his body seemed impossibly large as he advanced on her.

"Let go of my wife," he said, his voice a low, dangerous growl.

Hollywood raised his hands in surrender. "My bad," he said, the amusement dancing in his words making it clear he meant the opposite.

"Damn," Dani said, loud enough for Erica to hear her through both men's two-ways.

Jamie gave her one last hard look before turning in the direction Dani had gone. "What is it?" he asked.

"Rebar."

"Fuck. Can you get around it?"

"Not around, not over, not under. I'm going to have to go through it."

"What's your plan?"

Jamie's technical rescue team had some amazing tools, but how could Dani get through reinforced concrete? Erica listened anxiously to Dani's answer.

"It's a support column about fifteen feet long and four feet high by four feet deep. A chunk of cement from the center has already broken out and there are cracks extending out from there for about a foot on each side. If I can chip out the concrete, I can cut the rebar. The hole will be big enough to get the board through."

Visions of the column caving in on Dani and stranding Chloe alone on the other side made Erica sway. She grabbed Jamie's sleeve. When he looked down at her, his brow arched, she asked, "Will it hold after she cuts through it?"

He nodded. "She'll leave enough of the original structure on either side and above the hole to maintain the integrity of the column."

Releasing his arm, she breathed deeply and stepped back.

"Okay, do it," Jamie said to Dani.

"Roger that, LJ."

Dani gave them status updates as she loosened the concrete along the crack and cut several of the steel bars. "I need to do one more layer and then I should be good."

"Make sure there's enough space for an occupied board."

At the sound of Jamie's strangled voice, Erica looked up at him. His eyes were closed and a muscle jumped in his jaw. Her heart clenched with fear. He didn't think Chloe would be able to walk out. She must have whimpered because his eyes shot open and his gaze flew to hers. He didn't say a word, simply brushed his fingers along her cheek. But his eyes spoke of fear and regret.

"Hey, Jamie."

Erica looked up to see Drew and three other men approaching them, boots clomping over the debris, their heavy equipment jiggling and jangling. How such big men could move so fluidly with the amount of gear they carried amazed her. And their arrival thrilled her. Surely with the whole team here, they'd have Chloe out in no time.

"Erica, thank God you're okay." Drew grabbed her in a great bear hug.

She hugged him back, smiling. Of all Jamie's brothers, Drew had always been her favorite. "You should probably thank Jamie instead. He's the one who got me out from under the wall."

Drew stepped back and clapped Jamie on the shoulder. "Nah. They're one and the same."

Jamie pulled him into a chokehold, knocking his helmet off, then he rubbed the top of his brother's head with his knuckles. "Smartass."

Drew laughed, and all the men, including Jamie, joined in.

She'd often wondered why people joked in tense situations like this one. From an outsider's perspective, it had always seemed out of place to her. But now that she was here, in the middle of everything, she understood. When faced with the choice between laughing or crying to relieve the stress of a dangerous situation, laughter was easier to handle.

A sense of hope filled Erica's heart. She'd have her baby in her arms soon. Safe and sound.

Suddenly, everyone stopped, their expressions intent as they listened to someone speaking over the radio. Jamie unclipped the radio from his jacket and held it to his ear. She inched closer to him to hear better, but he shook his head and pulled away. "How bad is it?" he asked.

Her heart started a manic beat against her ribs. Oh God. Had something happened to Chloe? Her hands curled around Jamie's arm as she tried to climb higher. Drew gently disengaged her fingers from Jamie's turnout coat. When she lowered herself to the ground and stepped back, he put an arm around her shoulders and lightly squeezed her bicep.

"What's going on, Drew?"

A look passed between the two brothers. "Get her out of here," Jamie grunted.

What? "I'm not going anywhere. What's wrong, Jamie?" When he remained silent, she insisted. "Tell me. If this concerns Chloe, I have a right to know."

Ignoring her, he flicked his two-way. "Dani, stop all maneuvers until we get a readout."

No! She shrugged Drew's arm off and faced Jamie, desperation making her fierce. "What's the matter with you? You can't just leave our daughter to die under a stupid vending machine."

He narrowed his eyes at her. "I'm not leaving Chloe."

"But you—"

"Just calm down. This isn't helping our daughter. Can't you hear her crying? You're shouting and it's scaring her." He blew out in exasperation. "Give me a minute and I'll explain everything."

Her throat swollen with unspoken questions, she nodded and gave him some space. Surrounded by Jamie's grim-faced team, she waited and listened.

"How much time do we have?" he asked.

All the men swore when the answer came. If someone didn't answer her soon she was going to explode.

Jamie held out his hand. "Come here."

She took it and followed him to where he stopped a few yards away. If something had gone wrong with Chloe, she would… God, she had no idea what she would do. Tears filled her eyes and she searched Jamie's face for answers.

After a few moments, he cleared his throat. "I don't know how to say this."

"J-just say it."

"Okay. The aftershock caused a gas leak. Fumes are filtering up from the basement. We've got about twenty minutes before the levels on this floor become unsafe. We need to evacuate."

CHAPTER 5

Rickie's grip on Jamie's fingers was tight enough to break glass. In that moment, he'd have given anything to turn back the clock. Go back to five forty-five and pick Chloe up from the daycare himself. Go back a year to the day Rickie had sent him packing, the day that would forever be burned into his retinas. Hell, maybe he should go back to the day he'd first met Rickie. Not so he could avoid her, but so he could do everything right. He didn't for one minute regret having had Chloe, but he definitely could have worked on creating a better home for her and on building a stronger marriage with Rickie.

Her bottom lip trembled when she spoke. "What about Chloe?"

He wanted to tell her their daughter would be all right. How could he though? In a matter of minutes, the entire building would be one spark away from a bonfire. "I'll get to her. But you need to leave right now."

The wild shaking of Rickie's head sent her blonde hair whipping around her face. "No. Let me stay, Jamie."

"It's too dangerous." A sound like that of a trapped animal escaped her lips, making his heart break. Christ. Were their positions reversed, he'd want to stay too.

"At least until Dani reaches her. Please, Jamie. I need to stay."

The pain and humility in her tone did him in. Rickie had never been anything but authoritative and in control. It's what made her so great at her job. "When I say go, you go."

A tremulous smile flashed across her face, gone almost before he noticed it. "Understood."

When they rejoined the group, he asked for an update. "Gas levels?"

"Rising. Seventeen more minutes," Drew said.

"LJ, I've got a problem," Dani interrupted. "I need to use the saw to sever this last piece of rebar."

"No go. Use the bolt cutters."

"Already tried. They aren't big enough."

"Shit." He looked around at the men surrounding him. "If she turns that saw on, the place could blow." One by one, the men nodded. "If anyone wants to leave, go now. No hard feelings." One by one, the men shook their heads.

A lump the size of his fist formed in his throat. He had the best fucking team in the world. "Okay, Dani, do it. But be as quick as you can."

"Got it."

They all held their breaths at the sound of the saw powering up. Jamie held Rickie's hand and wrapped his arm around Drew's shoulders. Prayers from his childhood played in his mind. Was it too obnoxious to ask God for a favor now? He'd never know unless he tried. Bowing his head, he begged God to save his little girl.

Dani's whoop over the radios sounded like a heavenly aria when it came. "I'm through, LJ." Coco's excited barking joined the team's gleeful encouragement. "Coco's here. I told her to stay with Chloe, so I must be very close."

Since he hadn't wanted Chloe to be frightened by the team's radio chatter, he'd asked her to turn off the radio Coco had brought her. But now that his luck seemed to be turning, he wanted to tell his daughter that help was near. "Call to her. Ask her to turn the walkie-talkie on," he said.

A few seconds later, he heard a click and the sweetest softest voice. "Daddy?"

"I'm here, baby."

"Coco was barking. I got scared, but then I heard Dani."

"That's right. Dani's coming to get you. You be a big girl and do what she says. Okay?"

"Okay. I'm not going to die, am I, Daddy?"

The air left his lungs in one awful whoosh, as though the building had collapsed on his chest. Beside him, Rickie made a small keening sound. "No. Of course not," he said, more vehemently than he should have. Softening his tone, he asked, "Can you see Dani or Coco yet?"

"Coco came back." He heard slurping sounds accompanied by Chloe's giggles.

An ache started deep in his chest. "I love you, baby."

Dani's voice came over the air, calm and light. "I've got her, LJ."

"Good. Turn her radio off." He waited to hear the click, then spoke to Dani. "I'll try to ask questions you can answer without scaring her. What's on her? Is it the vending machine?"

"Yes."

"Can you lift it?"

"Yes."

"Can you pull her out from underneath at the same time?"

"Maybe."

"Too cramped?"

"Time is a bigger issue."

Shit. How could he have forgotten? If he didn't pull it together and keep a cool head, he'd get them all killed. "Levels?" he asked Drew.

"Almost critical. Ten minutes."

"We need to get SCBAs to them," Hollywood said.

"How?" asked Colin. "Dani's the only one who fits, and even that was a tight squeeze."

Jesus Fucking Christ. Had he really thought his luck was changing? He was a goddamn idiot. Now his child and one of his team members were essentially trapped without masks and instead of planning how to get equipment to them, he'd been praying.

"I'll do it."

He heard Rickie's words but couldn't make any sense of them. "Do what?"

"Bring tanks and masks to Dani and Chloe."

"Absolutely not." Civilians did not participate in rescue missions. Ever.

She rounded on him then, arms on her hips, eyes blazing. "Look, Jamie. I'm the only one who can do it. All of you are too big. I know I can fit; I'm smaller than Dani."

"Honey, you have no training. You'll just get hurt. And those tanks are heavy."

"Don't you 'honey' me, James Caldwell. I'm their only chance, and I'm a hell of a lot stronger than you think." Without looking back, she grabbed his SCBA from the ground and headed the way Dani had gone.

He lunged forward and grabbed her elbow. "At least let us outfit you properly. Evan, give her your trousers and extrication gloves." Given that he was almost a foot taller than his wife and outweighed her by a hundred pounds or so, his own turnout gear would be more hindrance than help.

Drew came up beside him, shrugging out of his jacket. "Take my jacket. With the sleeves rolled up, it should be okay."

Once she was dressed, Jamie helped her adjust the shoulder straps and waist belts of the SCBA, then he took off his helmet and secured it on her head along with the mask. "Click here to turn the radio on and off. There's an amplifier in the helmet."

Hollywood brought over another SCBA. "Try not to bang it around too much."

"Shouldn't I bring two extras?"

Jamie rubbed the back of his neck. Did she think she was Wonder Woman? "Each air cylinder weighs about twenty-five pounds. Think you can get through all that rubble lugging an extra seventy-five pounds?"

She gulped. "We'll share."

"Smart choice." When she turned to leave, he stopped her with a hand on her arm. She looked up and arched a brow. "Turn on the radio now. Dani will talk you through to her location."

Following his earlier instructions, she turned on the radio and started to leave. He stopped her again. She sighed. "Now what?"

"Be careful." He could convince himself he hadn't said the three words he most wanted to say so that he wouldn't upset her right before she started out. But that would be a lie. He hadn't said it because he was a coward. If they were all going to die, he'd rather die with the illusion that had he said those three words, Rickie would have said them back.

∞ ≋ ∞

Erica stared into Jamie's eyes, saw fear and resignation. He cared about her. It was obvious from his tone and his expression. But did he love her? Unless she heard the words, she wouldn't know. Too much had happened between them, and she couldn't trust her judgment or her instincts where he was concerned.

She nodded. "I'll follow Dani's instructions to the letter."

Her heart full of words and emotions she'd refused to let out for years, she picked up the second tank and mask and walked over to where she'd first seen Dani enter. "Dani?" she asked, checking to make sure the radio was working.

"Right here, Erica."

"I'm at the spot where you started—the big heating duct."

"Okay, you'll need to belly crawl through it. It'll be a tight fit with the SCBA on your back, but you can make it. Push the other tank in front of you."

With careful movements so as not to throw herself off balance, Erica got down on her knees and slid the tank into the duct. The interior was so dark, she needed the flashlight or she'd be fumbling around blindly.

"When you get to the end, the tank will bump into a wall," Dani continued. "You'll have to turn it to your left."

The bulkiness of the unfamiliar clothing made the distance to the other end seem interminable. Because her gloves were too large, she kept dropping the flashlight, and her bunker trousers kept sliding on the slippery material of the duct's surface. Like a child on a Slip 'N Slide, each time she pushed forward with her knees, she'd fall face first. Inch by inch, despite the new set of bruises on her legs, she pressed on and eventually the tank hit an obstacle.

Angling it in the direction Dani had instructed, she edged her way out of the duct only to end up squished between a wall and a downed support beam. God, how did Jamie and his team do this on a daily basis? She took a deep breath.

Suck. Hiss.

The uneven sound of her breathing in the faceplate was overwhelming and made her realize just how vulnerable she was. "I'm out," she said.

Dani must have heard the shakiness in her voice because unlike earlier, her tone was calm and encouraging. "You're doing great, Erica. Walk along the wall and the beam about ten yards until you get to a point where a second beam has fallen over the first. Oh, and lift up the second tank in that area. There's a lot of sharp metal on the ground there."

Wonderful. Erica looked down at her poor abused running shoes. This is when those thick fireman boots come in handy. Too bad she wasn't wearing any. She should be grateful though. There wasn't much room, but at least she could stand and walk more or less normally. Using the light from the helmet, she picked her way along the wall, avoiding whatever metal she managed to see. Unfortunately, the beam from the flashlight was narrow, and she didn't see the jagged edge of the filing cabinet in time. She stifled a scream as it cut through the rubber sole of her sneaker.

"Erica?"

Using the wall for support, she lifted up her foot and shined the light on it to examine the damage. The bottom of her shoe had a big gash in it. At least her foot had been spared. Sort of. Her heel burned and a few drops of blood oozed through the hole in the rubber.

"You okay, Erica?" Dani asked again, sounding anxious.

"Nothing I can't handle." She'd suffer through this and much worse for her daughter. Cautiously, she started walking again, following Dani's instructions.

After a few moments, Dani broke the silence. "So, how are things going with you and Jamie?"

Suck. Hiss.

Adrenaline surged through Erica's system at the question. It was bad enough her life and her daughter's depended on this woman. Did Dani have to rub in the fact that she was Jamie's girlfriend as well? Gritting her teeth, she spat out, "Seeing as how he's dating you, I'm sure you know exactly how well things are going." *Bitch.*

Dani laughed. Laughed!

Erica forced her feet to keep moving, reminding herself that Chloe—not Jamie or his other relationships—was the only thing that mattered. When she reached the overlapping beams, she reined in her anger and said, "I'm there. What now?"

"Crawl over the beams at the point where they intersect, then go right about forty-five degrees. If you're in the right place, in six yards, you should reach the failed support column I cut through."

Erica examined the beams, trying to figure out how she was going to get over their combined height. The beams reached her shoulders and without footholds or something to step on, there was no way she could pull herself and the extra fifty pounds of tanks she was carrying over. Despair dug serrated claws into her heart. Maybe Jamie was right. Maybe she'd let her pride override her abilities. She wasn't trained and she had no idea what to do. Inhaling deeply, she fought back the tears burning her eyes.

"Find something you can stand on to help you over," Dani added gently.

Why hadn't she thought of that? Mustering up her courage, she searched the nearby debris and located several large blocks of cement and some wooden planks.

"We're not dating, you know."

Erica paused in the act of organizing her findings into a table of sorts. "Jamie cancelled his evening with Chloe because he was going out with you. He told me himself."

"Well, he lied then," Dani said.

"Why would he do that?" Erica finished building her platform and tested it with one foot. A little wobbly, but it would have to do.

"To make you jealous, maybe?"

Standing on the platform, she lifted the second tank on top of the beams and settled it in the space between them. Then she hoisted herself up, pulling with all the strength in her arms. But the weight of the tank on her back dragged her back down. While one foot landed squarely on the platform, the injured one slipped off the edge. "Ow!"

"Everything okay over there?" Dani asked, her voice anxious.

Ignoring the woman's question, Erica asked one of her own as she massaged her ankle. Boots were definitely non-optional when traipsing through a minefield of obstacles as dangerous as this one. "Why should I believe you?"

"I'm not interested in Jamie."

That drew her up short. "Why not?" Erica blurted before she could stop herself. The man was gorgeous, smart, and made good money. Any woman in her right mind would want Jamie.

So why don't you?

Thankfully, Dani's response meant she could avoid her own question. "I'm in love with his brother."

"Drew?" she asked, unable to keep the incredulity from her voice. Two firefighters getting involved would be a disaster. She bounced with her knees and stretched her arms as far as she could, then jumped. Her hands hooked on the far beam. Swinging her feet to the side, she anchored one leg over the first beam. Tightening all her muscles, she pulled herself up and flattened herself on the beam to keep from falling.

Suck. Hiss.

Sweat streamed down her back between her shoulder blades. The temperature inside her turnout coat had to be at least one hundred and ten degrees. No wonder Jamie and his team didn't have an ounce of fat on them.

Dani's laughter rang out. "No way. Drew's like a brother to me. I meant Will."

Was it some sort of firefighter rule that they had to shorten everyone's name? "Does Jamie know?" Since the separation, Jamie had been living with William. Maybe Dani had been using one brother to get the other.

"Yes. He's been helping me out."

"Really?" Having regained her breath, Erica twisted her hips until she was aligned with the V of the intersecting wooden beams and let herself slide down, pulling the extra tank after her. Once her feet hit the ground with a solid painful thump, she scanned the area and identified the forty-five degree direction. Her limping steps were about half a yard each, so twelve or so should get her to the support column.

Dani sighed. "Jamie keeps finding excuses to invite me over. But Will has no idea I'm alive. As far as he's concerned, I'm just one of Jamie's work buddies."

Erica wasn't surprised. Of all the Caldwell brothers, William—the accountant—was the least likely to go for a tomboy like Dani. He harked back so thoroughly to the Caldwell's aristocratic British forebears that he should have an accent. If William even owned a pair of jeans, Erica would be truly shocked. "Good luck with that one. Okay, I've reached the cement beam."

"Push the spare tank through first, then follow. The hole is about two feet high and it might be a bit of a tight fit. When you reach the other side, go straight about ten feet until you reach a pile of junk."

A pile of junk? Okay. Shoving the tank in ahead of her, she concentrated on squeezing herself and the tank on her back into the two-foot hole. Once again she was entombed in complete inky darkness, save for the glow from her flashlight.

Suck. Hiss.

The sound of her breathing added to the creepiness of the cave-like hole. Her chest tightened, making it hard to squeeze air into her compressed lungs. All she needed now was to have a panic attack and get stuck here. Everyone she cared about would die.

"I walked in on Jamie today, sitting at the table in the lunchroom, staring at the divorce papers."

Dani must have noticed the change in her breathing. Erica laid her head on her arm, gripping the flashlight and the extra tank, while attempting to calm herself. "He told me he lost them."

"I don't think he wants to sign."

The cement was rough, with sharp edges that tugged at her trousers. The suspenders kept them from being pulled off, but the Velcro straps around her ankles did nothing to keep them from riding up her legs, exposing her skin. The jacket scrunched up under her arms and the sleeves pushed up to her elbows. Jagged cement tips tore through her turnout gear and scraped her lower legs, forearms, and belly. It felt like she was being dragged over a cheese grater, and each new cut stung as fresh sweat dripped into it. Nothing in her life had prepared her for this.

If Dani's goal with this conversation was to distract her from her mounting anxiety, it was working. "What makes you say that?" she asked, pushing with her feet to inch herself forward. Dust rose up and coated her facemask, blinding her. She stilled and wiped a gloved hand across it, listening, waiting for Dani's response.

"I figure if he'd wanted to sign them, he'd have done so already. When a guy wants free of the ball and chain, it doesn't take him three months to autograph a few sheets of paper."

Her stomach clenched—whether with hope or fear, she wasn't certain. Why hadn't Jamie said anything to her? When they'd met with their lawyers, he'd agreed to everything. She'd expected—hoped—he'd put up some sort of fight.

"So you want this divorce?" Dani asked.

As Erica reached for the spare tank, her sleeve snagged on a piece of rebar that stuck out from the cement. She tried to jiggle it free, but the metal was anchored deep. "That's not what I said."

"Maybe not, but that's what it sounds like."

"What do you mean?" Frustrated with her inability to free her sleeve as much as with Dani's comments, she yanked her arm as hard as she could and ripped the turnout jacket free. With her elbows, she hitched herself forward like a caterpillar until the hole narrowed and the tank on her back screeched against the cement. She rolled onto her side so there'd be more room for the tank, and with her feet anchored as best she could with her running shoes, she wiggled her hips and propelled herself forward. Soon the spare tank started to tip over the edge. Holding tightly, she slowly lowered it to the ground. Dani's answer came as Erica crawled out from inside the concrete support beam.

"Seems to me you've done everything possible to shove Jamie out of your life. Out of his daughter's life."

"It's what he wants."

"You sure about that?"

Something inside compelled her to give voice to her deepest concerns. But was Dani the right person to confide in? "There's no guarantee he'd be around anyway."

"What?"

"Isn't this situation answer enough? Jamie could be killed at any time."

"Look where you are, Erica. Right now, you're in more danger than he is. *Anyone* can die at any time."

There was a silence over the radio, but she had nothing to say. Her own father, an elementary school teacher, had died on his way home from work, killed by a drunk driver. There were no guarantees for any of them.

"But you know what, Erica?"

"What?"

"If you push him away now, he might as well be dead."

Suck. Hiss.

Oh God. She was such an idiot. She'd been so determined not to depend on Jamie, so determined to prove that she could raise her daughter alone, so determined not to be her mother, that she'd erased Jamie from their lives, depriving herself of a wonderful husband, and depriving her daughter of a loving father.

Assuming they survived this night, and assuming he still loved her, did their marriage even stand a chance? If they worked at it, could it survive as well?

Qué será, será. She couldn't dwell on this now. The only thing she needed to focus on was saving their daughter. She'd reached the pile of junk. "I'm at the pile. Where do I go from here?"

"Unfortunately, you're going to have to crawl over it."

Misgiving tightened her chest as she looked from her sneaker-clad feet to the mound of rubble. Steeling her spine, she cradled the spare tank in her arm and placed her foot on a sturdy-looking block. She pushed herself up, careful to keep her balance. After cresting the pile, she slid one foot forward until it caught on a piece of wood. She nudged it to see if it would hold and huffed out a breath when it did. She could do this. She would.

Like a tightrope walker, she held her free arm out and took a step. Her foot sank into the debris, pitching her forward. Everything happened in a flash. Within seconds, her body slammed into the ground, knocking the breath from her lungs.

She sucked in great gulps of air, stopping only when she began to feel lightheaded. On the verge of hyperventilation, she strained against the weight of the SCBA on her back and reached for the flashlight that had fallen a few feet away. Her only thought was to get on her feet. Time was running out.

Feeling like an astronaut in the heavy, bulky suit, she pulled her knees under her chest to give herself leverage. Pain stabbed in her thigh.

Muffling a cry, she rolled onto her butt and looked down to see a jagged piece of glass sticking out from her leg. With shaking fingers, she reached down and yanked it out. Drops of blood clung to the dirty glass. Nausea filled her throat. Almost desperately, she ripped open the mask's faceplate. All she needed now was to drown in her own vomit. Again and again, she swallowed and took shallow breaths through her nose.

She stared up into the darkness of what had been her workplace, and tears filled her eyes. Why had she thought she could do this?

She was going to let everyone down.

She was just like her mother.

CHAPTER 6

Jamie heard his wife's soft sobs through the radio, each one gouging his heart. Christ, sending Rickie in had been a big fucking mistake. But what choice had he had? She was their only hope for getting the SCBA to Chloe and Dani. And without her, Dani couldn't free Chloe from the vending machine. This rescue was turning into a major clusterfuck with the strongest members of the team standing around waiting, feeling like dumbasses. His years of experience meant nothing today. All he could do was help Rickie through this.

"Come on, babe. You can do this. Take a deep breath and tell me what happened."

He heard a gasp, then Rickie's shocked voice. "J-Jamie?"

"Yeah, it's me. What's wrong?"

"I fell and cut my thigh."

Shit. "Are you bleeding?" If she'd hit an artery, he'd have to blast his way to her. And risk blowing them all up in the process.

"Some."

Air rushed out of his lungs as relief threatened to overwhelm him. Still, better safe than sorry. "Use one of the straps we used to secure the pant legs around your ankles. Tie it as tightly as possible around your thigh above the cut. Can you do that, honey?"

He heard rustling sounds as she moved around.

"Done. Thank you, Jamie."

"For what?"

"For being there."

Always. She just didn't believe it yet. Unless Dani's words had sunk in. It'd been hard staying silent while Dani had been talking to Rickie about the divorce papers. But something had told him to stay out of it.

"You ready to keep going?" he asked, his tone unhurried. He didn't want to frighten her, but they were running out of time. The gas fumes would soon be reaching critical levels and not only was the risk of explosion very high, but Dani and Chloe were inhaling toxic air with every breath.

"I'm good. What do I do now?"

Dani's voice came on the line, cool and calm. "You're almost here, Erica. But this last part's a bit tricky. Ten yards to your left is a cement wall about five feet high. Jamie, did you give Erica the climbing rope?"

"Rickie, look at your belt. Attached on your right side is a rope. On one end is a grappling hook. You'll need to rotate the latch mechanism at the top a quarter turn. Once the claws pop out, rotate the latch another quarter turn to lock it in place. Then swing the hook over the wall. Can you do that?"

He heard her harsh breaths as she threw the rope, followed by a clunk as the claws hit the cement. "How do I get it to hook onto something?" she asked.

"Gently pull on the rope. As the hook moves up the wall, the claws should sink into a soft spot or a crevice."

"Oh! I think it worked."

A smile tugged at his lips. "Now give it a sharp yank to make sure it holds."

"Crap, it came all the way over."

"Stay calm and try it again. Throw the hook over the wall, then slowly pull it back."

A few seconds later, he heard her sigh. "I think I've got it now."

"Great. Do you remember that time we went mountain climbing and we had to go up a part that was pretty steep? It's just like that. Walk up the wall." That day would be forever etched in his mind as one of the happiest of his life. Rickie had finally agreed to go hiking with him. They'd climbed up the mountain and had a picnic near the top. For dessert, they'd had each other.

His body tightened as he remembered the softness of her skin warmed by the sun, the scent of her hair, the glorious feeling of slipping inside her. *Mind on the job, asshole*. "You can do this, Rickie."

"I'm glad you're so confident, Jamie," she said, her voice tinted with sarcasm.

"Chloe's counting on you. We both are."

"No pressure. Thanks."

He chuckled at her acerbic tone. "Rickie, you're the most capable, independent woman I've ever known. You can do anything you want."

She scoffed. "Whatever. Here goes nothing."

He listened attentively as she climbed the wall, the extra weight of the two oxygen units making her strain and grunt. "That's it, honey. Slow and easy."

When all he heard was her rasping breath, he knew she'd reached the top of the wall. "I bet you're wondering how you get down now."

"Something like that," she said between pants.

Dani broke in. "I left my rope in place. Look around. You'll see it."

"I see it," Rickie said even as he heard her move toward it. More shuffling, and then she said, "I'm down."

"I'm sending Coco to you. Just follow her. You'll be here in a minute," Dani said.

Jamie heard Coco's happy barking as she found Rickie. From her rapid breathing, he knew she was on the move again, following the dog to their daughter. His chest filled with warmth. Maybe they'd all survive this nightmare after all. Thanks to his courageous wife. "You're wrong, you know," he said softly, ignoring the fact that Dani and the entire team were listening in.

"About what?" Rickie asked, sounding guarded.

"I don't want the divorce." He had to tell her the truth. Make her understand. "I've wanted you from the moment I laid eyes on you at that party. I love our daughter and our family."

"Then why did you back out?"

Her angry words lashed at him. He could understand now how she could have misinterpreted his actions and intentions. "I knew you were afraid. That if I died on the job, you'd be left struggling like your mom."

"So what? You wanted me to be *prepared*?"

"I gave you the space I thought you needed."

"Ha! I didn't need *space*, I needed a husband. One who was there."

"Rickie, be honest with yourself. You pushed me so far away, I live in a different zip code."

But then she screamed and he heard scraping sounds, followed by a loud crash. Panic consumed him. "Rickie!"

"I-I'm okay. My shoe slipped and I tripped."

Running shoes were a damn sight better than the high heels she usually wore, but it was a wonder she hadn't lost her footing before. "Are you hurt?"

Her breathing sped up as she struggled to get back on her feet, the erratic hissing coming through the radio loud and clear. With each ragged inhale, his guilt increased. "Rickie, tell me if you're hurt," he said again.

"I'm just so tired of fighting with you, Jamie." Her voice hitched and he knew then and there that she still cared.

"I want things to be good between us again, babe. I miss you."

She laughed, the sound bitter. "When were things *good*, Jamie? When you married me out of an archaic sense of obligation?"

He gritted his teeth. Why couldn't she believe he'd married her because he loved her? "I wanted you."

"But did you love me? Did you ever love me, Jamie?"

"You know I did. I *do*. When Chloe was born, I thought I had it all. That if I died then, I'd die happy."

"And I'd have been left alone, a single mother with a fatherless child."

He remained silent for a moment, letting her words sink in. Finally, he cleared his throat. "Isn't that what you and Chloe are now?"

Coco's sharp barks and his wife's soft sob reached his ears.

"I'm not dead, Rickie. You're afraid of something that might never happen. You can't live life this way, never being happy, never letting your guard down because you're protecting yourself from anything that can go wrong."

"I can't be like you, Jamie. You never worry about anything."

"I'm worried about all of us right now." The lives of his family and his team were all on the line. And their chances of surviving diminished with each passing minute.

ಎ 🚒 ಅ

"Mommy! Mommy!"

The mix of pain, fear, and elation in her daughter's cry had Erica's body rushing with adrenaline. Ripping off her gloves, she knelt beside Chloe and began to gently feel her for injuries. "I'm here, sweetie. We're going to get you out," she said, turning to Dani with an expectant look.

Dani had already begun building a crib at the base of the vending machine. Erica estimated she'd already raised it three inches. Beads of perspiration rolled down her cheeks and her breathing was labored. Grabbing the second SCBA, Erica brought it to Dani. "You look like you could use some fresh air," she said so as not to alarm her daughter, who was looking on with large frightened eyes.

Nodding her thanks, Dani slipped the straps onto her shoulders and placed the mask over her face. For several moments, she did nothing but inhale deeply. Rickie hurried back to Chloe and transferred her own mask to her daughter's face. "Breathe slow and deep."

"While I raise this a couple more inches, can you arrange the stretcher so when you pull her out, she slides onto it?" Dani asked.

The void was small and cave-like. The panel of sheetrock above them had probably protected Chloe from some of the smaller, but no less deadly, debris that had fallen from the ceiling. Carefully, Erica cleared some space for the stretcher, placing the foot of it at Chloe's head. When she was done, she explained to Chloe what they were going to do, then took the mask back for a few fortifying gulps of air. After replacing the mask on Chloe's face, she gave Dani a thumbs up.

"Ladies, how's everything going?"

Jamie's confident voice settled her jumpy stomach. And her daughter's smile made her heart squeeze. If nothing else, she had to acknowledge that Jamie did love his daughter.

"Daddy! Mommy's here. She brought me a special mask."

"A special mask for my special girl," he said, and she could hear the amusement in his words. "Be sure to share with Mommy. She's pretty special too."

Her daughter laughed and for a moment, Erica imagined how happy they might be again if she and Jamie could get past this mountain in their path. But what if they couldn't? What if the wall between them was too high? The thought brought tears to her eyes.

"Erica?"

Dani touched her arm, and the worry in her eyes brought Erica back to the present. Back to the nightmare they were living. "Sorry. I'm okay."

"Good." Dani moved to the far side of the vending machine and grabbed the pole she was using as a lever. "When I say go, start pulling her out, very slowly. Once she's clear, let me know."

Erica grabbed Chloe under the arms and waited. Slowly, Dani pushed on the lever and the vending machine rose another inch. "Go," Dani said.

On her signal, Erica slowly tugged her daughter out from under the machine. Her gaze shot to Chloe's legs and a jolt stiffened her shoulders. The sharp edge of a bone was visible through the thin blood-soaked material of Chloe's cotton pants. Her little face scrunched in pain as Erica slid her onto the stretcher until her head rested on the neck support, but she didn't utter a single sound. Brave, just like her father. "Clear."

"Okay, now move the stretcher back a foot or two, as much as you have room for."

Erica maneuvered her daughter to safety and stroked her hair. Earlier Chloe had said she couldn't feel either of her legs. Hopefully, they'd just gone numb. "How are your legs, sweetie?"

"They hurt," she said, her voice thin, frightened.

"Both of them?"

Chloe's lip jutted out and her eyes welled.

"Shh, it's okay," Erica murmured, running her finger along Chloe's cheek. She didn't like her daughter being in pain, but it meant she wasn't paralyzed, and for that Erica was very grateful. "We'll be out of here soon."

Dani lowered the vending machine back onto the cribbing and released the lever. Her shoulders slumped and she inhaled deeply before speaking into her radio. "She's clear, Jamie."

Whoops of joy filled Erica's ears as everyone on the team congratulated them. "Did you hear that, baby girl?" Jamie said to Chloe.

"Am I going to be alright, Daddy?"

"You bet. Mommy and Dani are superheroes today."

"Like Wonder Woman?"

"Exactly like that. Okay, ladies. Are you ready for the trip back? The sooner we all get out of here the better."

Erica looked at Dani, who smiled. "Yep, we're heading back right now."

Dani crouched beside the stretcher and strapped Chloe into place. "Okay, kiddo. There might be some bumps, and you might feel like you're falling sometimes, but trust us, okay? We'll be out of here in no time."

Her lips pressed tightly together, Chloe nodded to Dani. Erica gently squeezed her daughter's hand then took another few gulps of air from the mask before giving it back to Chloe.

"From here on out, you share with me," Dani said. "I'm going to take the lead. When I get tired, we'll switch. You watch and help keep things stable."

"Okay," Erica said, moving to the foot of the stretcher.

Just as Dani began pulling the stretcher out of the small void, Coco bounded up to Dani, barking and pressing herself against the woman's side. "What's wrong, girl?" Dani asked, smoothing her hands over the dog's back. Coco howled and even from where she stood, Erica could see the dog's body tremble.

"Oh, shit!" Dani shouted, crouching over Chloe's face. "Get down, Erica. Cover your head with your arms."

The floor swayed as a powerful aftershock ripped through the building. Cracking and crashing filled the air as the already damaged building crumbled. Erica edged her way closer to Chloe and touched her leg, determined to be with her daughter in their last moments. She didn't have the oxygen mask on, but she did have the radio clipped to her turnout jacket. Pressing the button, she shouted, "Be safe, Jamie." *Come on, Erica. This might be your last chance.* "I love you."

As the words left her mouth, something enormous crashed on top of them. She couldn't hold back her shrieks as what looked like a steel I-beam cut through the sheetrock above her. It crashed onto the vending machine, partially embedded in the machine's frame. Would it stop there or crush them all? She had no way of knowing.

Lightly squeezing Chloe's leg, she prayed Jamie had heard her final words.

CHAPTER 7

Jamie and his team dropped to one knee as a violent aftershock shook the building. Time seemed to slow and Jamie's attention was drawn to a crack in the ceiling. *Christ, no!*

They were so close to victory. Let him be wrong.

The groaning of the building as it swayed was so loud, he almost missed his wife's frantic words over the radio. "Be safe, Jamie."

"Rickie, are you all right?"

He watched, his limbs paralyzed by horror, as a massive concrete support column from the north side of the building buckled. The I-beam it was holding up toppled with it, crashing down directly over the location of his wife and child.

Her loud scream filled his faceplate, and he knew he'd hear it until the day he died.

The connecting wall and ceiling crumbled and thousands of pounds of construction material pounded down over the area in the beam's wake. A roar tore through his throat as he imagined their bodies mangled and trapped under the weight. "Rickie! Chloe!"

When she didn't reply, his heart broke, unable to believe things would end this way. It couldn't be. This couldn't happen.

Then he heard it. So soft, so final. "I love you."

"Rickie!" he screamed again. "Rickie!" *Oh God. No.* Determined to get to her, to Chloe, he took off at a run, charging through the fallen structures.

Until strong arms dragged him back. "Jamie. It's too unstable.

Remember your training."

Drew's calm voice pissed him off. "Fuck my training. My family is there. I've got to save them."

"I know. They're my family too. But you can't do it this way."

Jamie looked down at his younger brother. He was solidly built, but not as tall as Jamie. "Who's going to stop me?"

A hand clasped his shoulder. "I will."

His heart sank. If push came to shove, Hollywood could probably take him. Fuck. "Come on, guys. You can't expect me to just stand here and wait for them to die. We're the damn technical rescue team. Let's do our jobs and rescue them."

Hollywood clapped him on the back. "Now you're talking. But we aren't charging in there like jackasses on meth."

Jamie looked around, considering the scene. Going forward was out. The north end was out. His gaze shifted upward to the gaping hole in the ceiling. He pointed. "That's it. I'm going in from the next floor. We'll use a pulley to move the beam."

Drew grabbed him by the neck and pulled his head down until their foreheads met. "I know how upset you are, Jamie. But we don't even know if they're alive."

Jamie shuddered as though he'd been shocked with a Taser. He struggled to pull away, but Drew just held him tighter. He had to make Drew understand. "But we don't know that they're dead either."

"Finally, a believer."

Dani's annoyed voice sounded like the singing of angels in that moment.

"Dani! Is everyone all right?" His stomach churned as he awaited her answer.

"A little shaken, a little stirred. But we're alive."

His legs wobbled, and he'd have fallen if Hollywood hadn't steadied him.

"Jamie?"

"Erica?" He silently thanked God for giving him another chance.

"Please, don't take any unnecessary risks," she said.

Had she been hit in the head? He'd die to save her and Chloe. "Don't worry about me, babe. Focus on yourself and Chloe. Try to keep her calm. Dani, what's the situation?"

"The machine we all bitched about saved our lives. The I-beam's jacked up against it. But the way out is blocked now. So you guys need to get your fantastic butts over here and get us out," Dani said.

"I second that," Rickie said, and he could hear the smile in her voice.

"I'm working on a plan." A grin ripped across his face. Maybe this time, luck would be on his side. "Okay, guys. Grab your gear and let's head up one floor."

They hauled all their gear up the stairs to the fourth floor and moved into position. Drew came up to him, worry on his face. "What is it?" he asked.

"Gas levels are rising faster. We need to get the security team out."

Jamie's brows furrowed. Fuck. He'd almost forgotten about the gas. He held his hand up and called the men to his side. "Things are getting very dangerous. Any minute, we could have an explosion or a full structural collapse. I know some of you have family and loved ones. Don't risk yours to save mine. Anyone who wants out, you're free to leave now." He met and held their gazes one by one. No one moved.

"No one will ever know," he insisted. Still no one left. "All right then. Let's do this. Colin and Evan, make sure the security guys leave the building. Then come back and be ready to get Chloe and Rickie out of the building." He paused and everyone waited for him to continue. "And call for a back-up medic unit. We're going to need it." The sooner they could get Chloe to the hospital, the better. Rickie's injuries weren't life-threatening, but he'd feel better if she was seen by a doctor. Then there was Dani. God only knew how much of the gas she'd inhaled.

"Right on it, LJ," Colin said as he and Evan headed for the stairwell.

Jamie stepped to the edge of the hole in the floor and looked down at the scene below. The steel I-beam that had nearly destroyed his family was clearly visible. Looking up, he pointed at an exposed area of the ceiling. "Get the rigging in place. One set for me and one set for the beam."

"You should let one of us do it," Gabe said.

He shook his head. "Nope. I have the most experience with rope rescues."

They made quick work of anchoring the ropes on the beams and setting up the pulley systems. Within minutes, Jamie was strapped into a harness and holding onto the simple web sling they'd use to raise the I-beam. They only needed to lift it up a foot or two, just enough for the women to slip out from under the debris and get Chloe's stretcher through. The quake had certainly disturbed things, so their path out might not be as easy as it had been going in. He only hoped they didn't encounter any obstacles that required drilling. With the gas levels so high, it would be suicide to even attempt it.

Hollywood double-checked the threading of the climbing rope through the figure eight descender and its attachment to the carabiner on Jamie's harness. Then he yanked on the ropes to test the strength of the anchor system while all the men held onto the ends of the ropes tug-of-war style. "Okay, LJ. Ready when you are."

Leaving the relative safety of the floor behind, Jamie swung into the void and rappelled down one level, using his hands on the rope to control his rate of descent. Seconds later, his feet touched the ground. "Dani, I'm here. Make sure everyone is in a protected position." When the I-beam lifted, the chances were very high that more shit would fall on them. "But be ready to move when I say go."

"Understood, LJ."

With light movements, he secured the sling around the beam and attached it to the master link at the end of the second rope. After double-checking the equipment, he alerted Hollywood. "Okay, lift it up. Smooth and steady." He kept his hands on the beam to stabilize it as it angled upward, inch by agonizing inch. "Get ready, Dani. A little more, Hollywood."

The large crossbeam they'd used as leverage for the sling creaked and groaned. Jamie jerked his head up, concerned. "Stop. Hollywood, get some binoculars. Check out the leverage pieces."

A few rustlings and curses later, Hollywood said, "We've got trouble. The load is too high and the beam is bending."

"How bad?"

"I'm seeing some edge cracks."

What had he said earlier about his luck holding out? Yeah. He'd fucking jinxed himself. "Well, we can't stop now."

"But if it breaks—"

"I'm well aware. Keep going." Under his hands, the I-beam pinning the women lifted another inch. "Dani? Everyone okay?"

"We're getting some fallout, but nothing too bad."

"Things might get rough, so try to move into position for exit."

He heard some quiet whispers and shuffling. "Need two more inches at least," Dani said.

"You got it." As the beam rose, he added his support beneath it, guiding it with his hands. "Easy does it, Hollywood. Almost there."

"That's good, LJ," Dani said. "We're moving out."

"Try to keep everyone calm and make sure Rickie gets her share of oxygen. Air's real bad."

"Will do. I'll let you know once we're clear."

As he listened to their movements, he heard a sharp snap from above, along with the shouts of his team. "LJ, the cracks are getting larger." Hollywood warned.

Without thought, Jamie moved under the beam, shoring it with his arms and shoulders. He pulled a knife from his belt, flipped it open and cut the ropes holding the beam. The last thing he needed was for the failing beam to fall on their heads. But the weight of the I-beam almost drove him to his knees. "Dani," he panted, widening his stance. "By all that's holy, run like the fucking wind and save my family."

"LJ! What—?"

Hollywood saved him from answering. "Dani, the anchor was about to rupture, so he cut the ropes. Get everyone out of there. Fast."

"Oh God." She didn't say any more to him, but Jamie heard her giving Rickie instructions.

He also heard Rickie's soft cries. He'd forgotten she had a radio too. His throat felt like a garotte was wrapped around it, but he pushed the words out. He had to say goodbye. "Everything will be all right, Rickie. Just know that I love you and Chloe. I always have. I always will."

"Jamie, no. Don't—"

"It's the only way, Rickie. Please just…" His voice broke and he stopped himself. This was not the time to be morbid. *Don't let our daughter forget me.* Sucking the words and thoughts down, he walled them off in a secret corner of his heart. "Go. Get to safety."

ം 🚒 ↶

"Is Daddy going to be okay?" Chloe asked. Her lower lip trembled and her beautiful blue Caldwell eyes pleaded for a positive answer.

Swallowing her tears, Erica forced herself to offer her daughter a smile. They had to get out fast. Jamie wouldn't be able to hold the beam up much longer. "Daddy's the best at his job, sweetie.

Remember that." She nodded to Dani, who turned and began pulling the stretcher out of the void Chloe had been trapped in. Coco went ahead, sniffing out the easiest path.

Despite her injured foot, the cut in her thigh, and the tourniquet she'd had to improvise, they managed to get Chloe in the stretcher over the wall, using the ropes she and Dani had left behind on their way in. Fortunately, nothing blocked the hole Dani had drilled through the reinforced concrete either. Erica had a brief moment of despair when she saw that the two beams crossed in a V were now covered in a mountain of pipes, plaster, and wood. But Coco ran to the left and barked until they followed. The shifting caused by the aftershock had opened a different path, a much easier one with far fewer obstacles. Without pausing, they raced away from Jamie and the fallen I-beam.

Away from the man she loved.

After what felt like hours but was really only a few minutes, they exited where they'd entered and found two members of the team, Colin and Evan, waiting for them. The men each grabbed an end of the stretcher and ran the remaining distance to the stairs.

As soon as they entered the shelter of the stairwell, Dani instructed the men to tuck the stretcher along the wall and told Erica to hunker down. "We're clear, LJ," she said to Jamie over the radio.

Erica's heart clenched as she realized what was about to happen. Ignoring Dani, she stood and peered out the door to where Jamie continued to single-handedly hold up the I-beam that had almost killed them all. God. How could he do it? Illuminated by strong spotlights from the fourth floor, she saw his muscles bulging. Sweat soaked his hair and dripped down over his mask.

He looked up and his gaze held hers. After a moment, he stepped back and let the beam fall. The entire building shook, the noise deafening. Her heart pounding, her mind reeling, she watched in frozen disbelief as the floor caved and Jamie disappeared. Her knees gave out and she sank to the ground, screaming, "Jamie! Jamie, no!"

Her cries ripped through her throat, her entire body suddenly cold. This couldn't be happening. Jamie was a survivor. The best at his job. It couldn't end this way. Scrambling to her feet, she started running back the way she'd come. Maybe she could get to him. Maybe he was still alive.

Before she'd gone three yards, she was tackled from behind and fell face first on top of a broken desk.

"Erica, calm down," Dani said. "You can't go there."

"But, Jamie—"

Dani turned Erica's head and pointed. Out of the haze of dust and plaster, Jamie's limp body rose out of the hole in the floor suspended from a rope. Joy filled her chest to overflowing. He was alive. Jamie was going to be okay. Only…

"Dani! What's wrong with him?" He hung unmoving in the harness as his team pulled him up to the fourth floor.

When she turned to Dani, she saw the woman's pale face and sad eyes. "Hollywood? How is he?" she asked into the radio.

Not waiting for an answer, Erica spun on her heel and ran back into the stairwell and pointed to the lower levels. "Get Chloe out of the building. Now," she shouted to the men. Then she tore off in the opposite direction, bounding up the steps to the next floor as fast as she could with her bum leg. Colin tried to catch her, but she twisted and evaded his hold, bursting through the doors to the fourth floor.

No one was going to stop her. She needed to be with her husband.

Like a mad woman, she dashed through the dark rubble-ridden halls, her flashlight bobbing wildly. She hurdled mounds of broken office furniture, stumbled, tripped, and picked herself up again. Every obstacle fed her need to overcome, her need to be with Jamie.

After what felt like a marathon, she arrived panting and bleeding in the ruined common area, which now featured a gaping hole in the floor. Her legs weakened at the sight of the team hovering over Jamie's prone body. She staggered forward, pushing through the men, and fell to her knees beside Hollywood, who was carefully disengaging Jamie's harness. "Is he?" she asked in a whisper, unable to give voice to her worst fear.

Hollywood gave her a crooked smile as he removed Jamie's mask. "I think his lordship just needs a kiss from his lady to wake him up."

Dropping to the ground beside Jamie, she ripped off her own mask and took his hand. It was warm. His chest rose and fell in even beats. She leaned over, hugging him, tears flowing freely down her cheeks. "Thank God." She kissed his lips. Wonderful soft lips that had haunted her nights for the last year. "Did you hear that, Jamie? You're going to be fine. We're all going to be fine."

"Well, he's going to have a pretty sore head for a few days, and he probably has a concussion. But yeah, he'll live."

Frowning, she rose up and touched the swelling on the side of

Jamie's head. His eyes popped open, and seeing her, he smiled. "Rickie."

"How are you feeling?" she asked gently.

"Glad to be alive."

"You got a nasty bump on your head. Why weren't you wearing your helmet?"

He reached his hand up and tapped her head with his knuckles, grinning.

Hearing the thud, she remembered. He'd given her his helmet. He'd wanted her to be safe. "I'm so sorry, Jamie."

"Shh… I did it because I wanted to. I'd give my life for yours."

"You almost did."

Hollywood coughed. "I hate to interrupt the reunion, but unless we get out of here ASAP, you still might."

Jamie struggled to sit up. Erica quickly tucked her shoulder under his and helped him to his feet.

After helping her put her mask back on, he smiled down at her. "Let's go see our daughter."

CHAPTER 8

Jamie sat on a stretcher at the foot of Medic 11, enduring his younger brother Chad's ministrations. He resisted and feigned annoyance like any older brother would do, but in reality, he was relieved to see Chad. Relieved to know his brother was safe. Chad had updated him on the rest of the family. William had been at his condo when the quake hit. That building, built to all the latest earthquake codes, had withstood the tremors without a single paint fleck. His parents and Victoria, Chad's twin, were also fine. Their older house in Queen Anne had sustained some damage, but they'd taken shelter in the reinforced bathroom he'd insisted they build.

Simmons and his security team gathered around Aid 44, where Colin and Evan cleaned wounds and bandaged injuries. Several people clearly in need of medical attention broke away from the crowd gathered in City Hall Park, next to the Courthouse, and approached the ambulances.

It was going to be a very long night.

Jamie looked over at the stretcher beside his where Rickie watched anxiously as Chad's partner, Liam, strapped Chloe's leg into a temporary brace while she kept a tight hold on her mother's hand. "How's she doing?" he asked.

Liam smiled at Chloe. "Leg's broken. But our little lass is taking it like her old man. She hasn't complained once," he said with a thick Irish brogue.

Chloe's face scrunched up and she giggled. "You sound funny, like a leprechaun."

Jamie slid off the stretcher and took her hand, winking. "Good thing he doesn't look like one though."

She studied Liam's face, then Chad's before nodding. "Good thing, 'cause Uncle Chad doesn't like leprechauns."

Everyone laughed. Except Hollywood. What was up with that? Whatever. Jamie had too much on his mind to worry about his friend's mood right now. He let go of Chloe's hand and moved back, giving Liam space to work, but still close enough to keep a watchful eye on his daughter. Rickie came to stand beside him and he laid a hand on her shoulder. "How are you doing?"

She leaned into him a little and looked up, her lips curving. "A lot better than I thought I would be an hour ago." Her smile fell and her bottom lip trembled. "I really thought we were all going to die."

He ran the back of his index finger along her cheek. "We wouldn't have all made it if you hadn't stepped in. You're one of the bravest women I've ever known."

She turned in his arms and laid her head on his chest. "About that trip…"

It took him a moment to figure out what she was talking about. The trip he'd suggested earlier. The trip she'd shot down. "What about it?"

"I think we should go."

"Sure. When Chloe's healed up, we can celebrate and take her to Disneyland. She'll love that."

Her chin lifted and she met his gaze. "I was thinking of something a little more adult."

Did she mean what he thought she meant? "Adult how?"

She ducked her head and tried to step out of his arms. He tightened his hold. No way was he letting her squirm out of this now. She'd started it, she was going to finish it. "I've got a concussion, Rickie. You're going to have to spell it out for me."

"I think we need some time alone. Like you said, some time to reconnect."

"So you want to go away for the weekend, something like that?"

"I was thinking something more along the lines of a proper honeymoon. We never did have one."

A honeymoon? Holy shit. Was she saying she wanted to get back together? His heart started hammering against his ribs and his breathing came in short huffs. *Take it easy, man. Don't scare her.* "What would we do with Chloe?" he asked, trying to sound casual.

She toyed with the fabric of his T-shirt. "I thought your mom might like to have her over for a visit."

Jamie stumbled and quickly covered it up by sitting on the bumper of the ambulance. "You sure you trust my mom to take care of Chloe while we're gone? It'll have to be at least a week."

Her gaze roamed from Jamie, to Drew and Chad. "I figure if she could cope with all you Caldwell boys, she can deal with Chloe."

Was he imagining all of this? If he was, he prayed never to wake up. But if this was real, then he had to clear up a few things. He'd made a lot of mistakes both in what he'd done and in what'd he'd accepted. He wasn't going to make the same mistakes again. He took her hand and pulled her down beside him. "If this is going to work, a few things need to change."

Her throat worked as she swallowed. "Like what?"

"Like I don't want to be an absentee father anymore. I want—no, I *need*—to be a part of Chloe's everyday life. A part of yours."

"I want that too."

"And you'll tell me if something I do bothers you?"

"Yes, and I'll expect you to do the same."

He put his arm around her shoulders and pulled her in for a kiss. As soon as her lips touched his, he knew he was in trouble. Love and lust surged through his veins, and he hardened almost to the point of pain. *Christ*, he wanted this woman. He wanted his *wife*. And after a long year of celibacy, he was finally going to have her. But not until they got home. Reluctantly, he softened the kiss and drew back. "Where do you want to go?"

"Go?"

Eyes glazed with arousal stared back at him. He grinned. "For our honeymoon."

"I don't much care." She smiled. "But no extreme adventure vacation please. I've had enough of that to last me a lifetime."

He tucked a loose strand of hair around her ear. "Come on. I'm sure you have some ideas." Rickie never proposed anything without having a clear idea of exactly what she wanted to do.

"Well, I've always wanted to visit London. I've already checked out all the tourist attractions."

He couldn't help the laugh that bubbled out of his chest. Rickie would change, but it would be a long road. "I bet you have an itinerary already planned."

A blush colored her cheeks. "Seven fun-filled days."

Unable to resist the show of vulnerability, he pressed his lips to hers once again. His hand slid into her hair and he held her neck, loving how she let him control the kiss. *Christ*, he'd missed her. Pulling back, he chuckled. "Seven fun-filled days in London sounds like an expedition to me. Remember how we talked about visiting Hawaii after Chloe was born?"

She ran her hand down his arm. "Sun, surf, drinks on the beach."

He slid his finger down her side, touching the curve of her breast. "Hot nights," he said, his voice husky.

"There are a few things I want to do if we go there."

His groin pulsed at the suggestion in her words. "Oh yeah? What?"

"Remember the first night we were together?"

He almost choked on his own tongue. That night had been magic for him. Something he'd never experienced before or since. He'd relived it thousands of times in his mind, always wishing he could relive it for real. But he'd always worried Rickie would run at the suggestion. "Are you saying that's something you'd like to try again?"

When she nodded, he swallowed. His voice was rough when he spoke. "You are a very cruel woman. How the hell am I going to survive until then?"

"Consider it an incentive." She threw him a saucy grin as she hopped to the ground, favoring her injured foot, and went to see their daughter.

Jamie returned the grin and slapped his hands together. Hot damn! He had his wife back. His woman. His hot *sexy* woman. And seven days wasn't going to be nearly long enough to show her how much he'd missed her. With any luck—and his and Rickie's grit—they'd have a lifetime to enjoy each other. That might just be enough time to explore everything he wanted to do to her. Might just be enough.

PART II

UNDER HIS COMMAND

BOOK 1 OF THE SIX-ALARM SEXY SERIES

CHAPTER 1

Seattle, five years ago

Jamie Caldwell shoved open the door to his apartment, tugging the woman along behind him. As soon as she cleared the door, he kicked it shut, then lifted her up and pressed her back against it. When she licked her lips, drawing his attention to their fleshy plumpness, lust turned his blood to lava. He couldn't wait another minute to taste her, to have her. "You're so fucking sexy," he growled against her throat.

The girl—she'd said her name was Rickie—tilted her head to the side and moaned. The sound vibrated through him, electrifying him. Sliding his leg between hers, he lowered her until she was riding his thigh, her heat scorching him even through his jeans. He pulled her blouse up over her face and paused for a moment, caught by the temptation to leave it across her eyes, before he yanked it off.

Her hips stopped their rocking motion and something flashed in her gaze. Uncertainty? He took her face in his hands and gently touched his lips to hers. No sense in scaring her off.

She wrapped her arms around his neck and pressed herself tightly against him. Taking that as a sign she wanted more, he twisted a hand in her blonde hair and used his grip to pull her head back before pushing his tongue into her mouth. She tasted sweet, like fruit. He'd bet anything she'd been drinking one of those girly vodka coolers at the party. On her, he liked it. Loved it, even.

When his tongue swept over hers, the groan that escaped her lips sent a jolt of arousal from his mouth to his cock. If he didn't get out of these jeans soon, he'd be stuck waiting for his hard-on to go away. And as long as she was around, that wasn't happening.

Setting her on the floor, he took her hand and drew her down the hall to his bedroom. He didn't have much in the way of furniture, but the sturdy four-poster custom-made king bed from Caldwell Fine Furnishings had been the first item he'd bought when he'd moved in. She eyed the bed curiously, then ran her hand over the smooth wooden footboard. "Wow, I didn't expect this."

What didn't she expect? Good furniture in a firefighter's house? Anger started to get the better of him, but then he remembered that she didn't even know what he did for a living. Before bringing her home, he'd made sure she wasn't a fire bunny. He'd had enough of those to last a lifetime. Taking a deep breath, he pushed the chip off his shoulder. "What do you mean?" he asked.

"I didn't expect to be making love on a Caldwell original." She grinned and turned to him. "My own bed is from IKEA. This is going to be a treat."

He wanted to smile, to respond to her teasing, but first, he needed to be sure she didn't know who he was. "How do you know it's a Caldwell?"

"My roommate. She couldn't stand the dorm beds, so she replaced it with hers from home. She literally spent hours telling me why Caldwells were the best and showing me how to identify them."

"So you're still in school. How old are you?" Shit. If she wasn't at least twenty-one, she was going home.

Her chin jutted out. "I'm old enough."

"How. Old."

"Almost twenty-two, okay?"

Phew. "What are you studying?" he asked, keeping his tone conversational. If the lady wanted some chitchat before they got serious, so be it.

"Pre-law, here at UW."

His brows flew up. "You want to be a lawyer?"

Her smile fell and she turned away. "Only if I can get in with a scholarship. The money I make working at the cafeteria certainly won't pay for law school." She chuckled then, but it sounded strained.

Jamie knew all about financial woes. The Caldwell clan had grown up happy, but they'd never had any excess cash. When Grandpa Bill died, Jamie's father had taken over as CEO of Caldwell Fine Furnishings. Unfortunately, he'd always been more interested in the latest chair design than in the bottom-line, so the company had struggled. Although Jamie's parents had encouraged him to get a degree, he'd dropped out and joined the SFD to pitch in with his younger brother William's tuition. Helping William become a CPA had been the right decision for the whole family and for the business. William was slowly whipping the company into shape, and when their dad eventually stepped down as CEO, everyone expected William to take his place.

Jamie slipped his hands around the girl's waist, enjoying the feel of her smooth flat stomach, and ran his tongue along the side of her neck. Her breath hitched and her nipples pebbled through the baby blue lace of her bra. "Maybe you just need to find yourself a rich husband who can make all your dreams come true," he murmured, using his breath to tickle her skin. Her shiver was his reward.

"Someone like you?" she asked and pushed her ass against him.

He snorted. "Hardly." After six years in the fire service, he made decent money, but no one would ever think of him as rich.

She squeezed her hand between their bodies and stroked his erection. "Speaking of hard…"

That was all the urging he needed. He spun her around and brought his mouth down on hers in a demanding kiss. The taste of her did crazy things to his body. His heart raced as though he'd just run up the practice tower in full gear, and he could barely think with wanting to be inside her.

He lifted his head and backed her up until her legs hit the bed frame. Before they started, he had to make something very clear, just in case there was some truth to their joking. "Tonight is for fun. No strings, no expectations, no limits. Agreed?"

Her eyes clouded for a moment before she nodded. "Agreed."

The word was barely out of her mouth when he gave her a little push to make her fall back on the bed. She was still gasping when he grabbed the waistband of her jeans and yanked them off her legs. The matching blue panties drew his attention. Placing his hands on her thighs, he drew them apart. She made a slight show of resistance, but gave that up when he frowned at her. Through the delicate material, he could see the shadowed outline of her folds, but no dark hair showed through. Was she truly blonde? Or shaved? Either would work. He grinned. "Take off your bra."

When she sat up, her legs drifted together. He tapped her right knee. "Keep your legs open."

Her eyes widened, but she did as he asked. The movement transfixed him like the unwrapping of a long-awaited gift. His gaze wandered up to her chest and focused there while she undid the bra clasp at her back. What tumbled out took his breath away. Perfectly pale, perfectly rose-tipped.

"Do you know how pretty you are?" he murmured.

She shook her head and started to close her legs again, but when she looked up at him, she stopped herself. Good, she was catching on.

"Lie back," he said. After she complied, he slid two fingers into the sides of her panties and tugged them down to expose her. The very narrow, very fine strip of pale hair left the outer pink lips clearly visible. How would she taste? He was more than eager to find out.

When he finished removing her panties, she immediately spread her legs wide. He smiled and rewarded her by kneeling between her thighs and tracing his finger along her silken folds. "You have a gorgeous pussy."

Her snort caught him by surprise. "You don't think so?" he asked.

"First, it's not gorgeous, and second, I hate that word."

"Pussy? What else should I call it? Crotch? Mound?" His mock-shudder made her laugh. The low throaty sound had him imagining what noises she'd make when she came. Christ. His cocked pulsed against his zipper.

"I guess there is no good word for it. But men use pussy in such a vulgar way. It's always turned me off."

With the tip of his finger, he massaged the V along both sides of her clit. The tender skin gleamed with her juices, and she writhed beneath his touch. "You don't seem turned off to me." A blush bloomed on her cheeks. She really was too cute. He continued his exploration. "Let's see. It's soft and warm and furry, and it likes to be petted. When you do it just right, you even hear it purr." He ran his finger up to her clit and circled around it.

"Mmm," she closed her eyes and moaned.

"Sounds like a pussy to me."

Her lids popped open and her gaze shot to his face. She answered his grin with one of her own. "You do have a way with... words,

Jamie." She licked her lips and arched her back. "But we'd better get this show on the road. I'm pretty close to the edge already."

Was she now? Little Rickie was going to learn that, with him, orgasms had to be earned, and she hadn't earned hers yet. Far from it. He stepped back from the bed and undid his jeans, letting his cock pop free. She sat up and watched as he wrapped his hand around it and stroked its length. "Want this?" he asked.

She swallowed and cleared her throat before answering. "Y-yes."

"Then come and get it."

Rising from the bed, she crossed the few feet over to him and stopped. When she reached out to touch him, he shook his head. "On your knees." The words tore out of his throat, thick and hoarse with need.

He waited for her to follow through on his command before removing his jeans and boxers. He tossed them onto the chair by the window then went back to her, placing the head of his cock so that it barely touched her glistening lips. A drop of pre-cum escaped. Her tongue peeked out from her alluring mouth and she licked up the bead with one broad swipe, a satisfied smile on her face. His knees shook with the strength of his arousal.

Who was this woman?

To hide his surprise, he wrapped a hank of her hair around his hand and tugged until her head fell back, then he moved in close. "Suck me. Deep."

෮ 🎥 ෬

This night was going to kill her.

Erica Madden gripped the sheets on Jamie's Caldwell original bed and turned her face into the pillow, clenching her teeth to muffle her screams—screams of ecstasy. She'd come so many times, she'd lost count. All she could do was lie there limp and satisfied.

But Jamie had other ideas.

He flipped her onto her stomach, then wrapped an arm around her waist and pulled her hips up so her ass was pressed against his cock. His still very hard cock. "On all fours, baby," he ground out, the raw hunger in his voice like the rasp of a tongue along her spine. She shivered and wondered how he could possibly expect her to keep going.

Something soft and cool slid over her eyes. "What's this?" she asked, reaching for it.

"Shh... It's just a blindfold. To heighten your senses."

Like she needed her senses heightened? He'd already taken her places she'd never been. "I'm not sure about—"

His hand smacking her butt cheek completely derailed her train of thought. "Did you just slap me?"

"That was a spank. Now turn around." He tied the scarf over her eyes, plunging her into darkness.

She really should resist, tell him to stop. Something. But she didn't. "Okay. Why should I let you spank me?" she asked. So far this night had been like nothing she'd expected. Jamie was skilled and unpredictable. And she was genuinely curious.

"Because you love it." His fingers trailed down the crease between her cheeks and dipped into her. Her body convulsed, pushing against his hand to take more of him. What was it about fingers that felt so darned good?

Another smack, this one a little harder, had her trembling. "See how wet you are? How good it feels?" he said.

He was so right. His hand, brushing her butt, was cool in comparison to her heated skin. And his fingers deep inside her found that most sensitive of spots, massaging it in tight circles.

With the scarf covering her eyes, she lost all perception of time, of place, of self, of everything except the enthralling sensation of his fingers stroking inside her and the low rumble of his voice. She could go on like this forever.

She moaned in protest when he pulled his fingers out of her, but she sighed in pleasure when he replaced them with his cock. He wrapped one hand around her hair and tugged until she arched her back, then he pulled her in tight against him with his other hand, his fingers grasping her hip.

In this position, he seemed even longer—impossibly long—as he glided in and out of her, the occasional swivel of his hips driving her crazy. Her breath hitched when he released her hair and his hands cupped her breasts. His strong fingers teased her nipples with light flicks of his nails before he caught the tips between his knuckles and squeezed. Gently at first. But as the speed of his thrusts increased, so did the pressure on her nipples.

"I can't take anymore!" she cried.

"You can and you will. You'll take everything I give you."

Yes! She clamped her lips together to keep from shouting out her answer as he tweaked and pulled on the tight peaks, making her walk that fine line between pleasure and pain. Yes, he was right. She would take it all, and if she didn't stop herself, she might even beg him for it.

Deprived as she was of sight, her sense of touch increased. Every slip, every slide, every heated caress became her only connection with the world, with reality. What was this man doing to her? She'd always enjoyed sex, but she'd never experienced anything like this before. It was a mind-blowing, full-body experience. Maybe even a life-changing one.

Tension coiled inside her. Eager now, almost desperate to reach the edge and jump over it, she rocked her hips against him, urging him to go deeper, faster. He spanked her again. Blood rushed to the spot, and her juices flowed. She groaned, the pleasure almost unbearable. What was wrong with her that she wanted him to do it again?

He pushed her face into the pillow and pressed a burning hand on her back to keep her in place. "Stay."

His gruffly spoken command echoed with his desire, his arousal. Jamie was clearly on the edge right beside her. As his cock slammed into her again and again, the pressure built higher and higher. Was this what heaven felt like?

Just as she thought she'd die from the intense sensations, she felt him swell inside her—could he really get any bigger? She contracted her pelvic muscles and screamed into the pillow as a powerful climax sent her soaring. Jamie continued to grip her hips and pound into her, extending her orgasm, catapulting her into another one.

He plunged into her several more times, shuddering with his own release. Her knees gave out under his weight and she dropped onto the mattress. He followed her down, but before she could be crushed under his weight, it was gone. Where was he?

"Come here," he whispered, rolling her over and pulling her into his arms.

༄ ༀ ༂

Erica woke feeling trapped. Something heavy pressed across her stomach and her legs. And even though her eyes were open, she couldn't see a thing. Her heart thundered in her chest as she tried to get her bearings and recall where she was, what had happened the previous night.

Jamie.

When she remembered what they'd done, her face burned and her *pussy* quivered. Maybe he was right about that word. The way he'd said it, the tone of his voice—the reverence—had made it sound almost... cute.

One of her hands seemed to be stuck, but the other was free. She brought it to her eyes and felt the silky material. Jamie had blindfolded her that last time they'd made love. Correction: they'd fucked. And she'd loved every minute.

Realizing she must still be at Jamie's apartment, she yanked off the blindfold. And there he lay: his dark hair too short to be ruffled, his closed lids hiding baby blues, and his jaw relaxed in sleep. He was tall, tanned, beautifully muscled, and sprawled over her, as though he wanted to keep her near. She shook off the stupid romantic notion. He'd made it clear last night—no strings, no expectations, no limits. They'd certainly managed that last requirement. Now it was time for her to fulfill the first two by leaving before he woke up. Mornings after were uncomfortable. Not that she'd had many, but this was one she preferred to avoid.

Maybe she could find out where he worked or where he hung out and arrange a chance encounter. If they met again under more normal circumstances, she'd see if he was still interested in her. Last night had been fantasy-shattering. She could only wonder what it would be like to get to know him, to take things slow and see where the relationship went.

Carefully, she eased his arm off her stomach and slid sideways, freeing her legs. When he made a noise, she froze and waited to see if he'd awaken. Luckily, he rolled onto his side, away from her, liberating her trapped arm in the process.

She paused for a moment to admire his sculpted back and what it had felt like to run her hands along all that restrained strength. This was the first time she'd slept with someone more than a year or two older than she was. Not that he was ancient or anything, but after him, every guy at school would seem like a boy. Jamie was a man in his prime and he'd proven that to her over and over again. Her entire body tingled just from the sight of him.

Spinning around, she grabbed her discarded clothes and tiptoed out of the bedroom to the sunny living room. Her shirt lay on the floor near the door. As she fastened her bra and pulled her blouse on, some pictures on the wall caught her attention. This might be her only chance to discover the identity of this man, this sexual paragon.

A photograph of Jamie in a spiffy navy blue uniform drew her like a magnet. Was he a cop? She peered at it closely and read the inscription on the badge. SFD. Jamie was a firefighter. In a rush, their conversation from the previous night came back to her. No wonder he'd been so insistent about knowing her age. He probably thought she was one of those women who threw herself at firefighters, hoping to land a husband. The men made good money and had great benefits. How could he not think she was one of them after what she'd said in response to his teasing about finding a rich husband to pay for her school? *Someone like you*, she'd said.

She needed to leave. Right away.

But as she stepped into her panties, she noticed a photo of Jamie with his arm around a young woman who gazed up at him, love shining in her eyes. The photo appeared recent. All residual arousal left her body in a cold rush. Did Jamie have a girlfriend? A wife? She twisted, taking in the rest of the room, searching for signs of a feminine touch. Her heart dropped when she spotted the plant on the coffee table, the colored cushions on the sofa.

Damn. Damn. How could she have been so stupid? Too busy drowning in her attraction to him, she hadn't even *asked* if he was involved with someone. *No strings, no expectations.* His words made perfect sense now. Fuming, she squirmed into her jeans. He'd used her. Good thing she'd told him her name was Rickie, and he didn't know her last name. He'd never be able to track her down, even if he bothered to try.

No matter how great he was in bed, she knew she'd never be— could never be—more than a one-night stand for someone like him. She deserved more. She deserved better.

CHAPTER 2

Seattle, present day (two weeks after the Seattle Quake of 2014)

Jamie dragged his tired ass into the fire station kitchen to grab a cup of hot coffee. Regular infusions of caffeine were the only way he'd make it through the rest of the night. Spotting Hollywood with his head in the fridge, he paused. "What're you doing here?" They'd all been working around the clock since the quake two weeks ago, but Hollywood was supposed to be off tonight.

"Captain asked me to come in and finish the paperwork on the inspections we did this week." Hollywood closed the fridge and set a carton of milk on the counter. "The mayor's breathing down the chief's neck and—"

"The captain's breathing down ours. Yeah, I know. I've got a mile-high stack of reports on my desk," Jamie finished. The quake that had almost killed Rickie and Chloe—that had almost killed them all—had left the city in shambles. The rescue team, all four shifts, was responsible for inspecting every building in the SoDo district. After that, they'd branch out and assist other teams throughout the city.

Hollywood angled his head, seeming to study him. Jamie wiped his mouth, wondering if he had something on it. "What?" he barked. Hollywood could be so fucking exasperating. When he stared that way, Jamie had no idea what he was thinking.

"Didn't you have the night off yesterday?" Hollywood asked.

"Yeah, why?"

"Cause you look like shit."

Feeling heat race up his neck, Jamie turned his back on his friend and got a mug out of the cupboard. He looked like shit because last night for the first time in almost a year—since Rickie had asked for a divorce—he'd made love to his wife.

Hollywood's chuckle had him reeling around. "I get it now," he said, slapping Jamie on the shoulder. "How does it feel to be back in the saddle, so to speak?"

"You're such an ass, Hollywood," Dani said as she entered the kitchen, cementing Jamie's embarrassment. His sex life was the last thing he wanted to discuss in front of Dani, even if she and the entire team had heard way more of the Caldwell family drama than they should have the night of the quake. Sex was something you just didn't discuss with female team members. Since he was Dani's lieutenant, it could even be considered harassment.

Hollywood shrugged. "I'm just trying to wake him up. He looks like the walking dead."

Jamie snorted and brushed past Dani. "I'll be in my office." As he walked down the hall to the officer's room, their bickering made him smile. Dani could shovel shit with the best. And Hollywood definitely qualified.

Setting his coffee on the desk, he dropped in his chair and stared out the window as images of last night filled his mind. Rickie had been so fucking sexy in the blue negligee she'd worn. After almost a year of doing the solo tango, he'd been so hot for her—so incredibly turned on—they hadn't even made it to the bedroom. Thankfully Chloe had been sleeping over at his parents' place.

His hardening cock had him shifting in his seat. Christ. He'd never get enough of Rickie. He loved her independence, her intelligence, her ability to do whatever she set her mind to. Ironically, these very qualities had led to their separation. But they were back together now. Things were *supposed* to be better between them. So why weren't they?

A knock on the door startled him and he almost spilled his coffee on the keyboard. "What?" he snapped.

"What's your fucking problem?" Hollywood grumbled as he crossed over to the second workstation and threw himself into the chair.

"Sorry. I guess I'm a little on edge."

"Why? You should be on cloud nine." Hollywood propped his feet on his desk, a frown creasing his brow. "Getting back with Erica was what you wanted, right?"

Jamie scrubbed the stubble on his cheeks and heaved a sigh. "It was. It *is*."

"Then what's the issue?"

"I think I already pissed her off."

Hollywood laughed. "Now that's not hard to believe." Then he sobered. "Is she mad that you've been working so much? If that's the case, maybe I can take a few of your shifts."

The big blond lug could be a real bastard sometimes, but he'd give his life to help a friend. And Jamie would do the same for him. He shook his head. "She understands that things are crazy right now. Chloe's only been out of the hospital for a few days, and Rickie's been spending all her time taking care of her." The earthquake had destroyed several floors of the King County Courthouse, including the offices of the Prosecutor's Family Support Division where Rickie worked, so getting the time off had been easy.

"Then what?"

"We had sex."

"No shit," Hollywood said, his tone slimy with sarcasm. "How do you fuck up make-up sex?"

Jamie groaned. "I don't know, man." But somehow he had. Royally. "I even apologized." Remembering the disappointment on her face made his chest hurt. She'd just stared at him, her eyes growing more and more distant.

Hollywood threw his head back, his deep laughter making his chair roll away from the desk. His feet hit the floor with a thud. Jamie balled up a sheet of paper and pitched it, hitting the asshole in the head. Hollywood leaned forward with his elbows on his knees, trying to catch his breath. "Did you have an early come-to-Papa moment?" Just asking the question had Hollywood's shoulders shaking with barely contained amusement. "Seriously though, I wouldn't blame you. I don't know how you made it through a year without even looking at another woman."

Heavy reliance on his hand and several tubes of lube. Not that he'd share that with anyone. "I made it up to her, though. Acted like her fucking sex slave." *Shit!* Definitely TMI.

"I'm not seeing the problem," Hollywood said, shaking his head.

Picking up a pencil that lay on his desk, Jamie twirled it between his fingers while he tried to put into words what was bothering him about last night. He'd made Rickie come, but... How did you admit to your best friend that your wife just wasn't that into you anymore? He swallowed and forced the words past his dry lips. "I don't think she enjoyed it."

What the fuck was wrong with him? He glanced up at Hollywood, expecting to see derision on the guy's face. Yeah, he knew he was acting like a girl.

"None of it?" Hollywood asked, his voice gentle.

Christ, now Hollywood was treating him like one. He held up his hands. "The first time was a complete"—disaster—"blur. I don't know how she took it."

After the earthquake, Rickie had hinted that she'd like to relive their first time together. So last night, he'd taken her up against the wall, hard and fast. But that had been all about him. He'd been too revved up by her suggestion, so blind with lust, with wanting to be buried deep inside her, that he didn't know, didn't care if she'd enjoyed it. He'd gone too far.

Hollywood rubbed his chin, making him look oddly analytical. "And then you apologized?"

Jamie wanted to disappear, to evaporate into the ether. He didn't talk about stuff like this. Ever. He pinched the bridge of his nose and exhaled. "Yeah."

"What did she say?"

And there was the kicker. "Nothing. She didn't say a fucking thing."

"How did she seem?"

"Annoyed, disappointed. Like I hadn't lived up to expectations."

Hollywood's hand came down on the desk with a loud thwack that made Jamie jump. "That's it!"

Jamie rolled his eyes. "Yeah, I know. That's why I said I was sorry."

"You're my friend and all, man, but sometimes you act dumber than shit. Now listen. I've had my share of women"—he shined his nails on his shirt—"so I'm a bit of an expert." Ignoring Jamie's loud snort, Hollywood continued. "Let's try this on for size. You have sex. It's fast and furious because you're so turned on by your wife, so hot to have her. Then after what was for you no doubt fan-fucking-tastic sex, you turn to her and beg her forgiveness."

Yep, that pretty much summed it up. Jamie nodded.

"Did you ever think maybe she *liked* that you wanted her so much you were out of your mind?"

No. He hadn't considered that at all. The second time had been all about her. Hard and fast became slow and easy, and he'd made sure she'd enjoyed herself. But Christ, it hadn't been easy, and he couldn't help but wonder why. Was she regretting her decision to call off the divorce? He massaged his chest. He couldn't go through that again. Rickie and Chloe were his life. "Even if that were the case," he said, frustration deepening his voice. "I treated her right the second time. She shouldn't be upset."

"Maybe she likes it rough."

Jamie scowled. "Watch your fucking mouth. That's my *wife* you're talking about."

Hollywood shrugged. "Just saying."

Closing his eyes, Jamie massaged his temples and reluctantly admitted the truth. Rickie *did* like it rough. Well, at least, she *had* liked it rough. "The night we first met, the sex was a little… wild. I know she liked it. But after we got together, she shut me down whenever I went there. I don't understand why." Seeing such an incredibly strong woman submit had taken him to a level of sexual fulfillment beyond anything in his experience. He knew she'd enjoyed it too. But for some reason, she'd rejected his attempts to dominate her after that first night. And she'd never explained her reasons.

"Some chicks think it's wrong to like it any way but slow and tender."

"Fuck."

"Yeah."

"Got any suggestions, Mr. Expert? I'm at a complete loss."

Hollywood grinned. "If at first you don't succeed, try, try, try again, my friend."

Swiveling his chair around, Jamie faced the window and lost himself in the view of Seattle's downtown. Maybe Hollywood was onto something. Although long repressed, Jamie's Dom instincts told him Erica had relished every moment of their first time together. But if she liked his dominant side, why had she gotten so upset the other night? He needed to sit her pretty ass down and have a much-needed chat. But the circumstances had to be right. It was time for their long-delayed honeymoon.

His cock jumped to attention at the possibilities. Images flashed in his mind of what he could do to Rickie, what he *had* done to

Rickie. As discreetly as possible, he adjusted the bulge at his crotch. Fucking Hollywood had better be fucking right. Their conversation had him wondering. And remembering.

೮♋ 🚌 ଓ

"And then the beautiful princess jumped on her motorcycle and pointed to the nerdy but handsome prince. 'Get on,' she told him. As soon as he sat behind her, she revved the engine and they sped off down the road, away from the evil queen."

Chloe clapped her hands. "And they lived happily ever after, right, Dani?"

Erica's heart squeezed, hearing the happiness in her daughter's voice. Her gaze rose, taking in the woman sitting next to Chloe. Dani. The woman who'd saved her daughter's life. The woman whose wistful tone indicated she was thinking of another nerdy but handsome man, Erica's brother-in-law, William.

"You bet they did, sweet pea," Dani said with a grin. She touched her finger to the tip of Chloe's nose then kissed her cheek. "Sleep well."

"Will I see you tomorrow?"

Erica stepped forward and tucked the blankets around Chloe's small body, careful not to jostle her leg. "You know Dani's busy at work with Daddy."

Chloe scrunched up her face. "But she tells good stories. I want to hear more."

Dani laughed. "I'll do my best. Okay, Chloe?"

Chloe smiled, but her eyes were already drooping. "Okay."

"Chloe..." Erica prodded.

"Oh, yeah. Thank you, Dani." Reaching up, Chloe curled her fingers around Erica's ears and kissed her nose, then her chin, each cheek, and ended with her forehead. When she was done, Erica did the same to her. It was their special goodnight ritual and Erica cherished it.

"Goodnight, sweetheart. I love you."

"I love you too, Mommy."

Dani stepped into the hall and Erica followed her, closing the door behind them. "Want some tea?"

"Got any coffee?" Dani asked, stifling a yawn. "This work schedule's killing me."

"Of course." Erica led the way to the kitchen and started a fresh pot while Dani took a seat at the table. "Have you had any time off since the earthquake?"

"I'm off tonight and Jamie made us all take a full day last week, even though he only took one night off himself. How are you holding up? You've had a lot to deal with on your own."

Pulling out a chair, Erica sat across from Dani and considered her answer. The night of the earthquake, Dani had probably learned far more about their marriage than she'd ever wanted to know. But the woman had been nothing but kind since then. She'd dropped in almost every day to tell Chloe a story and ask Erica if she needed anything.

Two weeks ago, Erica had mistakenly thought of Dani as the other woman. Now she thought of her as a friend. Something she badly needed. Sure, she had friends. But none of them had husbands whose work was as dangerous as Jamie's. Being a woman and a firefighter herself, Dani had special insight, and it was thanks to her that Jamie had moved back home. And that was a debt Erica could never fully repay.

"I'm okay," she said, projecting a joviality she didn't feel. "Chloe's doing much better. The doctor said she could start walking around on crutches in a few days."

"Do they make crutches that small?" Dani asked. "Seems like only yesterday she was crawling. Rug rats sure grow fast, don't they?"

"Tell me about it. Good thing she's light. If needed, we'll keep carrying her around until she gets a walking cast." The coffee maker buzzed, letting her know it had finished brewing. She got up and poured two cups before setting them on a tray along with cream and sugar.

When she placed the tray on the table, Dani picked up one of the pink Limoges cups with both hands. "Aren't you afraid to break these? They look like antiques."

Erica finished adding cream to her coffee with a chuckle. "Antiques or not, they're meant to be used. Stop worrying."

Still sporting a dubious expression, Dani blew on the hot liquid and took a sip. "This is good. Very good. Thanks." She took another sip then met Erica's gaze dead on. "I saw Jamie at work last night. He didn't look so hot."

Could she talk to Dani about this? She really wanted to. Erica averted her gaze, trying to hide her distress.

Dani covered Erica's hand and gave her a small smile. "I'm a good listener."

As though a faucet had been turned on, Erica's eyes filled with tears and all her pent-up fears spilled out. "I thought things would be different now. But they aren't. We're barely talking. We certainly aren't communicating. I really want our relationship to get better, but I don't even know where to start."

"Jamie wants this too. He was devastated when you asked for a divorce."

"Not because he loves me."

Dani frowned. "What other reason could there be?"

"He feels guilty."

"About what?" Dani asked. Then her lip curled and she grabbed Erica's arm. "Jamie didn't... he didn't... if he did, I'll kill him for you."

It took a moment for the implications of Dani's disjointed, unarticulated question to make sense. She gasped. "God no. Jamie would never hurt me." *Even when I want him to.*

Dani dropped her hand and sat back, visibly relieved. "Okay. Good. They say you never know a man until you live with him. So I had to be sure, you know, in case." She brought the cup to her lips and sucked down a big gulp.

Great. Some hostess she was. Now even the unflappable Dani was embarrassed. "We shouldn't talk about this."

"No. I'm sorry. I would have sided with you no matter how much I respect Jamie at work. Some lines can't be crossed."

Erica knew what Dani meant, but she wondered what the woman would think if she knew about *that* night, that night she'd been reliving in her dreams for five years.

"So what's this about Jamie feeling guilty? What did he do?" Dani asked.

It was time Dani knew the truth. Assuming Jamie hadn't already told her. "Did Jamie ever explain how we met?" When Dani shook her head, Erica continued. "Jamie only married me because he knocked me up. We knew nothing about each other beyond our names. Our first names, that is."

Eyes widening, Dani grinned. "Hot damn. You and LJ had a one-night stand."

"You don't have to look so shocked," Erica said.

"It's nothing against you, hon. It's just that you've always seemed so... proper." She waved her hand up and down, indicating Erica's outfit: beige silk blouse with navy slacks, three-inch pumps.

Okay, so she wasn't Lady Gaga. "Point taken," she said. "But in this case, the truth lies below the surface. As they say, you can take the girl out of the trailer park, but you can't take the trailer park out of the girl."

"Trailer park? Really? I can't imagine it."

"I did live in one. And it rubbed off on me. Look how I ended up: twenty-one and pregnant."

"Oh, come on, Erica. It was a mistake. You were just a kid. Jamie's what, six years older than you? If anyone is to blame, it's him."

"Which is why he feels guilty. He did his duty and made a respectable woman out of me. Unfortunately, we never had the happily-ever-after. Heck, we never even had the happy-right-now."

Dani pushed her cup to the corner of her placemat. "Let's back up a bit. You and Jamie met, had a night of fun"—she tapped her index finger on the table, punctuating each point—"and you ended up pregnant." She sat back and opened her arms. "Big deal. A lot of marriages start with an oopsie. And I know Jamie loves being a dad."

Regret made her stomach cramp. Chloe had always been a priority for Jamie. Until Erica had started pushing him out of their lives. No matter how much she wanted to, she could never give them back the time she'd stolen from both of them. "He's a wonderful father."

Dani threw her a sharp look. "You're not planning to kick him out again, are you?"

Erica shook her head. Even if Jamie didn't return her feelings, she'd never do anything to jeopardize his relationship with their daughter. "I won't do that to him—to them—again."

Dani shifted in her chair and supported her chin with her fists, her expression thoughtful. "Erica, what's going on? You both seemed so happy after the quake. I know Jamie's been working a lot, but we'll be going back to our regular shifts soon. Maybe you just need some time to get used to living together again."

A tear rolled down Erica's cheek and she hurried to wipe it away. She had no right to cry about this. Women would kill to share Jamie's bed, including that fire bunny bitch, Belinda.

"Oh, hon." Dani leaned over and hugged Erica, smoothing her hair like she always did to Chloe when she was crying. "What's got you so upset?"

"If I tell you this, you need to swear never to repeat it."

"What, like a blood oath? Better be juicy."

"Oh, it is."

Dani held up her right hand. "Cross my heart, hope to die. If I lie, stick a needle in my eye." She dropped her hand and smiled at Erica. "Is that good enough?"

Twisting her hands in her lap, Erica kept her eyes down. "When Jamie had the night off, we made love, and…" Her breath hitched and she couldn't continue.

"I promise. This is just between you and me."

The sympathy in Dani's voice only made Erica feel worse. But she knew Dani was right. Mountains always seemed more scalable with help. "It was our first time since we got back together. I was so happy, so hopeful. I wore something sexy and greeted Jamie at the door when he got home. And it was great at first. Better than great, even."

"Sounds awesome so far."

She probably shouldn't be talking about this with Dani since the woman did report to Jamie. But she really needed another woman's advice. She wanted her marriage to work. She took a deep breath and steeled herself to tell Dani the worst of it. "It was wonderful. Until he *apologized.*"

"Apologized? For not being around?"

Erica threw her hands up. "See, you're as confused as I was. He apologized for the sex. For being in a hurry. For 'nailing me against the wall' as he put it."

"Oh my." Dani tried to hide her laughter with her hands, but she couldn't keep the twinkle out of her eyes. "What did you say?"

"What could I say?" Frustration made Erica's voice sharp. She took a deep breath and let it out slowly. "I wanted to punch him, to scream, to leave. Anything so I wouldn't have to see his face and that damn contrite expression."

"Maybe he thought you didn't… uh… how can I put this? *Enjoy* it?"

Erica waved that away. "Oh, I know he didn't even realize when I uh… enjoyed it. He was so far out of his mind, we could have had another earthquake and he wouldn't have noticed." And that's what she'd liked so much about their encounter. Jamie had been hovering on the brink of his self-control, and she'd done that to him. She'd brought him to his knees. Not by making him do what she'd wanted, but by letting him do what he'd wanted.

"So why didn't you just tell him you'd had fun too?"

Erica traced the delicate hand-painted flower on her cup. "It's complicated."

"You lost me, hon. Complicated how?"

"You know how Jamie is a real take-charge guy at work?"

"Uh-huh. It's what makes him such a great lieutenant," Dani said.

Erica nodded as she continued to focus on the cup. "The night we met, he was like that... with me, if you know what I mean. And I liked it. No. I *loved* it." She snuck a glance at Dani in time to see the woman's brows rise to her hairline. Erica laughed. "Stop staring at me like that. It's not like I've shown you photos of the mayor's wife stripping at a peep show."

Dani's cheeks colored, but then she grinned. "So, Mrs. Caldwell has a naughty side, does she? Good for you, girl!"

Erica's own cheeks heated. It felt good to admit the truth, but she could never tell Jamie she'd told Dani about that night. He wouldn't understand. He might even be angry, though Dani seemed surprisingly okay with her revelation. It made her wonder what her new friend was into. Poor William didn't stand a chance once Dani had set her sights on him. The thought made her smile. "So you don't think I'm a mental case, then?"

"Do you?"

"I like things a little wild. That doesn't change who I am outside the bedroom."

"Jamie likes to boss you around, and you like to be bossed around. I don't see the problem with a little consensual kink."

Kink. Was Dani right? Was she kinky? She let out a sigh. "He might have a problem with it... now."

"Why? Most guys would kill for a wife who'd let them be dominant during sex."

"Even if that wife shut him down every time he tried?"

"Did you do that?"

Erica took a sip of her tepid tea and grimaced. "Things were really awkward when we first got together. We didn't know each other at all. So, we decided not to be intimate again until after we were married." She waved her hand. "Between preparations for the wedding, construction of our home, and my all-day morning sickness, neither of us had any energy for sex anyway."

"But after the wedding?"

"He seemed determined to treat me with kid gloves because of the pregnancy. After Chloe was born, we were both too tired to be adventurous. And then, I don't know, things changed."

"Changed how?"

"A few times, Jamie got a little excited, things got a little crazy, and I got... scared."

Dani frowned. "Scared? Why?"

"I don't know how much Jamie has told you about my past, but it wasn't pretty. After my father died, my mother had a string of boyfriends. Most were okay, but a few of them were mean bastards. Things always started out nice, but soon, they'd start ordering her around. Within weeks, they'd be smacking her if she didn't get them their beer fast enough. And the noises from the bedroom—" Her body shuddering, she cut herself off from the memories.

"You told me Jamie would never hurt you."

"I know that intellectually. But in the heat of the moment? I mean, what's to stop things from going too far?"

Reaching out, Dani patted her hand. "Erica, you have to trust your judgment. Not all men are like your mother's boyfriends."

Erica sniffed as a wave of regret submerged her. "The worst part is I miss him. I miss the man Jamie let me see that night. The man he tried to bring back before I pushed him away. I rejected him so often that now *he's* afraid to let himself go. And I don't just mean in the bedroom. He never argues. Never insists on anything." Her eyes filled with tears and a sob shook her shoulders. "I have no idea what Jamie sees in me."

Dani grabbed the box of tissues off countertop and placed it on the table. "So what do you think happened the other night? Obviously, you didn't shut him down that time."

"God, no." Erica took a tissue and patted under her eyes. "I thought that finally, finally, we had a chance to get things right, to have the relationship that we could have had. The relationship we *should* have had."

"And you think he apologized because he let go?"

"I've probably managed to convince him that I hate it." Her voice cracked. "God, I'm such a mess. I shouldn't be dumping all this on you."

Dani smiled. "Hey, it's okay. We're friends, right?" Her heart swelling, Erica nodded. "Look, who said women have to be satisfied with missionary style? Sex is just one more way that we express ourselves. You do whatever brings you the most happiness. To hell with anyone who tells you different."

"But what if that someone is your husband?"

"Jamie strikes me as a pretty tolerant guy. I think you're reading more into this than is there. You said it yourself, he just wants you to be happy." Dani pursed her lips. "I feel bad admitting this now, but the night of the quake I accused Jamie of walking on eggshells around you. He's always too careful not to offend you, going so far as to deny himself what he wants. I think this is just one more example of that."

Erica's brain wanted to explode with the truth of what Dani was saying. She'd made so many mistakes with Jamie. "What should I do now?"

"Tell him what you want. Make him tell you what he wants. Put all your cards on the table and see where you both stand."

After the quake, they'd talked about going on a honeymoon that was five years overdue. Maybe they could use that time away from everyone and everything to reconnect. She smiled at Dani. "With my luck, I'll be standing on the opposite side of the room."

Dani grinned back, a sparkle in her eyes. "Not unless he commands it."

ಬಿ 🚂 ೧ೆ

The slamming of the car door echoed in the quiet neighborhood. Jamie shouldered his duffle bag and hoped he hadn't woken anyone up. Hoped Rickie would be sleeping so he could have a little downtime before heading to bed. His mouth watered at the thought of a cold beer and a half hour of TV.

The outside light illuminated the three cement steps and the porch. As well as the deep cracks that bisected the steps. Had they been there before the earthquake? Sighing, he mentally added the repair job to his already long to-do list. He really needed a vacation. Good thing he'd already spoken to the captain about it. As soon as they went back to their regular shifts, he could take a week off. And since he'd finished the last of the reports for the SoDo district building inspections, that should happen in a matter of days.

Careful not to make any noise, he unlocked the door and pushed it open, grimacing when it made a loud squeak. One more task for his to-do list; put WD-40 on the hinges. He stepped inside and shut the door, pausing for the first time since he'd moved back in to absorb the sights, sounds, and smells of the house he'd bought right after learning he was going to be a father, the house he hadn't lived in for almost a year. It felt strangely familiar and foreign all at once.

Most of the family photos that had lined the staircase leading to the second floor had been replaced with pictures of Erica and Chloe. In the living room, his favorite chair, an old recliner he'd rescued when his parents had remodeled their house, was still there. But Erica had done some remodeling of her own. His chair, which had enjoyed a prime spot right in front of the TV, was now pushed up against the wall, squeezed into a corner. Worse, there wasn't even a line-of-sight to the set.

His chest tightened a little when he noticed one of Chloe's picture books and her Little Mermaid blanket lying on the seat, evidence that his daughter had missed him as much as he'd missed her.

Rickie had made other changes as well. Some subtle, others not so much. Most of the rooms had been repainted and she'd hung artsy prints, doing away with their vintage movie posters.

In the dining room, she'd gotten rid of the new china cabinet he'd given her on their third anniversary. In its place stood an antique Caldwell cabinet. For all he knew, it had been crafted by the first James Caldwell himself. Looking at the collection of fragile teacups and pots that filled the shelves, he felt like an overgrown, undereducated gorilla.

The house was cool and classy. Just like Rickie. *Christ.* The woman had erased him almost completely. At least she'd kept the bed. Then again, she'd admired it from that first night. His cock jumped at the memory, and he groaned.

"Jamie?"

Head shooting up, he spun around and tried to pretend he hadn't just been imagining her naked.

Erica stood in the doorway to the kitchen, a dishtowel in her hands, a smile absent from her pretty face. "I didn't expect you home tonight," she said, her tone cautious. Distant.

Fire raced through him, galvanizing his veins. Was she with someone? "Am I interrupting something?"

Erica scowled and bunched the towel in her hands. "You can be such a jerk."

Before he could reply, she showed him her back and marched to the sink. Her movements were stiff and jerky as she finished drying a pot and placed it in a lower cabinet. After shutting the door with a bang, she threw the towel on the counter and leaned against it, hanging her head.

The sight of her, so upset, sent guilt slithering over his skin like dirty oil. He went to her and put a hand on her shoulder. "I shouldn't have said that."

She sighed and turned to face him. "No. It's good that you asked. It's bad that you think I would cheat on you." When he opened his mouth to deny it, she put her finger on his lips. "And just for the record, since meeting you, I haven't slept with another man. Heck, I haven't even kissed anyone else."

Thank God. Every day of the year they'd been apart, he'd worried that she'd find someone else, someone better.

Removing her finger, she cocked her brow. "Can you say the same?"

The loaded question boomeranged him right back into the guilt-zone. They'd never discussed what either of them had done during the month between when they'd met and when she'd shown up on his doorstep, pregnant. He shoved his hands into his pockets, and tightened his jaw. "No. I can't."

Her eyes filled with hurt. "I suspected as much. But I really hoped I was wrong. Who was it? Oh!" Her eyes flashed and her hand flew to her chest. "I really shouldn't assume it was in the past."

What was she talking about? "I swear to God, Rickie. I've *never* cheated on you."

The tension lines in her forehead eased, and he was able to breathe again. "What did you mean, then?" she asked.

"After you left that first time, I tried to track you down, to see if you might be interested in more. But only knowing you as Rickie, and not knowing your last name, I didn't get far. When I couldn't find you… I went on with my life. Then you came back, and since then, there's been no one else."

"I can live with that," she said, and her smile filled his chest with warmth.

He ran his fingers through her hair, stopping to caress the curve of her ear. "Me too." Tonight, God had given him what he'd needed by making him talk with Rickie and not what he'd wanted by letting him escape with TV and a beer. And he couldn't be more grateful. He leaned in to give Rickie a kiss. With Hollywood's advice in mind, maybe he could make up for their disastrous reunion night.

Before his lips touched hers, she pushed against his chest with both hands. "Jamie. We need to talk."

Stepping away from her, he raked his fingers over his scalp, trying to massage away his problems. He let out a bitter laugh. "Didn't we just do that?"

She gripped the countertop on either side of her hips and her gaze hardened. That particular expression had always meant Erica was digging her heels in. She was going to rip him a new one. "We managed to iron out one issue from five years ago. You really think that all our problems are solved now?"

At this rate, he'd die of old age before they got to their current problems. Jamie crossed his arms and widened his stance to keep from crumbling under the weight of her disappointment. It sapped his energy like running up forty flights of stairs in full gear. "I'm too fucking tired to rehash our entire lives tonight."

Just the thought of facing off with her made him feel sick. He swung open the fridge and reached for his long overdue beer. When his hand closed on air, he leaned in to look. Shit. That's all he'd wanted tonight: one goddamn beer. He shut the door to check the magnetic notepad they'd always used to make the grocery list. Sure enough; the top sheet was gone. "Where's the Redhook? I know I put it on the list."

"Oh. It's in the garage."

She'd left his beer in the heat? "Why on earth would you put it there?"

Her expression fell and she smoothed imaginary wrinkles on her blouse. "I... I didn't like how it cluttered up the shelf." When she wrapped a strand of hair around her ear, the one he'd been caressing mere minutes ago, he saw her fingers tremble. "I know. That sounds incredibly selfish. Here, let me get the box."

Before she could leave, he stopped her with a hand on her arm. "Don't bother. Warm beer tastes like piss."

She yanked her arm out of his hold. "I said I was sorry."

Actually, she hadn't. But making her feel bad wasn't what he wanted. "Listen. That didn't come out right. I'm dead on my feet, and I'm acting like a Neanderthal. How about we get a second fridge and put it in the garage? That way, all the bottles and extra stuff can stay there."

"We don't have to do that," she said, hugging her waist. "I'm just being a baby."

Maybe a bit of a perfectionist, but it was one of the things he liked about her. It balanced his complete lack of order. "I love that you alphabetize the cans and shelve things in the fridge by height."

The prettiest shade of pink tinted her cheeks. "You're teasing me."

He ran the back of his hand along her jaw. "Maybe a little."

"Can I get you something else?" she asked with a smile. "You probably want to relax in front of the TV for a bit before bed."

"What do we have?"

"Coffee, tea, hot chocolate, white wine, red wine." She hesitated in her enumeration when he grimaced. "Uh… I think we still have some of that root beer you used to like. Although I don't know what's the shelf life on that."

"It'll be fine with some ice."

"Are you hungry?" she asked, opening the fridge. "I could make you a sandwich."

Was it bad that he was enjoying having Rickie serve him? It felt wrong and so damn right at the same time. "That would be nice. Real nice."

She shooed him toward the living room. "Go settle in while I get this ready."

"No hurry," he said, walking back through the dining room to the attached living room. Dropping onto the couch, he set his feet on the coffee table. The chrome edges dug into his calves, so he tucked a cushion under them. Much better. He palmed the remote, then sat back. Not good. His neck arched over the top of the couch and his head rested on the hard wall. He groaned and looked longingly at his recliner, which at the moment, seemed like a symbol of his manhood: out-of-place and relegated to a distant corner.

The night of the earthquake, he'd told Rickie things would have to change if they got back together. He knew one of those things was him. As Dani had so artfully put it, he needed to man-up. If he continued to bottle up his wants and needs, and let Rickie control everything, they'd be right back where they'd started.

In a flash, he was on his feet. He pushed the love seat that had taken the place of his recliner over to the far wall, opposite the couch. Then he carefully set Chloe's book and blanket on the coffee table and picked up his chair, setting it back in its rightful place—dead center on the flat screen.

With a satisfied sigh, he grabbed the remote off the couch and stretched out in the recliner, even raising the footrest. After punching in the channel numbers for ESPN, he put his hands behind his head and moaned with unadulterated pleasure. He was so fucking happy to be home. To be in his chair, watching his television.

A few minutes later, Rickie appeared beside him, tray in hand. Her head turned as she scanned the room, obviously none too pleased with the changes he'd made. He cleared his throat. "I rearranged the furniture a bit."

"I can see that."

"Does it bother you?" It pissed him off to even ask, but if this marriage was going to get a fair shake, he and Rickie needed to start communicating.

She surveyed the room before meeting his gaze. "I like that you put your chair back. This is where it belongs. Where *you* belong."

"But...?" She hadn't said the word, but he knew it was hiding there, like the missing piece of a puzzle that changed everything.

She pointed to the loveseat. "I don't like the loveseat there." Turning, she indicated the front wall with the large bay window. "Maybe we could try it over here?"

His relief left him feeling like a wuss. So to prove his manliness, if only to himself, he jumped to his feet and in a matter of seconds, he'd moved the loveseat. Together, they stood back to admire their efforts. In the silence, his heart began to race. When she finally said, "I like it," he gripped her around the waist and pulled her down onto the recliner with him.

She laughed and the sweet sound of it started to fill the emptiness that had plagued him for the past year. He tightened his hold on her waist and smoothed his hand up the outside of her leg. "Now that we're done decorating, there's something I want to discuss with you."

"I thought you said you were too tired." She gave him a freezing look.

"Too tired to fight."

Her lips thinned. "I see."

He shifted her on his lap and pressed her head against his shoulder. "You'll like this."

"Just a minute." She picked up his root beer from the tray and took a sip. With a grimace, she handed him the glass. "I hope I like what you want to discuss better than I like this crap."

He laughed, then downed half the root beer, enjoying the cool mix of vanilla and spices. It wasn't Redhook, but it would do in a pinch. Okay, enough stalling. He set the glass down on the corner table. "Remember you said you wanted to go on a honeymoon?"

Mid-way to reaching for his sandwich plate, she stilled. After taking a sharp breath, she grabbed the plate and sat up. "I remember."

"Captain said I could take my vacation."

"When?"

"In a few days."

"So soon?" A spark of anxiety flashed in her gaze. Was she having second thoughts?

"Any reason why not?"

She stared at the plate in her hands. "Chloe's not walking yet."

"I'm sure my mother can take care of her. You're still okay with that, aren't you?" The night of the quake, she'd agreed to let his parents watch Chloe more often, including when they went on their trip.

"Of course. But check with your mom. It may be more trouble than she'd anticipated when she agreed."

"No problem." He knew his parents would be thrilled to have Chloe stay with them for a week. They'd consider it a chance to make up for some of the time they'd lost when Erica had refused to let them help out.

He took a bite of his sandwich and watched the thoughts play out on her face. "What's got that sweet forehead of yours scrunched up like that?"

"Are we still going to Hawaii?"

"Oahu. A full week of fun in the sun. I'll make all the reservations." He was pushing her boundaries by taking control of the planning. He studied her reaction.

She bit her lip and toyed with a piece of crust that had broken off from the sandwich. "What are we going to do there?"

He slid his hand up her hip. "Have lots and lots of sex." His stomach fluttered. *Christ.* He felt as giddy as a little girl.

When she glanced away, the fluttering turned to cramping and the sandwich threatened to come back up. He took the plate from her hands and set it on the table beside his root beer. "Talk to me."

"What happened the other night..."

He turned her face, forcing her to meet his gaze. "I already apologized for that."

Her eyes welled, and he felt like shit. Could Hollywood possibly be right?

She ran her hand along his jaw, the rasp letting him know he had far more than a five o'clock shadow. "The sex. It's one of the issues we need to talk about."

"So talk." The roughness of his voice shocked him. *Christ, Caldwell. Get a handle on your ego before you drive her away.* Rickie pushed off his lap, the cold emptiness reminding him of the year he'd spent without her.

He rose from his chair and stopped in front of her, bending at the knees so they were eye level. "I really want things to be okay between us, babe."

"I know. But this isn't the right time to get into this discussion. You're tired and I'm too emotional."

"Fair enough. When?" It had better be soon. For a year he'd been starving without her, and that one night they'd shared had barely been an appetizer.

"On the trip. We'll be alone then. Rested. No excuses."

"No excuses," he agreed, the words grating his throat. If they could get through this, their honeymoon would be a week in paradise.

If they couldn't, it would be a week in hell.

CHAPTER 3

"This is so beautiful." Erica spun in a circle, taking in the beach cottage Jamie had rented for their stay. They entered into a large sitting area. Up one step, there was a large four-poster bed and a matching dresser. The bathroom was beautifully tiled and had a great sunken bathtub and separate glass shower. It was the perfect spot for their five-years late honeymoon.

Jamie walked to the end of the room to open the glass doors that led to the gorgeous private lanai. She raced past him to see the magnificent view of the ocean. They could have breakfast here every morning while being serenaded by the music of the waves. He came up behind her and circled her waist with his arms. "You like it?"

"I thought we'd be staying in some big stuffy hotel. I never imagined we'd have a cottage right on the water."

"Most of the cottages in this resort are double, but I managed to get us the only remaining *private* one."

His emphasis on the word "private" sent a thrill up her spine as she pictured what they could do here, far from any neighbors. If any place was worthy of a new beginning, this was it. "What do you want to do first?" she asked, her voice breathy.

He chuckled and pressed his erection against her bottom. "Do you really need to ask?"

"I guess not. But shouldn't we—"

Spinning her around, he cut off her words with a hard demanding kiss. He tasted of the cocktails they'd been served upon arriving at the resort. She was running her tongue along his bottom lip, seeking more of the sweetness, when he surprised her by sucking her tongue into his hot mouth. Usually their positions were reversed, with her sucking his tongue. The sensation of being inside someone else's body was exquisite. Was this how Jamie felt when he was inside her?

Jamie groaned in his throat. Without breaking the kiss, he gripped her thighs and lifted her up. Instinctively, she wrapped her legs around his waist and tightened her hold on his neck as he carried her into their room.

When she saw he was heading for the bed, she pulled away. "The curtains."

"Right." He carried her over to the doors where she released the long diaphanous material from the tasseled rope that held it to the side.

With one hand, he undid the buttons on her blouse and pushed down the cup covering one breast. When his firm fingers closed on her nipple, she gasped. Arousal arrowed through her, dampening her panties. She arched her neck and spotted the curtains, still half-open. "Jamie."

He continued to toy with her breast, sucking, nibbling. Driving her crazy, making her throb. They had to close the curtains before it was too late. Before they had sex in front of the people on the beach. "Jamie. Wait."

Releasing her, he raised his head. His eyes were sharp with desire. A shiver shimmied through her.

"What?" he asked. The husky tone of his voice almost had her melting against him and forgetting all about her need for privacy.

She pointed to the gap in the curtains. "We should close them all the way." He blinked as though she'd been speaking Elvish. "People can see us," she added, feeling like an idiot.

Jaw tight, he shook his head and carried her to the far side of the room. He yanked the curtain closed. "Okay, now?"

He hadn't shouted, but she'd detected the undertone of annoyance. Great. This was what she wanted most in her life, and she was going to ruin the moment because of her prudishness.

"Perfect." To get them back on track, she smiled and massaged the base of Jamie's skull in the way she knew excited him.

As expected, he closed his eyes and moaned. "That feels so good."

She nipped his lips and drank in the sounds of his pleasure. His hands seemed to relax as well, and feeling herself slip, she let out an involuntary squeal. Eyes snapping open, he dug his fingers into her legs to catch her, and hiked her up higher. The suddenness of his actions caught her off-guard. "Oh!" she gasped.

Immediately, he loosened his grip. "Did I hurt you? I'll be more careful."

"I'm fine," she murmured against his lips. He spun around and slammed her against the wall. It seemed like a replay of their first night together so many years in the past and of the beginning of their reunion night just a few days ago. She'd hoped Jamie would let her see this assertive side of himself again. And now it was happening. Like the mercury in a thermometer on a hot day, her excitement shot to one hundred in an instant.

He thrust his hips against hers, and the power of it made her head bounce against the wall.

"Fuck," he ground out. His voice was rough, like sand on tender feet. Like a tongue on her engorged clit. She shook and trembled, awaiting his next move. His hand threaded through her hair and delicious little quakes rocketed through her entire body. Was this it? Was he finally going to let himself go?

Tilting her head, he leaned in close, his lips brushing her ear. She quivered and throbbed with need. "Are you okay?" he whispered.

What? His soft-spoken question, so out of place, had her reeling. Everything inside her was screaming for him to quit being so damn solicitous, to get the hell on with it.

"Did I hurt you?" he asked again.

Her patience snapped. "Jamie, please just stop talking."

He pulled back and studied her face for a long moment. She tensed, waiting for his response. How he reacted would set the tone for the rest of their honeymoon.

Her heart started to do a happy dance when he pulled her blouse off and shoved the bra up higher on her chest. Not liking that it impeded his path from her mouth to her breasts, a path she hoped his tongue would take again and again, she let go of his neck and undid her bra, tossing it to the floor.

He remained silent, although he did shoot her a blistering glare that made her panties even wetter. Would he ever get to that part of her they hid? God she hoped so.

When she reached for the snap of his shorts, his hand closed on her wrist like a manacle. Shaking his head, he raised her arm and pinned her hand to the wall above her. Her pulse thudded through her veins, drowning out the sound of the waves crashing onshore. Her insides burned with a fire only he could put out.

His tongue lashed her nipples, circling each one before picking one and latching on, sucking deep. She leaned forward to watch. The sight of her nipple and then part of her breast disappearing between his kiss-roughened lips made the fire roar. She bucked her hips against him, wanting—needing—to feel him inside. Her body cried for him to fill it.

When he moved to her other breast and bit her nipple, she let out a deep moan. His head jerked, colliding with her chin. "Ow!"

"Shit. I'm sorry, Rickie," he said, his eyes filled with concern. "I got carried away and… I didn't mean to hurt you."

Erica wanted to cry. But not in front of him. Jamie wasn't letting go at all. He'd been listening to her every sound, evaluating her pleasure or displeasure. And getting it all *wrong*. Had she brought him to a place where he didn't trust his own instincts anymore?

This had been a mistake. She shouldn't have let herself get caught up in the moment, in the place, in Jamie. She should have insisted they talk and sort out their problems before even attempting to have sex again. "Put me down."

He brushed her hair off her face. "Rickie, I said I was sorry. I won't do it again."

Anger fled and disappointment took its place. He really didn't get it. She shook her head and felt as though she were turning to ash inside. "God, Jamie. Stop. I can't take you treating me like a damn doll anymore."

She pushed on his chest until he released her thighs. Sliding down his body, she noticed his erection was gone. A sob rose in her throat as an immense sadness set anchor in her heart. Could they ever get past this?

As soon as her feet hit the floor, she stumbled over to where her shirt lay, a rumpled rag, and grabbed it. He caught her elbow. "Rickie, stop."

She twisted away and thrust her arms into the sleeves of her blouse, her fingers fumbling with the buttons. "I—I need to get some air."

"I'll go with you."

She held up a hand to stop him. "No. I need some time to think."

"I don't get the doll comment." His expression stony, he turned and walked up the step to sit on the bed. "Just tell me what I did wrong."

"It's not what you did, Jamie," she said, her voice breaking like her heart. "It's what you *didn't* do." With that, she turned and fled from the hero of her dreams, from the star of her nightmares.

ॐ 🎬 ॐ

The thin curtain fluttered back into place, and Rickie's retreating form disappeared from view. Jamie fell back on the bed and closed his eyes, hitting his forehead with his palms.

Fuck. Fuck. Fuck!

He'd done it again. Ruined everything. The bitch of it was, he'd really didn't get how. *It's not what you did, Jamie. It's what you didn't do.* What the hell did that even mean? Enough with the riddles, already! Why couldn't she just tell him plain and simple?

One thing was sure—he was going to kill Hollywood. She liked it rough, did she? He'd repeated exactly what he'd done on their reunion night when he'd taken her against the wall. Right before she'd run off, she'd been melting in his hands. But something had gone wrong. When she'd made that fucking doll comment, maybe she'd meant a rag doll. Maybe he'd been *too* rough. Or maybe he just didn't understand a damn thing about Rickie and what she wanted.

Pushing off the bed, he grabbed a beer from the mini-bar and popped it open. It wasn't Redhook, and he hated drinking from a can, but he certainly wasn't going to get drunk on those frou-frou drinks they served in coconuts with umbrellas. He chugged the can of watery-tasting shit and popped open a second one before dropping onto the couch.

The curtains shifted and for a moment he thought she'd come back, but it was only a breeze bringing in the salty ocean air. Where had Rickie gone? They were on their honeymoon, in one of the most beautiful places on Earth, and they were fighting instead of having blow-your-mind sex. It just wasn't right. Had she expected more romance? Had he come on too strong, too soon?

He took another long swig of his beer. Yeah, he probably should have taken Rickie out for a nice dinner and dancing before bringing her back to the cottage for some mattress mambo. But as soon as their plane had landed, all he'd been able to think about was getting his hands on her lush ass, and sinking his cock into her hot pussy—

Fuck!

Just the thought of taking her made him hard as a damn fire axe. Maybe if he took the edge off, he'd have better control of himself, wouldn't be so damn desperate. Through his cotton shorts, he wrapped his hand around his hard-on and pushed back. He groaned and a shudder shook his body. It felt good. But it wasn't what he wanted.

With a snort of disgust, he let go and raised the can of beer to his forehead. If he could get sex off his mind, he might be able to figure out a way to talk to Rickie. His eyes went to the curtain. Had she expected him to go after her? Shit. One more mark against him.

He stood and started to pace the room, pausing to toe off his sandals. The cool wood felt like heaven on his bare feet. This situation was making him crazy. Even as a teenage boy, he'd never felt this insecure with a female. He rubbed the back of his neck, stiff with tension. Dani was right—he'd changed. Being with Rickie had changed him, and not for the better. The more she'd pushed him away, the more he'd let her. He'd gone against every instinct he had, just to try to make her happy. Some Dom he was.

He'd done this to himself, and it was up to him to find a fix. But introspection had never been his forte, and the idea of visiting the fire-service shrink made him nauseated. If word got out… He didn't even want to think about what would happen.

But there was someone else, someone who knew him better than he knew himself. Reaching back, he fished his cell phone out of his pocket and dialed. "Hey, Mom," he said when she answered on the second ring.

"Jamie?" She sounded confused, surprised. He hadn't expected to be calling his mother during the first hours of his honeymoon either.

"Just wanted you to know we arrived safely. And to check on Chloe."

"Ah. Did Erica ask you to call? Is she regretting leaving Chloe with us?"

"Not at all. In fact, she went for a walk on the beach."

Silence.

"Mom?" He pulled the phone away from his ear to check if they were still connected. They were. "You there?"

"First, Chloe's fine, and she's sleeping. It *is* past nine here."

Shit. His mind was so wrapped up in the fight with Rickie, he'd completely forgotten about the time difference. He glanced at his watch, which he'd set to local time in the plane. Six fifteen. In an hour or so the sun would set. If Rickie wasn't back by then, he'd go searching for her. "That's—" he started.

"And second," she said, cutting him off. "Why aren't you on the beach with her?"

"She... uh...." Like an idiot, he'd walked right into that one. His mother was far too perceptive—and inquisitive—to let his comment slide.

"Something's wrong. I know it."

He started to pace again, and finished off his beer while he did mental gymnastics trying to come up with an answer that wouldn't set off her bullshit detector. "Nothing's wrong, Mom." *Yeah, that should do it, dickhead.*

His mother's amusement came through loud and clear. "You've always been too direct to be a good liar, son. But thanks for the entertainment. Now tell me what's going on."

He pushed the curtain aside and secured it with the tasseled rope. Watching the huge waves rolling in, he felt small, petty even. Why couldn't he and Rickie just talk? After taking a deep breath, he pushed the truth out. "We had a fight."

"Already?"

His chuckle sounded bitter, harsh. So unlike him. "Must be some kind of record, huh? I should call the folks at Guinness. Get into their next book."

"Oh, Jamie. I know how much you want things to work out with Erica. What happened?"

Rubbing the line of pain that reached from his gut to his throat, he stepped out onto the lanai. "That's just it, Mom. I don't know. I do something. I think she hates it, so I do something else. She gets mad. I do the first thing again, thinking she'll be happy. But no. She's mad. Again."

"I'm not sure I want to know the specifics of what you're talking about." He could hear the affection and humor in her voice. Caroline Caldwell deserved a nomination to sainthood for having raised four boys and an incredibly contrary girl.

"Have I changed much since meeting Rickie?"

Empty air filled the line again.

He sat on the foot of one of the padded chaise longue. "It's okay to tell me. I did ask."

She sighed. "You've matured a great deal. You've accepted your responsibilities and settled down. Those are all good things."

"Sure, but by your tone, there's more. Like maybe not all the changes are good ones."

"They aren't."

"Talk to me, Mom. I'm a desperate man."

"And right there is the problem, isn't it?"

Leaning forward, elbows on his knees, he raked his free hand through his hair, as a headache began to pound his brain like a boxer in the ring. Everyone seemed to be talking in tongues. Maybe he was having an aneurysm. "I want Rickie to be happy. That's not a bad thing."

"It's exactly what a husband should want. But why are you so desperate for her happiness, even at the cost of your own?"

"Because I love her."

"There's more to it than that."

"There really isn't. I love my wife. I want her to be happy. End of story."

"Jamie. Lie to me, but don't lie to yourself. There's more to it. Think hard."

"Because I owe her." His voice sounded strangled.

"Now we're getting somewhere." His mother would have made a great psychiatrist. Or military interrogator. "Why do you owe her?" she asked.

His mouth slammed shut and his molars ground together. It would take the Jaws of Life to free the words trapped in his throat.

Seeming to grasp his current inability to speak, she began to fill the silence. "I never mentioned this to you before, even during the divorce, because I didn't think you wanted to know. Perhaps you weren't ready to admit it to yourself. But you know what, Jamie? I think you're ready now, so I'm just going to say my piece. If you want to make things work with Erica—and I believe you do—you need to understand and acknowledge your role in what's happened. So tell me—what do you owe her?"

"Everything!" he blurted. "Christ, Mom. I ruined the girl's life." His volume had risen to a shout. He shot a furtive glance at the area surrounding the cottage, then headed inside. No need to let all of Oahu in on his problems.

"Does she feel the same?"

"Yes." Had they actually ever discussed it? There'd been so much going on at the time, he wasn't sure. He cleared his throat. "I don't know."

"In the five years you've been together, you've never talked about how getting pregnant impacted her life? So you actually don't know anything."

"She had plans, Mom. She was going to be a lawyer. The pregnancy changed all of that. But my life? It continued pretty much according to schedule."

"And you feel guilty about that."

"I'm not a sociopath. Of course, I do."

"Enough to mold yourself into the man you think she wants?"

He thought about that for a moment, then shook his head even though she couldn't see him. "No. Into the man she deserved." His mother's sigh hit his heart like a battering ram. "Whatever you're thinking, I'm not pussy-whipped."

"I never said you were, dear."

If defending yourself against your own accusations meant anything, he was so fucking pussy-whipped. And he'd done it all to himself. *Stupid bastard.* "How the hell am I supposed to fix this?"

"Well, you start by introducing yourself to her. Let her get to know the man you really are."

"I'm not sure I know who that is anymore."

"This might sound harsh, but stop judging yourself by Erica's standards. Because you obviously have no idea what she's thinking or what she wants. Do what feels right and good to *you*. If she likes it or she doesn't, she'll tell you. Don't assume anything."

He leaned his head against the wall and groaned. "That's not going to help. Even when I ask her, I don't understand the answer. The words are all English, but they don't make any damn sense."

Her laughter eased some of the pain in his head, some of the ache in his chest. "Erica is a good woman. Listen to what she doesn't say and you'll be just fine."

Christ. He'd gone and jinxed himself. Why were women so fucking complicated?

༄ 🚌 ༃

Erica approached the cottage from the side. As she rounded the corner and the lanai came into view, she froze. Her heart gave a hard thump, then contracted painfully.

Dressed in black shorts and an unbuttoned short-sleeved shirt, Jamie sat at one of the deck chairs, a sight to behold. The setting sun sent rays dancing over his golden skin, creating caramel highlights in his mahogany-colored hair. Like a fine wine, her husband had only improved with the passing years. Age and hard physical work had enhanced the edginess in his features: the cut jawline and the sharp blade of his aristocratic nose, a reminder of his British ancestry. The whiteness of his shirt against his tanned skin emphasized the breadth of his shoulders and the strength of his chest muscles.

Her gaze flowed down to his flat stomach and ridged abs. Abs that begged to be licked. She swallowed and ran her tongue over her dry lips.

Legs stretched out before him, he lounged in the deck chair. The position put on display his powerful thighs and calves, the result of vigorous exercise and innumerable trips up and down the practice tower.

With reluctance, she brought her gaze back up to his face. Dark sunglasses denied her his amazing Caldwell blue eyes, but saved her from his piercing—no doubt, accusing—glare.

Steeling her resolve, she stepped up onto the lanai. Jamie's only acknowledgement of her arrival was a slight tightening of his lips. She pulled out a chair across from him and sat on the edge, her hands cradled in her lap. She hadn't been this nervous around him since that day she'd sought him out, pregnant and alone. He'd had all the power. Had he chosen, he could have turned her away. Many men in his position would have.

This time, things were different. This time, she had all the power. But only if she grabbed control of the conversation. Inhaling deeply, she filled her lungs to capacity, before slowly releasing her breath. Jamie continued to stare out at the ocean, ignoring her. "Jamie, can we talk?" Okay, not quite the power play she'd envisioned. She tried again. "I mean, we *need* to talk." There that was better.

He slowly turned to her, the tinted lenses making it impossible for her to read his mood. On the other hand, the stiffness of his posture and the turning in of his lips told her plenty.

She pushed some more. "We need to talk about what just happened. About what happened on our reunion night."

His face as unmoving as a statue, he made a tiny "go-ahead" gesture with his hand, as if she weren't worth the effort of movement or conversation.

She huffed in annoyance. "I can't do this alone."

"No?" His brow arched over the rim of his glasses and his mouth curved into a smirk. "You've proven you're quite good at doing things alone."

Erica closed her eyes. She deserved that dig. Jamie was tough, but she'd pushed him, hurt him, over and over this past year. But despite everything, he'd only shown his pain to her twice—the night of the earthquake and right now. "I've handled a lot of things very badly where you're concerned, Jamie. I'm sorry about that. But it doesn't change the fact that we have serious problems. Problems that have to be resolved before we can move forward." She flicked a glance at him. He was watching the water, his manner dispassionate, disinterested. It made her blood pressure rise. "Problems that aren't all mine," she finished, her tone sharp.

"Ah, so this is going to be a what's-wrong-with-Jamie lecture. No thanks."

She threw her hands in the air. "That's not it at all. I just want us to talk, *really* talk. No judgment, no recriminations. Let's lay everything on the table so we can figure out how we can fix"—she waved her hand between them—"us. And this isn't just about what happened in there. The sex is just a symptom, a casualty, of the fact that we can't seem to communicate anymore. If we ever even did."

Steepling his hands in front of him, he ran a finger over his lips. "You want to talk? Fine. You want us to put our cards on the table? Fine. But I go first."

"Fine." She folded her arms across her chest. When he flicked off his sunglasses and stared at her arms pointedly, she sighed and laid them on the armrests.

He picked up his beer and tilted his head back as he finished it off. When he lowered his face, she was caught off-guard, floored by the turmoil boiling in the depths of his eyes, as impenetrable as the ocean. "Let me start by saying that I'm fully aware that getting pregnant on our one-night-stand ruined your life. Don't get me wrong, I love our daughter, but if I had to do that night over again, I'd have made sure to protect you better."

Two sentences that said more than he'd said in the entire duration of their marriage. "You didn't ruin anything. I got pregnant, that wasn't your fault. We used condoms, and neither of us noticed one break."

"But did we use one every time? I honestly don't know." He pinned her with his gaze. "You made me so crazy. All I could focus on was you."

When she blinked, he turned away.

Her heart stuttered, then took off at a harrowing pace in her chest. The intensity of his stare had robbed her of breath. "Uh... it was the same for me."

He jerked his eyes back to hers. "Explain."

"Seriously? I came so many times, I almost went blind."

A sexy grin softened his expression, melting her insides. "If I recall correctly, you *were* blind at the end."

Heat raced to her cheeks, but she couldn't keep from smiling back. She'd cherished the memory of their night together. Replayed it so many times in her dreams. Sometimes when she and Jamie were making love, she'd fantasized about the blindfold he'd tied over her eyes. Wishing he'd do it again. It had been a guaranteed orgasm. She squeezed her trembling thighs together and became aware that his grin had fallen. Her continued silence seemed to unnerve him. It was now or never. "It was the best night of my life."

"Because of Chloe, you mean."

She shook her head. "Because of you."

He laughed, sounding pained. "You can't possibly mean that. Hooking up with me that night was probably the dumbest thing you ever did."

"You really have no idea, do you?"

"None whatsoever." He scrubbed his stubbled cheek. "Afterward, I kept wondering if you'd been drunk and I just hadn't noticed."

"I was stone-cold sober. Why would you have thought otherwise?"

His lips quirked up for just a moment before flattening again. "Rickie, you were studying to be a lawyer. I'm just an idiot who runs into fires and falling buildings. You're a proper lady. You have style and organization. I'm loud, crass, and it's a hallmark day when I can find the remote without tearing the living room apart."

Snorting, she sat back and crossed her arms. This time when he glared at her, she ignored him. "A proper lady? What is this—the nineteenth century? I grew up in trailer parks and people's basements, anywhere my mother could stash me while she went on another bender."

He leaned forward and started to extend his hand as though he wanted to take hers. But then he let out a breath and straightened. "That's just circumstances and poor choices on the part of the adults who were supposed to take care of you. The person you are now? That's who you were meant to be, minus the law degree."

"You make it sound like we're two different species. If I'd known you felt this way, I'd have made a point of leaving wet towels on the floor."

"Sarcasm doesn't sound good on you, *honey*."

"I did my best to compromise."

"Maybe. But the house looks just like you now. There's nothing of me left."

"I kept the recliner."

He snorted. "How kind."

She rubbed her forehead. This conversation wasn't going how she'd intended. "Do what you want with the house. I don't care about any of that."

"What do you care about, then?"

"Us, Jamie. I care about us. I care about Chloe having two parents who love each other."

"Do you, Rickie? Do you love me? You said you did, but emotions were running high after the earthquake. And honestly, I'm not seeing it."

"What are you seeing?" His gaze turned to the ocean, and a terrible fear clutched her heart.

"I'm seeing a woman who is very confused about what she feels and what she wants. A woman who pushes me away with one hand and pulls me to her with the other. A woman who now claims that the first time we had sex was the best of her life, but froze up like a popsicle stick whenever I acted even remotely the same way."

"I… No, Jamie… I…"

"What do you want from me, Rickie?" He sighed, a horrible tired sound that echoed the depths of his frustration.

She blew out a breath, prepared to take the blame she deserved. All of this was her mess, her fault. "I want you to love me. Not because I got pregnant and gave you Chloe. But because you like who I am. Even if I am neurotic."

"I love your brand of crazy. I love *you*."

"You keep saying that."

"Because it's the truth."

"No. It isn't. It can't be."

His hand curled into a fist on the tabletop. "I wouldn't say it if I didn't mean it. Besides my family, I've never said that to another woman."

"I don't understand how you can love me."

"That's your problem, not mine, Erica." His use of her full name took her aback. Anger seethed from his pores and coated his words. "The real problem is and always has been that you don't trust me. I understood that in the beginning. You had no reason to trust me back then. But I've worked hard to be a good husband and a good father. And until I went to Indonesia on that search-and-rescue mission, I thought our marriage was pretty damn great."

His admission had butterflies fluttering in her belly. "It would have been great, Jamie, if you had trusted *me*."

"I did. I do."

"You can't possibly trust me after everything I've done."

"The night of the earthquake, I trusted you enough to let you take the place of a firefighter and save our daughter."

"Those were extenuating circumstances. You didn't really have a choice."

Reaching out, he ran his fingers over her hand. The gentleness of his touch had hope welling in her chest. "Maybe what's really going on here is that you don't trust yourself," he said.

She frowned at him and shook her head. He was wrong. "God, Jamie. You took me in when I had nothing and no one. And what did I do to repay you? I made you feel bad about who you are. How can you love or trust me after all that?"

Yanking his hand away, he growled. "What the fuck are you talking about? I don't feel bad about who I am."

She flinched at the curse and instantly regretted it. Jamie thought her enough of a prude already. "That first night, you let me see a side of you I've rarely seen since. That's on me."

"It was supposed to be a one-time deal." He shrugged as though to brush it off, but his features hardened.

"How does that matter?" she asked.

"No woman wants to marry a man like that."

"I thought you weren't ashamed of who you were."

"I wasn't. Not until—" He clammed up.

"Until I pushed you away. And that's my fault."

"I should have been more sensitive, once I knew your background." He pressed his palms against his eyes for a moment. When he lowered them, he asked, "Had you ever done anything like that before?"

"I wasn't a *virgin*."

"What we did wasn't vanilla, and you know it. Was it the first time or not?"

"Yes. Okay? Yes, it was. So what?"

"You were young, naïve, and horny. A very combustible combination." He smirked. "You experimented, let yourself go *because* you never expected to see me again."

Ever the hero. Always taking the blame. "You didn't force me to do anything, Jamie."

He raised his brows. "I never gave you much choice."

"Listen. First time or not, if I hadn't wanted to do the things we did, I wouldn't have. I stopped you today, didn't I?" There, that ought to be clear enough, even for him.

"Yes. Let's talk about that."

"Gah! Are you really this dense or are you just being difficult?"

"Use real simple words," he said, his jaw tight.

"You are such a frustrating man. Let me be very clear. I stopped you because you were being too nice. I might like fine china, but that doesn't mean I want to be treated like it! I *like* sex a little rough, a little bit"—she swallowed and decided to use Dani's word—"kinky. Deal."

Jamie pushed his chair back and stood, looking at her like he didn't recognize her. "I don't fucking believe this."

Erica watched, utterly bewildered as he turned his back on her and marched inside the cottage, taking her heart and her hope with him.

ಸಿ 🚋 ಲ

Of all the things he could have imagined, hearing Rickie say she *liked sex a little rough, a little bit kinky*, was dead last. In fact, it wasn't even on the list. After that first night, every time he'd acted the least bit dominant with her, she'd stiffened and fear had crept over her features, making him feel like a goddamn rapist. And now she was telling him she liked it rough? Liked it kinky? Fuck.

He strode into the bathroom and locked the door behind him. *Kinky.* As soon as the word had left her lips, his cock had instantly given her a salute. A movie reel of all the adventures they could have shared over the years played in front of his eyes, making him pant. Sweat beaded his forehead and a most incredible sensation wound in his belly, a building pressure that signaled he was spiraling out of control. *Take it down a notch, Caldwell.*

His hand drifted down to the bulge in his shorts. He needed to rub one off right now before he burst through the door and drove her into the mattress.

A knock on the door.

"Jamie? Are you okay?"

Like a teen caught charming the one-eyed snake, he dropped his hand to his side. "I'm fine," he said, his voice rough. Guilty.

"Are you... um... coming out?"

Hell yeah, he wanted to come out. In. So deep inside she'd feel him push against her heart. "Give me a minute. I'll be right there."

After listening to her walk back to the sitting area and switch on the television, he opened the tap and splashed cold water on his face, willing his loose jimmy away. He took his time, even used the toothbrush and toothpaste provided by the resort. He'd been so anxious to have Rickie, and then after she left, he hadn't felt like unpacking. All he'd wanted was a beer and time to think. He'd resolved to follow his mother's advice—tell Rickie how he felt about his own responsibility, beg her to give him another chance, and try to rediscover who he was. Who he'd become.

Kinky. With that one word, Rickie had thrown a Halligan bar into his carefully thought-out plans. With that one word, who he was, the man he was—it all became crystal clear. She'd set the stage and he needed to act. If he went about this the right way, he could have everything he'd always wanted.

He had to take it slow. Draw her in with care. His poor wife had no idea what she'd set in motion, but he'd make sure she never regretted it.

His face dry, his dick in its place, he rolled his shoulders and opened the door. With a few steps, he was in the sitting area. He stopped in front of Rickie. She switched off the set, but made no other move.

All right. Good start.

He was so excited, so fucking joyful, it was all he could do not to grin like a boy in the Nerf section of a toy store. *Slow down, Caldwell.*

"If that first time was so damn special, why did you nun-up every time I got a little demanding with you?" Until they had this figured out, there was no way he was going any further. He wasn't risking that kind of hurt again.

She crossed her arms and rubbed her throat with one hand. "I was scared."

Christ. He recoiled in horror. "Of me?"

She dropped her head forward. Her hair shielded her face, and he didn't like that. He lifted her chin up. "Eyes on me."

Swallowing hard, she met his gaze. "I was afraid that you'd turn into Mr. Asshole."

"Mr. Who?"

"That's the name I used for my mother's boyfriends." Her eyes blazed and whiteness ringed her mouth. "At least the violent ones. The ones who'd talk dirty and slap her around. Who'd punish her with kicks and punches whenever she was too slow or did something they didn't like."

Jesus. He'd known things had been difficult for her growing up, but he hadn't known her mother had been abused. Then a sickening thought speared though his gut. He crouched down in front of her. "Did any of them ever... *touch* you?" He'd kill any fucker who'd so much as laid a finger on her.

She squeezed her lids closed and shook her head. "It came close a time or two, but Mom always managed to distract them."

Thank God. Patting her knee, he stood back up. "This certainly explains a lot. I wish you'd told me earlier."

"It wouldn't have mattered. I don't think I was as afraid of you turning into Mr. Asshole, as I was of me turning into my mother. She *let* them do those things to her."

He walked back to the couch and sat beside her. "Your mother was a substance abuser. She let them hurt her because they fed her addiction, not because she liked it."

"But that's just it, Jamie. I liked it. I *liked* when you spanked me. I'm exactly the same as her. Maybe she started out liking it too. And then things went too far and she couldn't stop it anymore."

Pulling her against his chest, he stroked her back, her hair, her arms. He could feel her body tremble beneath his hands. "What those men did had nothing to do with pleasure and everything to do with power. I'd never do anything you didn't want. And I'd never let things go too far. With me, you don't have to be afraid of what you like and what you want."

She clung to him as though he were a life raft. "I really want to believe you, Jamie. I want to trust you."

"And yourself."

"And myself."

"I have an idea that might help us get there." But first, he had to make sure they were on the same page. Her kinky might be his vanilla. "Tell me. What exactly about that night did you like?"

She looked up at him, her eyes wide and innocent, so much like they'd been the night they'd met. And despite the seriousness of what they'd just discussed, his cock hardened.

"I liked what we did," she whispered.

Could she be more cryptic? "Give me specifics."

"It wasn't so much the 'what'. It was more the 'how.'"

"Details, Rickie." His tone was firm. Low. Exactly the tone he'd used with his subs in the past.

She sat back and jutted her chin out, and he almost smiled at the show of resistance. "I liked the way you spoke, the words you used, the way you touched me."

He stood up and took a few steps. "Do you know what BDSM is?"

Her eyes flicked to her suitcase before returning to him. Hmm. He'd have to find out what she had in there later. "Whips and chains? People who like pain when they have sex?"

"Uh... not quite. It's a combination of bondage and discipline, dominance and submission, and sadomasochism. They're lumped together like that because many times, people who like one, like them all. I'm different. I'm not into the last one. But the rest?" He stepped closer and leaned over her, boxing her in with his arm on the side of the couch. When he was an inch from her ear, he murmured, "Those are a definite turn-on."

He felt her shiver as much as he saw it. He stepped back, pleased to see the spark of arousal in her eyes. She licked her lips and his belly flipped. Rickie was even sexier now than she'd been when they'd met. She'd gone from a girl to a woman, and he loved every inch of her.

"You have experience with all of that?" she asked, her voice shaky.

Pulling one of the chairs closer, he sat, his knees touching hers. If he wanted her trust, he had to be honest with her. Bare his past. Bare his soul. "There's a lot you don't know about me, about the time before I met you. About my... women." He'd almost said subs, but she wasn't ready for that. Not until he explained about the lifestyle and why he was no longer a part of it.

"I know you had your pick of fire bunnies." Her lip curled up just a bit at the end. Just enough to let him know she didn't like that idea at all.

Biting back a grin, he said, "I wouldn't say that."

"Come on. You're a hot, hunky firefighter. That's why I was so surprised when you hit on me at that party."

"So you think I'm hot?" The question made her blush, and the grin he'd been trying to hide burst out.

She bent her neck, hiding her face with her hair again. "You know I do."

With his finger under her chin, he raised her face. "You have no idea how beautiful you are." He murmured the words while winding a strand of her hair behind her ear. He loved her ears, so delicate and perfect, with the little diamond studs she preferred.

After giving him a small smile, she pulled away. "Tell me about the women."

"You sure you want to hear this?"

"Well not all the gory details. Just what's relevant to our discussion."

Twisting sideways on the couch, he studied her. He was going to have to tell her about Andrea. That was the only way she'd really understand where he was coming from. And his limits. "I've been involved in D/s relationships before. Most were short-lived. But one was more serious."

"D... s?"

Step-by-step. He had to remember she was new to all of this, and the last thing he wanted was to scare her off. "Dominant and submissive."

"Obviously, you were the dominant."

He smiled. "The only time I've ever been even remotely submissive has been with you."

"Why would you do that?"

"It's because of what we talked about before. I felt guilty for what happened, for getting you pregnant, and I wanted to make you happy."

She sighed and shook her head. "I liked you just fine that night. I think our relationship would have gone a lot better if you hadn't tried to change for me. Tried to become someone you aren't. I know I pushed you a lot, but I expected you to fight back, to show that you cared. But you just seemed to check out."

"I'm starting to get that."

"So, about these dominant and submissive relationships?"

"I'm telling you this because I want you to understand what I like and what I'm willing to do. After, we'll need to talk about your side of things." When she nodded, he continued. "I met Andrea at a club that specializes in BDSM. We hit it off right away. We agreed on some conditions and after signing the contract, I became her Dom."

"Hold on. A contract?"

"I don't know how legal these things are, but a lot of people in the lifestyle like the idea of a contract, because it forces the Dom and sub to make everything clear. It establishes a framework for the relationship that both parties feel comfortable with."

"Contract, framework, parties. I don't hear anything about love in all that."

"D/s relationships aren't usually about love, Rickie. They are about two people getting what they need, sexually."

"I see. Is that what you wanted with me that night?"

He laughed. "No. I could never see you as part of the lifestyle. You're way too pure."

When her expression turned mulish, he laughed again. "No need to be insulting," she said.

"Believe me, I meant that in the best way possible. I like you exactly the way you are. The world of BDSM can be very ugly. It isn't for people who just want to experiment. You have to *be* the lifestyle, not act it."

"Did you see any of this ugliness?"

"I'd never judge anyone. People have different needs and what's right for one might not be for the other. That's what went wrong with Andrea. I like—no, I love—controlling my partner's sexual gratification. It turns me on like nothing else. But part of a true D/s relationship also involves punishment. If the submissive doesn't follow the rules, her Dom has to punish her. Now don't get me wrong, I'm not against inflicting pain when the return in pleasure is greater. But I just can't hurt someone for the purpose of giving them pain."

"Is that what she wanted, this woman?"

"It is. Andrea was a masochist."

"So by hurting her, you were giving her pleasure?"

"That's what she said. But it wasn't the kind of thing I like to do. *I* wasn't getting any pleasure from it. The final straw was when she had me whip her with a Viper. She'd had it specially made with blood knots and metal tips." He rubbed his stomach. Just the memory of that day made him feel sick. "I'll never forget the welts across her back and legs, her stomach and her breasts." *The blood.*

Rickie pressed a hand to her mouth. Clearly the idea didn't seem all that appetizing to her either. Thank God. He wasn't sure what he'd have done if she'd seemed excited by this. "Why would she do that?" she asked.

"She wanted me to mark her. Some subs like having marks that remind them of their Doms when they're apart. Again, I'm not judging. It's just not for me."

"So this is one of your limits?"

"Absolutely. I gave my subs just enough pain to push their limits, but always to increase their pleasure."

"But if you never punish, how did you make them do what you want?"

"I'm a great believer in positive reinforcement. When that's not enough, a little orgasm denial goes a long way."

Her eyes rounded. "That's what you did to me that night!"

"It was. And it worked."

She gave him a wide smile. "If we do this, do we need a contract?"

"Babe, we already have one. It's called a marriage."

"How do you want to handle it then?"

"I don't want a true D/s relationship with you, Rickie. When I was with Andrea, she wanted a full-on D/s relationship. Even though we didn't live together, she expected me to dictate everything she did, everything she ate, even what she wore. Let me tell you, it was exhausting. She'd call me when I was dragging my ass to bed after twenty-four hours straight on the job to ask if she should wear her red skirt or her brown slacks. Do you know how little I give a shit what someone wears to work?"

They shared a smile, a memory. "You even let Chloe pick her clothes when she was a toddler," Rickie said.

A load of anxiety rolled off his shoulders. He took her hand, running his thumb over the blue veins visible through the thin skin at her wrist. "We'll play this by ear, and I'll give you information as we go so you aren't overloaded and overwhelmed. The key is trust. You need to trust that I'll never do anything you don't want to do, or that I don't want to do. And I have to trust that you'll tell me if I push you too far. Without trust, this won't work. Our marriage won't work."

"When do we start?" she asked, giving him a coy glance.

Lust coiled in his groin and his cock wanted him to shout, "Now. Right the fuck now." But before they could start, he had some shopping to do.

Plan your work and work your plan.

He pushed up from his chair and got his night clothes from his suitcase. "We start tomorrow."

And if his plan was going to mean diddly-squat, he needed a cold shower. He caught a glance of Rickie lost in thought. Her eyes were bright, her color high. His cock shot to full attention, reiterating its earlier mantra: Now. Right the fuck now.

The water had better be ice cold, because he was fucking volcano hot.

CHAPTER 4

"Housekeeping."

Stretching her hands above her head, Erica luxuriated in Jamie's touch. His hand moved up her leg, igniting little flames with every inch closer to her thigh. Almost involuntarily, her knees spread in invitation. She kept her mouth closed, knowing he'd prefer it that way. But her mind screamed for him to hurry, to touch her where she needed him most.

"Housekeeping."

The insistent voice distracted her and the spinning in her belly unwound, the moment ruined. With a groan, she patted the bed beside her, refusing to open her eyes. "Jamie? Someone's at the door."

When there was no response, she sat up and rubbed the last remnant of sleep from her eyes. Seeing the empty space beside her, she frowned. Where was Jamie? She felt fingers on her leg again. Her eyes shot to her thigh, where a small brown lizard-like animal was making steady progress northward. "Ahhh!" she screamed, knocking it off her leg and jumping to the floor. "Oh, my God! Jamie!"

Knock. Knock. "Housekeeping! Ma'am, are you okay?"

Adrenaline sending her heart into overdrive, she scooped up her robe and raced to the door, pausing only a moment to peek through the peephole. A middle-aged woman in uniform stood outside. Erica swung the door open, holding the robe against her chest. 'There… there was something in my bed," she said, trying to catch her breath.

The woman marched over to the bed and smiled. She picked up the beast and held it so Erica could see. "Just a little house gecko, ma'am. They eat bugs, not people."

"Good to know." Now that the critter was safely in the woman's hand, Erica could admit it was kind of cute, with its big unblinking eyes and bright red tongue. In a reptilian kind of way.

"I'll take him outside while I get your tray."

"My tray? There must be a mistake. I haven't ordered anything."

The woman pulled a notepad out of her pocket. "Caldwell, cottage six?"

"Yes. Okay, my husband must have ordered." The bathroom door was ajar, and the room clearly empty. Why would Jamie order breakfast, then leave?

Returning with a cart, the woman rolled it into the sitting area and pushed open the thick night curtains. "Would you like to eat on the lanai?"

"That would be lovely," Erica said, opening the glass doors. "It's so beautiful out here."

After setting the tray on the table, the woman wheeled the cart back inside. She pointed to Jamie's pillow and grinned. "Looks like your husband left you a love note."

Nearly tripping over her robe, Erica rushed across the room to grab the note. As she unfolded the paper, the woman said, "Enjoy your breakfast, ma'am. I'll be back later to collect the tray and clean the room." With that, she made her exit, shutting the door behind her.

Note in hand, Erica sat on the edge of the bed and read.

Mrs. Caldwell,

I've ordered you a light breakfast. Eat, have a bath. Do your hair and make-up. You are to wear only a loose sundress, and strappy heels. Nothing else.

Take your time getting ready, but meet me at exactly 12:30 in the gardens by the resort lobby. Use your sunscreen. We're going for lunch and a walk on the beach.

Don't be late.
—J.

He'd addressed the note to Mrs. Caldwell. Why? She'd have to ask him about that later. Walking out to the lanai, she removed the lid from her plate, revealing small muffins and a mound of fruit. Her mouth watered at the array of exotic scents and colors. A thermos of hot coffee accompanied the breakfast. She poured herself a cup and mixed in some milk and sugar, her mind returning to Jamie's note.

Given its authoritative tone and that fact that he'd given her no choice in their plans, Jamie had already slipped into his new role. And he'd expect her to slip into that of a submissive. Should she balk or go along with it? It had been her idea, and the payoff would be extraordinary if she could have the old Jamie back.

She didn't really mind him telling her to have a bath and wash her hair. She'd have done that anyway. But what was the bit about the dress? Last night, he'd been abundantly clear that he didn't want to be in charge of her clothes. That he didn't care what she wore. The cup mid-way to her mouth, she hesitated as she replayed his earlier words in her mind. Correction: he'd said he didn't care what she wore to work. This wasn't *work*. She shivered in anticipation. No. This was *play*.

The dress and heels. Only. The very idea of wearing nothing under her sundress made her wet. Did Jamie know she'd react this way? Probably. What else did he know? She couldn't wait to find out.

Before the adult games could begin, she had a child to check up on. Retrieving her cell phone from her purse, she dialed the number to Jamie's parents' house. Her mother-in-law answered with a laugh. "Jamie, honey. I already told you. Everything is fine."

A smile teased Erica's lips. More evidence of what a wonderful father her husband was. "Caroline, it's me, Erica."

"Erica. I'm sorry. I saw Caldwell on the caller ID and well, I didn't expect..." She trailed off.

Erica could count on one hand the number of times she'd called Jamie's parents. She'd pushed them away, like she'd pushed their son away. "Caroline, I want to apologize again to you and Liam. Regardless of what was going on between me and Jamie, I shouldn't have let it affect your relationship with Chloe. I hope someday you can forgive me."

Dead silence had Erica squirming in her seat. Had she made things worse by bringing up the past? She could have ignored it and gone from there. It was more her style. But she was turning over a new leaf, and ignoring the past had always done her more harm than good. She opened her mouth to explain further when Caroline cleared her throat.

"I won't deny that I was hurt when you wouldn't let us see Chloe. She's my only grandchild, and I missed out on more than a few of her milestones. From the day Jamie brought you home, all I've wanted was for you to feel included, a part of the family. I'm sorry that we didn't succeed. But let's try to change that. I'm here for you, whenever you need me."

A tear rolled down Erica's cheek. Those were words she'd never heard, would never hear from her own mother. But now she had Caroline, and with some work, maybe they could be friends. She picked up the linen napkin and wiped her cheeks dry, then took a deep breath to ease the constriction in her chest. "I've learned some things about myself recently, things I don't like very much. Things I'm trying to change. If you'll allow it, I'd like for us to be closer. Maybe we could go on an all-girls shopping trip with Chloe and Victoria."

"I'm ready whenever you are, honey," Caroline said, her voice rough with emotion.

"Thank you." Chloe was so lucky to have Caroline as an example of what a strong, capable woman should be. They were all lucky. "So is my daughter being a good girl for you?" She took a bite of mango, the sweet juice easing her raw throat.

"Ah, she's an angel. Don't worry about a thing. Her leg is looking good, and I'm following all your instructions to the last letter."

Erica choked on the mango, and in her grab for the napkin, she almost knocked Jamie's note onto the wooden floor of the lanai. Apparently, he wasn't the only one who liked to give out orders. "Listen, Caroline. I don't know what I was thinking. Please just throw those out. You raised five children; you don't need me telling you how to handle Chloe."

Caroline laughed. "Liam will be happy to hear that. He was just about to make copies of your instructions and the hourly schedule and post them in every room of the house so we didn't mess up."

Groaning, Erica set the napkin on the table. Jamie's parents had to think she was certifiable. And maybe she had been. But not anymore. She was turning a corner. When she and Jamie returned to Seattle, everyone would see the new and improved Erica. "Please tell Liam I'm sorry."

"Believe it or not, Erica, I understand. When Jamie was little, I went through something similar. But then William came along, and I was just too darn busy to keep fussing."

"You know Jamie and I are working through some things. Any advice?"

"The Caldwell men aren't an easy bunch. No matter how smart they are about other things, when it comes to understanding women, they don't have a clue. Jamie's a good man, but the poor boy is just like his father. He needs direction. Be patient with him and crystal clear. If you let him guess, he'll guess wrong."

Interesting. She was scrambling for some sort of response to Caroline's advice, when her mother-in-law said, "Hey sweet pea. Guess who's on the phone?"

Erica smiled at Chloe's squeal. "Mommy! I'm having so much fun with Grandma and Grandpa."

"Are you being a good girl?"

"I'm *always* a good girl."

Amused, Erica said, "You're right, sweetheart. How are you getting on with the crutches?"

"It's kind of hard. So when I need to go upstairs or to the car, Grandpa or Uncle Chad carries me."

"Uncle Chad is there?"

"Yeah. He said he missed me. Uncle Drew and Auntie Tori are here too. And Uncle William has to work, but he's coming for supper tonight. And Mommy, everyone gave me presents! Is it my birthday?"

A bittersweet ache gripped Erica's chest. She really hadn't been fair to Jamie's family or to her daughter. She'd talk to Jamie later and figure out a way to make it up to them. "It's not your birthday. They're all so happy to see you and to know that you're going to be okay. They want to celebrate with you. Just enjoy it. And remember to say please and thank you."

"I know that. I'm not a baby."

"You'll always be my baby, sweetheart," Erica said, her voice breaking.

"Are you crying, Mommy?"

"Maybe a little. But only because I'm happy you're having such a good time."

"I miss you and Daddy," Chloe whispered.

"We miss you too. But Daddy and I really need this time together to work through a few things so we can be a family."

"Daddy's not going to leave us again, is he?"

The anxiety in Chloe's voice felt like salt on a wound. She couldn't let her daughter keep thinking Jamie had walked out on them. "Daddy didn't leave because he wanted to. He left because I asked him to."

"You didn't like him anymore?"

How could she explain this to a child when she barely understood it herself? "There were some things I didn't like, but I know now that Mommy and Daddy were confused."

"I don't want Daddy to ever leave again."

Neither did she. "I'm doing everything I can to make sure that doesn't happen. Ever. So have fun with everyone, and listen to Grandma and Grandpa. We want your leg to heal quickly so we can go on that trip to Disneyland. Remember?"

"All three of us?"

"All three of us."

"Yay!"

"I'll talk to you again in a few days. I love you, sweetheart."

"I love you too. And Daddy."

Erica blew Chloe a kiss and hung up the phone. The breakfast Jamie had ordered sat virtually untouched. Picking up the fork, she speared a chunk of bright green kiwi. The mix of sweet and tart livened up her taste buds and made her stomach growl.

She polished off the fruit and muffins, thinking about Jamie. She loved him, but would that be enough to cement their relationship? It hadn't been before. When he'd mentioned that woman—Andrea—and his other women, his subs, he'd admitted that love had never factored into those relationships. Despite that, those women had given him something he needed: control. If she gave him that, would it be enough? He had a lot of experience with BDSM, and she had none, other than the fictionalized accounts she'd read in erotic novels. Reading about it had been exciting. Titillating. Would it be that way in reality as well? What if it wasn't? She didn't want to go back to how they'd been, both of them isolated and dissatisfied.

Did they even really know each other as people? Right now, they didn't seem to have much of a connection beyond the physical. Although he cared for her, he hadn't chosen their marriage any more than she had. He'd done his duty, honored his responsibilities, and loved their daughter. But she and Jamie were essentially strangers. Could this BDSM adventure help them build the trust and understanding they lacked? She hoped so. She wanted a happy, healthy relationship with the man she loved.

A breeze blew in from the ocean, carrying the scent of salt, cooling her heated skin. Jamie's note drifted off the table. She leaned over the arm of her chair to grab it before it was blown away and lost. What had he planned? Her belly tightened with a heady mix of excitement and fear. Jamie had done things with his subs that he'd liked. What if some of those things were things she couldn't do? Things she couldn't give him? Things she *wouldn't* give him. They'd talked about some of his limits—no pain for pain's sake. And no blood. She shuddered at the thought. If he'd said he wanted to whip her until she bled, would she have allowed it? Could she have? For him, maybe. Her complete lack of experience meant she had no idea what she'd like and what she wouldn't. She didn't even know what was out there. What he might want.

Sipping on the last of the coffee, she tried to reassure herself. Jamie had made a point—several times—that she should never do anything she didn't enjoy. That doing something just to please him was bad for their relationship. If she wanted this to work, she'd have to follow Caroline's advice and be upfront with him if he asked her to do something she didn't want to do. He trusted her to say no.

That was empowering.

As her Dom—she could almost hear the uppercase D when he'd said the word—Jamie might be directing their activities, but she was the one with the power. If she said no, that was it. Game over.

With that thought in mind, she went to execute Jamie's orders and get ready for her first date with her Dom.

౸ 🚘 ౸

Jamie maneuvered the black Mustang convertible he'd rented for the week into an open parking spot. The sun was shining, a light breeze was blowing, and it was a perfect day to take his wife out for lunch and a drive along the coast of Oahu. The black leather interior was gorgeous, but to keep the bugs out and prevent the car from becoming too hot, he closed the roof. As he waited for it to click into place, his recent purchases taunted him from the bag on the passenger seat. He couldn't wait to try them out on Rickie. The idea excited him so much, he had to keep reminding himself that she was a novice, that he had to ease her into their new arrangement.

In the five years of their marriage, toys had never been part of their sex life. But they were a crucial part of any BDSM relationship.

A part he was anxious to get back to. His cock stirred in agreement. Five years was a very long time to go without.

Grabbing the bag, he got out of the car and tossed it in the trunk. As he was closing the lid, he hesitated. Should he? Yes! He reopened the lid and, after rummaging through the bag, tucked his little surprise in his pocket. Just the thought of it between Rickie's legs made him half-hard. Thank fuck he was wearing loose pants.

He slammed the trunk closed and walked toward the resort lobby, careful to keep his pace unhurried. A Dom had to appear in control. Cool, calm, and collected. At least until that final moment when he let himself go. God, he couldn't wait to have that with Rickie again.

I like sex a little rough, a little bit kinky. Deal. He chuckled, remembering her words. His wife deserved kudos for instigating the whole thing. If she hadn't brought it up, he sure as shit wouldn't have. The woman had spunk. He liked that. It would make getting her to submit to him all that much more of a challenge. And he loved a good challenge. Especially one that would end in limitless pleasure for both of them.

Her lack of experience might be an issue, at least in the beginning. She had no idea what she'd put in motion. No idea how far BDSM could go. So, he'd be fair, and before they did anything, they'd have a nice long chat. He'd lay it all out for her, make sure she understood her rights. The last thing he wanted was for Rickie to feel used, to clam up and shut him out again. He couldn't relive the last five years. He had to bind her to him—physically and emotionally, and he only had a week to do it. By the time they returned to Seattle, she'd be his, body and soul.

But only if he didn't fuck it up by acting like a horny teen and going off half-cocked.

Entering the lush gardens, he saw her standing by a hibiscus plant with large yellow flowers. He only knew what it was because when they'd arrived yesterday, Rickie had shown him one and explained that the hibiscus was the Hawaiian state flower. The bright yellow blooms were pretty, but next to her radiant beauty, they could have been weeds.

Her sundress billowed in the warm breeze, fluttering around her knees. After her pregnancy and months nursing Chloe, Rickie's breasts had softened. When she bent to inhale the flower's perfume, they swayed gently, evidence that she'd followed his instructions. His hand tightened around his surprise. Had she left off the panties too?

Hearing his steps on the stone pathway, she straightened and shaded her eyes with her hand. The sun reflected off her blonde hair, turning it gold. From that first night, he'd been drawn to her hair, its color, its texture, its feel when he gripped it in his fist.

With slow purpose, his gaze wandered down her body, taking in the curves beneath her dress. His hands itched to touch her sun-warmed skin. He'd bet good money she didn't know that in the sun, her dress was almost see-through. When he raised his gaze to her face, her naughty smile stopped his heart. Maybe he'd have lost that bet.

Closing the distance between them, he caught her in his arms and kissed her. Lightly. Sweetly. When he pulled back, her puzzled expression thrilled him. Keeping her off-balance was one of his new life goals.

His hand on her elbow, he guided her to a more secluded section of the garden, where he could give her his surprise. He hadn't minded other men seeing his subs before, he'd even liked going to BDSM clubs and putting on a show. But with Rickie, everything was different. If another man so much as glanced at her.... Yeah, he was just too damn possessive where she was concerned. His wife's body was for his eyes only.

They stopped on a small bridge from where they could see the ocean. In silence, he turned her toward the water, away from him. He pressed his chest against her back and slid his hands under her dress, caressing the globes of her ass. He'd always loved Rickie's ass—so round, so firm. So perfect.

She hung a hand on his neck and arched her back, pressing herself against his hardening cock. He lowered his head and whispered in her ear, his first words since the previous evening. "I'm pleased you agreed to proceed with this change to our relationship, Mrs. Caldwell." Just saying her name like that ratcheted up his lust.

Looking at him over her shoulder, she frowned. "You called me that in the note too. Why?"

"It's a sign to you that I'm in character. I'm turning on the D/s part of our relationship. When I do that, you need to take on your role as my sub and do whatever I say."

"Anywhere?"

"Anywhere. Anytime."

"But—"

"I'll never do anything to embarrass you. Or hurt you. Much." He grinned. "Whatever I do or make you do, we'll *both* enjoy it."

"Uh... okay." Her voice shook, betraying her nerves. But he could see the wheels turning in her head. See her connect the dots. "Can *I* turn it on too?"

He nodded. "Call me Mr. Caldwell."

"Anytime? Anywhere?"

"Yes. But if I call you Rickie in response, it means I'm not playing."

Her forehead creased as she seemed to process the information. "So, if I call you Jamie, it means I'm not playing?"

"No. You can't *not play*. A sub must always be available for her Dom."

"Hmmm." Her expression hardened and she ran her tongue along her teeth; Rickie was going to balk. He'd expected nothing less. "That doesn't seem fair," she said.

Time to lay down the law. "This isn't about fair. It's about pleasure. If I'm not in the right mood, the right frame of mind, I won't be a good Dom to you. I might even be a bad one." He narrowed his eyes at her. "And we wouldn't want that."

"What if I'm not in the mood to be your sex slave?"

"You will submit to me, even when you might not want to. The reward will be all the better. But, as your Dom, it's my responsibility to know when your resistance is part of the game, and when it's real. If you aren't into something, it won't be good for either of us."

"So I have to trust that you'll take my feelings and my needs into consideration."

"Trust is the key." He stroked her arm, moving up to her shoulders, and back down to her belly. His hand cupped her pussy through the cotton of her sundress, her warmth heating his palm. He bunched up the dress, so he could feel her, skin on skin. She was so soft, so wet.

"I'm working on that," she said, undulating against him.

He slid his finger between her pussy lips, coating them with her own juices. "There are two safewords."

"Safewords?" She tried to turn, but he held her firmly against him with his free arm. If he didn't crave more than a quick fuck, he'd bend her over the railing and slam his cock into her tight pussy, right here. Right fucking now.

He had to clear his throat, and his mind, before he could speak intelligibly. "The first safeword is 'yellow.' It's like a caution sign. If

I'm pushing you too close to the limit of your fear or pain tolerance, use it. I'll back off."

"And the second one?"

Continuing to caress her with his fingers, he said, "Red. It means we've hit a hard limit that maybe you didn't know about. That's okay. I need to trust you'll tell me if I go too far." He removed his hand from her, knowing it would heighten the impact of what he was about to say. "That word stops everything. Don't use it unless you really mean it."

She gripped the railing and leaned against him. "D-do you have any hard limits? Besides blood, I mean."

Sliding his hand back under her dress, he thrust his pulsing cock against her ass, and knew he'd have to have it as soon as she was fully prepared.

"After lunch, we'll talk about hard and soft limits. And must-haves."

"Must-haves. I like the sound of that." She rolled her hips and moaned when he circled her clit, then trailed his finger down to her entrance and plunged it deep into her wet heat. She was ready for her surprise.

Pulling his hands away from her, he moved a step back. Not too far, just enough for her to feel the loss along her back. He took his surprise from his pocket and when she turned to face him, a question in her eyes, he dangled the G-string from his forefinger. When he'd spotted the miracle of white pearl-sized metal beads, he'd pounced on it.

Rickie scowled. "What is it?"

"A G-string."

"Seriously?"

"Put it on, Mrs. Caldwell," he said, his tone firm. Unyielding.

"Here?"

"Now." Rickie swiped the G-string from his hand and fiddled with it, trying to figure out how it worked. "Need help?" he asked. It was a real challenge to keep from grinning.

"No!" she snapped. Fire sparked in her eyes as she stepped into the loops and pulled up the G-string. "Why beads?"

Taking her arm, he led her in the direction of the Mustang. "You'll see."

He was able to pinpoint the exact moment when she did see. Her step faltered and she gripped his arm, nails digging into his flesh.

"Oh!" she gasped, her cheeks flushing a beautiful shade of pink. The same pink as her nipples.

"You like?"

Licking her lips, she turned to him. The mix of Madonna and Magdalene in the smile she offered him turned his knees to jelly and his cock to stone.

Delayed gratification was going to kill him. His lovely wife was going to kill him.

Kill him with pleasure.

CHAPTER 5

Naughty, sinfully delicious sensations coursed through Erica's body. With each step, with each glide of the beaded G-string, a fresh rush of tingles fanned her arousal. The knowing grin on Jamie's handsome face made her want to jump in his arms and beg him to take her, to plunge deep inside her, to ease the ache building between her thighs.

But that wasn't how this game was played. He would draw this out until she broke. And she would, but not until he was ready to break too.

They neared the sleek convertible, and ever the gentleman, Jamie opened the passenger door for her. It would almost be a relief not to feel the to-and-fro of the beads against her sensitized flesh for a while.

As she sank into the deep seat, the extent of her error became clear. The row of beads snuck in, deep and tight against her. Her grip on Jamie's hand tightened as an orgasm tore through her, startling her with its suddenness. She arched her back, the motion bringing on another long glide, propelling her into a second climax before the first even ebbed. The world, the car, Jamie's face—everything blurred as her body soared.

When she finally stopped quivering, she slumped against the seat back and opened her lids, blinking to bring her surroundings into focus. Jamie's smile and the fire sparkling in his eyes almost stopped her heart. "This is going to be a great day," he said, closing her door.

Erica tried to regain her breath while Jamie rounded the hood and sat behind the wheel. "Where"—she swallowed to moisten her dry throat—"where are we going?"

He turned on the car and opened the roof. "The clerk at the resort recommended this little seafood restaurant in Kaaawa. Sound good?"

"Wonderful." She shifted to adjust the seatbelt and winced when a wayward bead dug into her butt. "Am I going to keep this on?"

"This?"

She sighed. "The G-string. Do I have to keep it on?"

"You'll keep it on until I tell you to take it off." His words were clipped, like he was commanding his team.

A thought nailed her to the seat. What if she came in the restaurant? In front of other people? She'd want to die. "Jamie, I—"

He laid his hand on her thigh and squeezed it lightly. "I said I'd never do anything to embarrass you."

"It's not like I can control this." She motioned awkwardly toward her middle. Discussing sex had never been comfortable for her.

"This? You'll have to be more specific, Mrs. Caldwell."

Jamie turned the car onto the two-lane highway and accelerated. The purring of the engine made the metal beads vibrate. She felt as though hundreds of fingers were massaging her at once. "Oh, God," she said, moaning.

"I'm glad you think so highly of me. But I'm not God."

Damn him. He was enjoying her struggle. She gripped the edge of the seat, and ground her teeth together. "I'm going to come again." Her voice rose to a shrill pitch.

"You will not." He let a moment pass. "Not until I give you permission. As your Dom, *I* say when and where you can come."

Was he out of his mind? No one could control an orgasm. "And how do you propose I stop it?"

"Count sheep." She closed her eyes as a tornado built deep inside her. Jamie sucked in a harsh breath and grabbed her wrist. "Self-pleasuring is *not* permitted. Unless *I* order it."

What was he talking about? She wasn't— The thought died as she looked down. Her dress was hiked up to her waist and her right hand was between her legs, rolling the beads against her swollen folds. Hissing, she tore her hand away and shoved her dress back in place. He was turning her into a sex addict!

Jamie's loud laugh startled her. She jerked her head up and seeing the humor dancing in his eyes, her cheeks flamed. "Did I say that out loud?" Dropping her face into her hands, she groaned. "Oh, God. I did."

With a sideways glance, Jamie wound his hand in her hair and tugged. "Sit back."

The guttural scrape of his voice put her on instant alert. Desire etched his features, sharpened his jaw and cheekbones. The tingles between her legs turned to sizzles. Who would break first? Since she'd already climaxed twice, logic would dictate that it would be him. But everything about Jamie defied logic. The unexpectedness of her previous orgasms had astounded her, and left her primed and ready for more.

What had he said earlier? Count sheep? It was certainly worth a try. Closing her eyes, she pictured fluffy little lambs jumping over a fence. *One sheep. Two sheep.*

Jamie tugged on her hair again. "Open your eyes."

Not fair. Keeping her head down, she resisted. How could she count sheep if she couldn't see them? When he tugged harder, she snapped her eyes open. His clenched jaw jumped and she had the sudden urge to run her tongue along the edge of it. The pulsing between her legs flared and she tore her gaze away from him.

"Lift up your dress."

Her eyes narrowed. "Here?"

"Yes. Now."

Happy that she'd worn her favorite no-wrinkle dress, she raised the hem, folding it neatly at her waist. When the hem passed her mound, exposing her, he said, "That's it. Show me your pretty pussy."

Pussy. The word ripped through her memories, bringing that first night back to her in high-definition. Every sound, every scent, every touch. It all came back in a rush. Simply remembering the way he'd spread her legs and studied her most private place triggered a fresh wave of desire.

He pushed on the back of her head. "See how wet you are? How your juices gleam in the sun? Describe it to me."

God, that was gross. Why did he want her to do that? Keeping her head down, she glanced at him out of the corner of her eye. Oh, right. He *was* still driving. She swallowed, stalling. "You lied."

Frowning, he shot her a questioning look. "I've been more honest with you in the last day than ever before in our marriage."

"You said you'd never make me do anything embarrassing."

"No. I said I'd never embarrass you or make you do anything embarrassing in public. But that's beside the point. Describing yourself shouldn't be any more embarrassing than describing a picture or a painting. Now do it."

Her husband had lost his mind. Letting out a long breath, she tilted her hips so she could have a better view of the area in question. "Um... well... it's pink and shiny."

"Sounds like you're describing a newborn pig. Pretend I've never seen a pussy before. Tell me *everything* you see."

She snorted. "It's not at all nice to look at. I may just turn you off women forever."

Reaching between her legs, he fondled her with his fingers, dipping one inside her. Stunned, she barely had time to register what he'd done before it was over. He brought his hand to his mouth, and sucked his fingers. His action, so carnal, so hot, stole her breath.

"Your pussy is beautiful and so are you. Every inch of you makes me crazy. Now try again, and see yourself through my eyes."

Did he really believe that? Only truth showed on his face. After years of hearing her mother's boyfriends calling both of them filthy cunts, it was hard for her to block that out, to think of that part of herself as anything but dirty. Growing up, she'd often wished she'd had a penis, long and wide. Men were proud of their bodies in a way few women were of theirs. For Jamie, for the sake of their marriage, she'd try.

Placing a hand on her stomach, she edged her fingers lower until they touched the trimmed hair at the apex of her thighs. She was a little obsessive about keeping it neat. "Okay. The hair... it's short and a little curly."

After a moment, he prompted her. "Color?"

"Blonde. So pale, I can see my skin through it."

"What color is your skin?"

Carefully, she pushed aside the row of beads. Good thing the hair was short or Jamie's little surprise could have been a painful one. "It's light pink here."

"And lower?"

She trailed her finger down to her outer folds, still swollen from her earlier passion. Touching herself like this in front of Jamie felt... wrong. She took another breath before answering his question. "It's darker. Closer to fuchsia."

"Open yourself."

Was he trying to prove something with all this? *Come on, Erica. Be honest.* Yes. There was something exciting and sexy about exposing herself in broad daylight. Did Jamie know that? She guessed that he did.

Forcing herself to follow his orders, she used both hands to push back the swollen lips and reveal the smaller folds. Folds that glistened with moisture. Jamie sucked in a breath, drawing her attention to his hands gripping the steering wheel, his knuckles white against the black leather. "Tell me what you see."

This little game was affecting him as much as her. Stimulated by the visual proof of his arousal, desire spun tight in her belly. She returned her gaze to her mound and the new moisture that coated it. "I see a flower. A flower touched by the morning dew."

The car swerved sharply off the road, and Jamie pulled it to a stop on the shoulder. She smothered her smile, but a curious warming sensation filled her chest. He unbuckled his seatbelt and twisted toward her, his body boxing her in. "Repeat what you said."

"All of it?"

"Just the last part," he said with an impatient shake of his head.

"It… uh… it looks like a flower touched by the morning dew."

"Good. You see what I see now."

She bit her lip and nodded, her heart swelling. He'd done this for her. "Thank you," she whispered, ducking her head.

He hooked a finger under her chin. "Never be ashamed of your body or how you feel." He pressed his lips against hers. "Accept it, and it will reward you."

For a moment, much too short, she lost herself in blue eyes that shone with sincerity and something else. Was it love? Whatever it was, she was grateful to him for what he'd done. What he was doing. Already she felt their connection growing stronger. "I will," she said, and meant it.

"Now, let's make it look like a flower after the rain." He pulled on the G-string, rolling the beads back and forth. Her belly clenched hungrily as the smooth balls slipped between her wet folds, the pressure on her nub perfect. Then as though he'd completed his demonstration, he indicated for her to take over.

Replacing his hand with hers, she continued the motion. As her desire mounted, she increased the rhythm—faster, harder. Her ragged breathing turning to gasps, she thrust her hips forward in an attempt to increase the pressure against the beads. Blood pounded in her ears. She was so close. Just a few more—

He stilled her hand. "Stop."

"But I need—"

"I *know* what you need." With slow controlled movements, so at odds with the tempest wreaking havoc on her own body, he put the car in gear and got back on the highway. Her mind reeled and all she could focus on was reaching her climax. All it would take were a few touches. His eyes were on the street. He wouldn't see if she extended her finger a little…

The rumble in his chest squashed that idea. He smiled. "Patience, Mrs. Caldwell."

Dropping her head against the seatback, she huffed out a breath. Patience had never been one of her virtues.

After a few minutes of silence, he said, "Slip the straps off your shoulders."

"But my dress will fall down." She was wearing a simple sheath dress. The entire thing was held up by narrow spaghetti straps.

He gestured with his hand. "We're alone."

The resort had been milling with people, but Jamie had managed to find the only deserted stretch of road on the island of Oahu. Go figure. "Okay. But if someone sees me, you're in big trouble, mister."

Her fingers shaking, she slid the straps off and let the top of her sundress fall to her waist. Naked except for the fabric across her stomach, she shivered in the warm sun.

"Are you cold?" he asked, concern furrowing his brow. "I can put the roof up."

"No." Could she tell him the real reason she'd shivered? That being alone with him, naked when he was fully dressed, made her feel sexier, more vulnerable, than anything else in her life had. That it left her more aroused than she'd ever been?

He groaned and she followed the direction of his eyes to her *pussy*, her juices making it glisten. "Touch your breasts," he growled, tearing his gaze away and back to the road.

Bringing her hands to her chest, she cupped each breast, kneading them the way Jamie did.

"That's it. Now pinch your nipples."

With her thumbs and index fingers, she captured each peak and squeezed. A moan escaped her lips as a spark of pain ignited the sensitive tips.

"Do it again. Pull at the same time," he ordered.

The tingles were so intense, so exhilarating that she hurried to comply. Pinching again, she tugged on her nipples, stretching her breasts, enjoying the pull on her skin.

"Tell me how it feels."

"Like I'm being suspended by the tips of my breasts."

"We might have to try that someday."

"Not on your life," she said, tensing up.

"Hard limit. Got it."

Hearing the humor in his voice, she relaxed and continued to massage her breasts, her gaze fixed on his face. Wishing his hands would replace hers.

"Pinch. Harder than before. And pull farther. Do both until you're on the edge of pain."

She breathed deeply. There was no reason to worry. She was in control. These were her hands on her breasts. If it hurt too much, she'd stop. Squeezing her thumbs and index fingers together until pain enveloped the elongated peaks, she pulled. Pulled until the stretching of her skin and breast tissue made her yelp.

"Easy now. Let up a little. Then do it again."

Was he crazy? As she prepared to follow his command, she knew she was the one who was crazy. After several rounds of the squeeze-pull routine, she began to pinch harder, pull farther, trying to reach the same flashpoint of pleasure and pain she'd hit the first time.

"That's it babe. Roll your hips."

With each thrust, the beads stroked her, all of her. She arched her back to increase the pull on her breasts and the pressure against her pussy. Her toes were at the edge of a magnificent precipice and she was ready to jump off. If he stopped her now, she'd die.

"Good. Now—"

"Jamie. Please."

"Please, what, Mrs. Caldwell? Remember, you need to be specific."

She lifted her eyes to him. Was that a smirk of satisfaction on his lips? He looked like a hunter who'd just captured his prey. "I want to… finish."

"Finish, Mrs. Caldwell?"

"I'm glad you're having so much fun with this," she grumbled. "I want to *come*."

"Badly enough to beg?"

"Yes, dammit."

He motioned vaguely with his hand. "Do your best."

Rethinking their exchange, she wasn't certain what he meant. At this point, she didn't much care if he wanted her to come or not. She was so close. A few Kegel exercises might just do the trick. On the other hand, she didn't want to ruin the moment. She was starting to see the real Jamie, and the last thing she wanted was to disappoint him. "Do my best to come?"

"No. To beg."

She'd never been good at begging, and now on the verge of climax, her mind careened into a void. What did he want her to say? Her vocabulary seemed to have vacated her mind. "Please, Jamie. I want to come." There, that was good. Sounded submissive, didn't it?

"Sir."

"What?" If Jamie changed the rules on her, she'd turn to ashes. The burning in her belly intensified and she moaned.

"Please, *Sir*," he said.

Erica wet her lips and reminded herself this was a game. Pulling on the submissive mantle, she lowered her voice and her eyes. "Please, Sir, allow me to come."

In a flash, he pressed his hand against the beads between her legs. "Again," he said, his voice husky and far from unaffected.

Her submissive mantle had worked. And his hand between her legs was working as well. "Please. Oh God. Sir, please. Let me come." Her hips pistoned against his hand. Her fingers pinched and tugged on her nipples. Her actions were almost violent, like a sex-deprived woman. Or was that like a depraved woman? How could she be so desperate for satisfaction when she'd achieved it twice in the last half hour?

He pressed harder with his palm and pushed a finger into her, stroking the bundle of nerves far inside her. She ground against his hand, swiveling her hips until the beads bit into her flesh. Pleasure spiraled and bright colors flashed on the perimeter of her vision. Death would ensue if he tried to stop her now. "Sir, Jamie. Please. Oh! Please, tell me to come. *I beg you.*"

"Well done, Mrs. Caldwell." He flattened his thumb against her clitoris. "Come. Now."

Without even a conscious thought on her part, sensation exploded low in her belly. Her eyes closed as her body convulsed, tightening around Jamie's finger. She clamped her legs shut, trapping his hand, willing the waves of ecstasy to go on forever.

Awareness filtered slowly back. She released her aching breasts and parting her knees, slouched against the seat. Sated.

Jamie slid his finger out and she felt empty again. Like she'd felt for the past year. Melancholy replaced the satisfaction. As though sensing her change in mood, he patted her leg. "Hey, this is just the beginning."

She really hoped so. Jamie and Chloe were her world, her reason to live. Without her family, nothing meant anything. She understood that now.

"Fix your dress. We're almost there."

Almost there? Just ahead was a small town. With people! Fumbling with the straps, she pulled up the bodice and covered her breasts, then she pushed the skirt down. When they arrived at a quaint main street with shops lining either side of the road, she was fully covered. Thank goodness.

Jamie turned into a narrow alley that led to a private parking lot. Checking her watch, she realized how much time had passed. It was already two o'clock, which explained why there were only a few cars in the lot.

"Hope you're ready to eat," Jamie said, his tone lighter and happier than she'd ever heard it.

Her stomach growled at the scent of cooking in the air. Coming three times in thirty minutes, had given her quite an appetite. "Famished." She ran her tongue over her lips, letting him know she was hungry for much more than food.

෴🚆෴

Jamie shifted in his seat and surreptitiously adjusted his pants in an attempt to stave off imminent castration.

Rickie moaned as her lips closed around another forkful of butter mochi. He gritted his teeth to hold back a groan as his cock hammered against his zipper. Seeing the tines of the fork disappear between her lips was killing him. Maybe it was the fact he hadn't had a blowjob in over a year. He couldn't help remembering how it had looked, how it had felt to have her swallow him like that.

Christ. Sweat broke out on his forehead.

One sheep. Two sheep. Jump, fucker! Three sheep.

Her low laugh reached him through the haze of lust. His eyes lasered in on her face. "What's so funny?" he snapped.

"You. You look like you're going to blow an artery."

Something was going to blow all right. Or rather someone. "Are you done?"

Setting her fork down neatly across her plate, she took a last sip of her tea and nodded. "Whenever you are."

His heart crashing against his ribs, he stood in a rush, barely catching his chair when it almost toppled over. After tossing enough cash onto the table to cover the bill and tip, he stepped around to help Rickie out of her seat. *Get a grip, Caldwell.* He was acting like a fucking moron.

Rickie's lips quivered as she got to her feet, smoothing down her dress. When her hands brushed her ass, desire shot through him—from his head to his other head. Clasping her wrist, he dragged her out of the restaurant, through the parking lot straight to their car. But instead of opening the passenger door, he backed her against it, caging her between the car and his body. Something flickered in her eyes. Fear? His pulse skyrocketed. "Had fun?" he asked, keeping his voice low and even.

"Yes. The food was great."

"Did you enjoy teasing me?" he ground out. He watched her throat work as she swallowed. His body swayed toward her, and his mouth opened. He caught himself a moment before his lips met her creamy skin. He was dying to scrape his teeth along the sensitive tendons of her neck. The move had always driven her to her knees. The image of her red lips closing around his throbbing cock flashed in his mind again. *Christ Almighty.* "Answer the question, Mrs. Caldwell."

Staring at his shoulder, she whispered, "Yes."

He shifted and brought his face to the other side of her neck, inhaling deeply, the scent of her perfume making his eyes roll back in his head. He took her hand and brought it to his groin. "Did you enjoy doing *this* to me?"

She angled her head, giving him full access to the tender flesh at her throat. "Yes."

The word vibrated against his lips and straight to his cock. *Fuck.* He was the Dom. She would not win. *She* would not control *him*. He lifted his head away from her to study her expression. "You've been a naughty girl. Do you know what happens to naughty girls, Mrs. Caldwell?"

Interest gleamed in her eyes. "They're punished?"

"Playing with fire might get you burned."

Her hand tightened on his cock. "I'm counting on it," she said, desire making her voice hoarse.

He didn't want to, but his body leaned into her touch. Glancing around the parking lot, he made sure they were alone and unseen. Witnesses would ruin the mood, at least for him. He'd never asked Rickie about her preferences when it came to exhibitionism, and he never would. She was his and his alone.

With his hands on her hips, he spun her around and pressed her up against the car. Before she could utter more than a shocked "Oh!" he pulled up the hem of her dress and bared one creamy cheek.

She struggled against him, tried to turn around. "Stop," he said, his voice sharp. When she froze, he knew he had her. "That's better."

Now that she was still, he could admire the sweet curve of her ass, the color of her skin. He itched to have it under his hand. Reining himself in, he caressed her hip and ran his fingers along the beads bisecting her butt. "How do these feel here?"

"Different." She sounded breathless. Sexy as hell.

He tugged on the string. "Good different or bad different?"

"Good."

"I'm going to have this lovely ass soon." Tracing the puckered skin, he added, "I'm going to sink my cock in this tight little hole. And you're going to love it."

"I wouldn't count on that," she smirked.

His stomach dropped, collapsing like a ceiling cave-in. "Is that a hard limit?"

"What if it is?"

"Then we have a problem."

Her forehead wrinkled as she glanced at him over her shoulder. "Why?"

"Because your ass is one of my must-haves."

"Oh."

"So, is it? A hard limit?" Before he got any more caught up in his dream of the perfect relationship with Rickie, he had to know. If it was a hard limit, he'd have some thinking to do.

Turning away from him, she leaned her forehead on her forearms against the car. "Why is it suddenly so important to you? You've never brought this up before."

He trailed his fingers along the pale curve, enjoying the sight of his tanned hand against her white skin. "I never thought you'd accept it before." He laughed, the sound like gravel against his throat. "I was on such thin ice with you. The last thing you needed was proof that I was a perv. I couldn't risk it."

She raised her head. "Because you thought I'd use it against you. To keep you away from Chloe."

"Yes."

"I'm so sorry I made you feel that way, Jamie. It's not a hard limit. I'm not sure I'll like it, but I'm willing to try."

"Fair enough." Relief and pride poured through him.

Meeting his gaze, she smiled. "What now?"

"Now it's time for your punishment." Rickie's eyes widened. He tried to hide his grin, but he wasn't sure he was all that successful.

"What are you going to do?" she asked. Her breath came in small pants that betrayed her excitement.

"Remember the safeword. Use it if necessary." He palmed one of her breasts through the thin material of her dress, capturing the nipple between his fingers. With his other hand, he stroked her exposed ass. Her moan as she pressed into his hand sent a thrill humming through his body. He lifted his itchy palm and brought it back down in a quick hard smack. The satisfying sound of flesh against flesh and her small yelp almost drove him to his knees. He'd waited so fucking long for this.

He caressed the mark on her ass cheek, easing the sting. Her cry had held more pleasure than pain. Still, he had to make sure she was really onboard. "Do you have something to say to me?"

"Thank you?" she said, licking her lips.

Her answer surprised a chuckle from him. "No." He brought his hand down again, enjoying the sound of her breath catching and the moan that escaped her plump lips as he rubbed the now rosy skin. "Try again," he ordered.

"Mmm... I'm sorry?"

"When a sub speaks to her Dom, she needs to show appropriate respect."

"So I should call you Mr. Caldwell now?"

"Or Sir."

"Is that what your subs called you?"

"No."

"Tell me. I want to know."

"They called me Master."

"Oh." She swallowed and he waited, knowing she had more to

say. "But you don't want me to call you that?"

"No."

"Why?"

He turned her around so they were face to face, so she was clear about what he was going to say. "Because I love you. Because we're equals. Because you're my wife, Rickie, not my slave or servant."

A blush colored her cheeks as a smile played at the corner of her lips. "You know, I'm starting to believe that."

Hauling her against his chest, he crushed his mouth over hers, drinking in her gasp as she melted into him. When her lips parted, he plunged his tongue inside, relishing her heat, the taste of the mochi she'd had for dessert. Desire swept through him like an electric river in his veins, sparking every nerve ending in its way. His chest pumping like a bellows, he spun her around, flattening her against the convertible. "Let's start that again. Do you have something to say to me, Mrs. Caldwell?"

One hand closed on her nipple, the other found its way to her ass. She pressed herself against him and arched her back. "I… I'm sorry, Sir."

His stomach clenched and everything south of his waist turned to rebar. "That's much better." As light as he could, he brushed his hand over her reddened skin. She rolled her hips. "Is there something you want?"

"Please do it again, Sir."

"You really must be more specific, Mrs. Caldwell."

She sucked on her lower lip for a moment. Had he pushed her too far? He watched nearly paralyzed as she inhaled deeply. Then her lips opened. "Spank me, Mr. Caldwell. Please, spank me again."

Tingles raced up his spine. Had he died and gone to heaven? Surely Rickie was an angel, a gift from God. With his hand on her breast, he pulled her tight against his chest, careful to leave her bare cheek unhindered. Bringing his hand back, he sent it forward and raked his teeth along the fragile bones of her neck. His hand hit her bottom, his fingers splayed so the tip of his middle finger brushed her pussy. Her groan, low and carnal, arrowed through him like lightening. He spanked her again and twice more.

She turned her face to him. "Oh, I'm c—" He covered her mouth with his own, sealing in her cries as her body convulsed with the power of her orgasm. She was so goddamned beautiful.

Letting go of her breast, he slid his hand between her face and the car. She leaned into his palm and pressed her lips to it in a gentle kiss. "Thank you, Mr. Caldwell," she murmured, a sexy smile curving her mouth.

Still shaking with the struggle to fight off his own orgasm, he gave her bottom one last lingering stroke before tugging her dress back in place. He kissed her nose, then opened the car door and stepped aside. "The pleasure was all mine, Mrs. Caldwell."

As she leaned down to get into the low-slung vehicle, her ass nudged the tent in his pants. "Didn't know you enjoyed having blue balls, Mr. Caldwell," she said, her voice a sassy lilt.

Something told him Rickie would do her best to earn herself more punishments. A smile cracked his face. His prim and proper wife was turning out to be quite the wildcat.

༂ 🚂 ༃

Rickie's silence as he drove unnerved Jamie. Was she having regrets? Second thoughts? He'd seen it happen before. *Had* it happen to him before. He remembered one sub who'd kept pushing him to go further, harder. She'd screamed as she'd come. Five minutes later, she was puking in the toilet, ashamed by what they'd done, by the pleasure it had given her. What would he do if Rickie reacted the same way?

Resigned, he took the turnoff to go back to the resort instead of continuing on to Laniakea Beach to see the turtles as he'd originally planned. She continued to stare out the window. When he stopped the Mustang in the parking lot near their cottage, she jerked her head toward him, blinking as though waking up from a nap. "Why are we here? I thought we were going to discuss terms."

"You've had enough for one day."

She smiled and held her hand out to him. "Well, maybe. But I'm not too tired to talk."

Clasping her fingers in his, he kissed her wrist, making her giggle. The joyous tinkle washed away some of his dread. She was just tired, not turned off. "Walk with me on the beach?"

"Of course."

Jamie hopped out of the car and around to her side. He opened the door and helped her out. She patted his chest and kissed his lips lightly. "Such a gentleman."

He crooked his arm. "Always."

Bursting into laughter, she hooked her arm around his. "That was no gentleman who spanked my bottom at the restaurant."

"Are you sorry you let me do that?" he asked, his stomach cramping. Like the burned-out husk of a building, his life would be destroyed if she said yes.

She stopped walking and cupped his jaw in her palm. "No. Not at all. Why would you think that?"

"You were so quiet in the car."

"It's just a lot to take in," she said, her voice low, confidential. "I've never been one to act lightly, Jamie. I'm trying to understand why I liked it."

"And what else you might enjoy."

Her gaze softened. "Exactly."

Before stepping onto the sand, they removed their shoes. She stuck hers in her purse and raced to the water's edge while he tied his together and slung them over his shoulder. He joined her, savoring her carefree laughter and the glee lighting her eyes as she splashed around in the waves. Had he ever seen her looking so vibrant, so alive? He shook his head in silent denial. They'd really done a number on each other these past five years.

She bent down and fished around in the wet sand. When she stood, she waved a shell in her hand, a proud grin on her face. "Chloe will love this."

"We could have it made into a necklace for her," he suggested. She gaped at him. He frowned. "What?"

"That's just so... sweet."

His frown deepened. "I can be sweet."

Toying with the strap of her purse, she began to stroll along the water. He caught up to her and threw her a questioning look. She shrugged. "I just don't know what to expect from you now."

Ah, so that's what had been bugging her. He put his arm around her shoulders and pulled her to his side as they walked. "Was I too rough?" He held his breath as he waited for her response.

She rolled her eyes. "You know you weren't. But I don't think I could live with your Dom side all the time. He's a little... intense."

Relaxing, he smiled down at her. "We'll only bring him out on special occasions. Okay?"

"Will I see him again on this trip?"

"Do you want to?"

Humor lit her eyes. "Please."

"Let's get the rest of the discussion out of the way first," he said, kissing the top of her head. The breeze from the ocean blew a few silky strands of her hair across his cheek, soft as a flogger. The thought made his cock stand up and cheer. Good thing he'd thought to buy one on his shopping spree that morning.

"What's that grin on your face for?"

Using his finger, he trailed a path down her spine to the curve of her ass. He couldn't help smiling when she shivered. "You'll find out soon enough. Business first."

"Okay. You said we'd talk about hard and soft limits, and must-haves."

"You already know blood is a hard limit for me."

"And my butt is a must-have for you."

"That it is." He swatted the 'it' in question and laughed when she yelped. "Do you have any hard limits?"

She twisted a strand of hair as she thought about his question. "I'm so new to all of this. Can you name some things you want to do? That might help."

Ease into it, Caldwell. "We've established that spanking with my hand is okay. What about spanking with something like a ruler or a paddle? Remember, you can always safeword."

"Okay. You can do that."

He blew out a breath. "A flogger?"

"As long as it doesn't cut my skin."

"Never," he said, shaking his head. "Whips? Canes?"

"Won't that leave bruises?"

"Not if I do it right. Which I would." Her teeth left marks on her lip, proof of her nerves. "Okay, let's put that in the soft limit category."

"I get hard limit, but what's a soft limit?"

"It means that, for now, I'll treat whips and canes as a hard limit, but as you get more used to things, we can talk about it again."

"Okay, I can agree to that."

"What about restraints? Ropes, handcuffs?"

"You want to tie me up?"

His groin clenched at her innocent question. "More than you know," he said, his voice hoarse.

"Oh. Okay then. As long as I'm not covered in rope burns or left there for hours."

"Hours, definitely not." She shot him a perplexed glance. But she must have read his desire because her eyes widened and her cheeks bloomed with color. He wouldn't leave her tied up alone for hours, but anticipation was most certainly part of the game. "How do you feel about toys?"

"Toys? Like vibrators?"

"Vibrators, dildos, balls, butt plugs, nipple clamps, genital clamps, things like that."

"I've never tried any of those things."

He stopped and turned, running a finger along the side of her face. "Oh honey. You've never had a vibrator? What did you do the year we were apart?"

She pursed her lips. "I used my hand."

"And when we were together?"

"Nothing. If we didn't have sex, then I did nothing."

His heart swelled. God, she was more than perfect. "Let's keep it that way. Remember, I want all your orgasms."

She closed her eyes and nodded. "Since I don't know how any of those will feel, we can try them."

"I have to trust you to tell me if there's anything you don't like."

"I will."

"Blindfolds, we know you like those. What about hoods? Gags? Ball gags? Masks?"

Smiling, she said, "I did like the blindfold. The others I don't know. I'm not too good with closed-in spaces."

"We'll go slowly with those then. Last thing for now—vaginal and anal fisting." She hissed in a breath and blanched. "Okay," he said, quickly. "Hard limit."

She sighed, her relief visible. "Other than the fact that you want my butt, do you have any other must-haves?"

BDSM was wide and varied and there were many other things they could try. But everything else was too hardcore for her. For them. Except… "How do you feel about double penetration?"

Her eyes widened. "Like two men at a time?"

"Fuck no!" He scowled at her. "You want that?" If she said yes, he was in serious fucking trouble. It wasn't that he had something against threesomes. People who live in glass houses and all that. But the idea of another man touching Rickie, making love to her—made him rabid.

She rubbed her fingers between his brows and smiled. "Relax, Jamie. I don't want anyone but you."

Tension drained from his shoulders as he studied her expression, open and honest. He wrapped his arms around her and hugged her tightly. Then framing her face, he pressed his lips to hers in a possessive kiss. He poured everything into it—his love for her, his need to protect her, to keep her safe, to make her his. When he pulled back, they were both breathing hard. "It's just you and me, Rickie. No one else. Ever."

Her expression clouded. "How can you be so sure? We still have a long way to go. Not everything's been resolved."

Christ. He felt like he'd been hit in the gut with a sledgehammer. "You're still thinking of leaving me?"

"No. Of course not. You're the only man I want. I realize that I haven't been the wife you deserve, but I'm trying to change that. I feel like we're finally communicating, like we're both working hard to make this marriage a success." She ran her hand over his chest muscles and sent him a shy smile as she raked her nails over his nipple. "We've made a great start."

A groan in his throat, he caught her hand and brought it to his mouth. Baring his teeth, he nipped her index finger. Her pupils dilated despite the bright sun.

She cleared her throat. "So… uh… what did you mean about the double…" When he grinned, she left the question unfinished.

"Interested in that, are you, Mrs. Caldwell?" He snaked his hand over her hip to her delectable backside. "I can take your pretty pussy and your tight ass at the same time with a little help from a toy."

She nibbled her lip and lifted her eyes to his, so sexy and playful that he wanted to tumble her onto the sand and take her right there in front of all the beachgoers. "Any other orifices you'd like to fill?" she asked.

"Just this one," he said, tracing her lips. Her tongue darted out and touched his finger. He caught his breath.

She stepped in to him, and her hand roamed down his chest to his groin. "We still haven't taken care of this."

In a heart's beat, his half-hard cock was ready for action. When he thrust into her palm, she smiled. "What are you suggesting, Mrs. Caldwell?"

"A little *quid pro quo?*"

"You've got yourself a deal." He had it bad; even her use of Latin legal terms turned him on. Taking her hand, he turned her toward the parking lot. They'd go to the cottage, but first he had to get his bag of toys.

CHAPTER 6

Erica's belly fluttered as they walked up the path from the beach. Why had she pushed Jamie? He'd seemed ready to call it a day, even though up to now, everything had been about her. She'd caught a glimpse of his wild side in the restaurant parking lot, but she really wanted to see him let go. It was clear now that to do that, she was going to have to show him that it was okay to test the limits. If not, he'd stay in the safe zone and in control. While this dominant Jamie was sexy as heck, he was capable of far more.

The fluttering turned to flipping as the truth came to her. She pressed her hand to her stomach, willing it to settle. If she wanted Jamie to let go, she'd have to let go as well. Did she trust him enough to do that? Did she trust him enough to let herself be vulnerable?

Jamie touched her shoulder. "Hey, you okay?" His voice was laden with concern.

She faked a bright smile. "I'm fine. You?"

He hesitated for a moment as though he wanted to say something but wasn't sure he should. Finally he blew out a breath. "Scared shitless."

What? Stopping in her tracks, she spun around to face him and peered into his beautiful eyes, which were filled with fear and trepidation. Her heart warmed. Wordlessly, she slipped her arms around his waist and rested her cheek on his solid chest.

Stroking her back, he held her close and nuzzled her hair. "Rickie, we have all our lives to work on this. Let's slow down. The last thing

I want is for you to be afraid of me or what I might do to you."

"Is that what you're scared about? That I'll fear you?"

"Yes. I've seen it before, that frightened deer look."

"From one of your subs?" He dropped his hands and shoved them into his pockets, staring down at his bare feet. A shudder worked its way up her spine and she wrapped her arms around herself. She might not like what he had to tell her, but he needed to say it and she needed to hear it. "Tell me what happened," she said softly, the way she'd ask Chloe to share a bad dream.

He filled his lungs, then exhaled, the sound surprisingly loud despite the crashing of the waves on the beach. Still avoiding her gaze, he said, "It was years ago, with my first sub. I was so young, so cocksure. Neither of us really knew what we were doing." Raising his head, he met her stare. "I hurt her. Badly."

Folding his arms across his chest, he turned away from her and took a few steps toward the water. Her chest tight, she followed. "Was it an accident?"

"Whips, canes, clamps, even a crop or flogger can be dangerous in the wrong hands. But I didn't want her to know how little experience I had. I treated her like a guinea pig."

"Why didn't she stop you, or at least tell you she was hurting?"

"I betrayed her trust by lying about my expertise, and she lied about how much pain she could tolerate."

"I take it you figured it out."

"She had bruises on her body, some cuts and burns. She'd always explain them away—she'd fallen or burned herself taking food out of the oven. I believed her, convinced myself to believe her. But then she started getting *that* look in her eyes whenever we—" His mouth straightened into a thin hard line.

Wow. The way he described it, his sub sounded like an abused spouse. She couldn't imagine Jamie intentionally hurting anyone. For heaven's sake, he risked his life every day to rescue strangers. He wouldn't knowingly injure someone he cared about. She touched his forearm. "That must have been hard on you."

He barked out an angry laugh. "Not as hard as it was on her."

"Stop it, Jamie. I know you. If she'd told you or even if you'd only suspected that she didn't like what was going on, you'd have stopped, safeword or no safeword."

He uncrossed his arms and leaned forward until their noses were only an inch apart. He was so close, his breath brushed her lips. "Are you sure about that?"

"Yes."

"How sure?"

"Sure enough to let you do it to me. Right now."

His face paled and he jerked backward. He stabbed his fingers into his short hair and dropped his head. "I don't know, Rickie. We can play around, but when it comes to the rest… I don't think I can risk it."

"Risk what?"

"You lying to me too."

She shook her head to emphasize her point. "I won't."

"You say that. But women have a tendency to let men go too far, to put their own needs and wants aside for their lover's pleasure. I want your surrender, Rickie. Not your sacrifice." His voice broke. "You've already given up too much because of me."

Not that again. The man was so frustrating, she wanted to stamp her foot. "I thought we were past that. We've both made mistakes. We've both kept secrets. But we've also both made a decision to be honest with each other." She smoothed her fingers over his stubbly jaw, trying to soothe away his mulish expression. "I promise to tell you if I don't want to do something."

"You'll use the safeword if it hurts or you're too scared."

"I will. And in return you have to promise to be yourself. Don't be afraid, and don't decide for me what I want or don't want."

He smoothed a lock of hair behind her ear. "What do you want right now?"

"You. I want to feel you inside me."

"Vanilla?"

"No. I want the Dark Knight, not Prince Charming."

"Be careful what you ask for."

"I'm up for it, Mr. Caldwell. Are you?"

His eyes darkened, his features shifting subtly, becoming harder, more intense. She'd awakened a fire-breathing dragon. The Master was back.

෩ 🚂 ෬

Gripping his bag of sex toys with one hand and Rickie with the other, Jamie marched into the cottage. Adrenaline raced through his system, triggered by a mix of terror and exhilaration, a rush he usually only experienced when facing a potentially life-threatening situation.

To some extent the comparison was apt. His life wasn't on the line, but his marriage was.

He ushered Rickie through the door and locked it behind them. She entered and stopped by the bed, watching him in silence as he closed the curtains and turned on lights. Her eyes were wide and anxious, but her lips were curved in an encouraging smile.

Shit. Could she tell how nervous he was? If he didn't appear confident and self-assured, she wouldn't trust him to know what he was doing. And he wouldn't blame her. Hardening his expression, he nodded toward the bathroom. "Take off your dress and put on a bra and some panties. Then bring me your body lotion." Spanking her behind had been incredibly gratifying, but now he needed to take care of it so she didn't hurt. He kept his promises.

When the bathroom door clicked shut, he let out a long breath before rolling his shoulders and shaking out his arms. A tense upper body would make his movements stiff and jerky. He wanted—and Rickie needed—everything he did to be fluid and controlled.

More relaxed, he reached into the shopping bag of props he'd bought that morning and began to set the scene. He pulled out some scented candles and gave them a sniff. Not bad. The clerk at the store had recommended them, said they were reputed to help increase orgasm strength. He snorted and placed them around the room in strategic locations. Far be it for him to turn down any assistance. After lighting each one and ensuring that there were no fire risks even if they fell asleep, he turned off the lights and moved to the television. It took him a few moments to find an all-music station with a steady stream of rock. Some of his subs had preferred soft or classical music, but those did nothing for him. The solid rhythmic beat of the song thrummed through his veins, ideal for dancing—and fucking. He hoped his lovely wife agreed. Hmm... now he was having second thoughts.

The bathroom door opened and Rickie stepped out, a vision in a lacy blue bra and boy shorts. An image flickered in his mind, an image of their first night together. She'd being wearing very similar lingerie. It had turned him on then as much as it did now. "You look amazing, babe," he said before he could think better of it. Yeah, he exuded dominance tonight. But when she blushed and sent him a shy smile, he forgave himself. "Come here."

She took his extended hand and stepped down into the living room, her legs a mile long in the matching high-heeled slipper mules.

Everything about his wife was a contradiction. "Do you want me to give you a massage?" she asked, handing him the lotion.

"Not tonight." He shook his head at her guileless expression. "Are you sure about this, Rickie?"

"Positive."

Okay, then. Let the games begin. "Lean over and place your palms flat on the coffee table, Mrs. Caldwell."

She blinked. He nodded.

After a brief pause, she turned and started to go into a crouch. "Legs straight," he admonished her.

Her eyes flared in understanding. Moments later she was in position and Jamie stood transfixed by the sight of Rickie's lace-covered ass offered up in such a breathtaking display. The boy shorts rode up a little, outlining her pussy beautifully. His cock transformed into a battering ram, eager to pound her walls. He stepped behind her and grasped her panties. In a slow, tantalizing striptease, he tugged them down her legs, crouching when he reached her ankles. He lifted her feet free, then had her spread her legs.

Because he'd barely had a taste of her in almost a year, he rocked forward and licked her pussy from behind. She gasped. "Jamie?"

"Shh," he murmured, getting in another, longer, swipe. She tasted amazing, sweeter than any nectar. How had he lasted a year without her? The truth was painfully obvious—he hadn't being living, he'd been existing.

His fingers curled around her thighs as he delved deeper, thrusting inside her with his tongue. Mmm… he moaned. Her legs trembled and her breath came in quick little pants. The position might have shocked her, but she'd gotten over it quickly enough. He hoped she'd be like that about all the new things he planned to introduce her to.

Reluctantly, he pulled back. It wasn't time for either of them yet. Rickie's loud groan and the dirty look she shot him had him biting back a grin. "All good things come to those who wait, Mrs. Caldwell." After pushing to his feet, he picked up the bottle of lotion and squeezed out a handful. He warmed it up in his hands, then cupped her bottom and gently massaged the thick cream into skin that still bore faint marks of her earlier spanking.

Starting on the outside, he made small kneading motions, working his way inward. She dropped her head and closed her eyes, enjoyment clear on her face. When he smoothed two fingers down the seam of her ass, she moaned. "That feels so good, Jamie."

Perfect. His cue that she was ready. "Don't move," he ordered and let go of her. He twisted around and went to the couch where he'd left the bag. A smile tugged at the corner of his mouth when he caught Ricking trying to see what he was doing. "Mrs. Caldwell, a spanking is not what I have in mind right now. But if you insist on disobeying me, I'll bend you over my knee and teach you how a proper sub should behave. Understood?"

Her eyes widened, but she regained her original position without argument. *Progress.* To tease her, he made as much noise as he could rooting through the bag for the toy and the special, thicker lubricant he needed. After shoving the toy in his pocket, he squirted some lube on his fingers, then set the tube on the table. Eager to continue, he returned to his favorite position and spread the lubricant on the puckered skin, circling her tight hole. "Oh!" she said, jerking away.

"Problem?" he asked. He kept his tone mellow, only mildly inquisitive, but inside he was gripped with worry that she was going to stop him.

"N-nothing," she stuttered. "I just didn't think we were going to do that so soon."

Relieved, he patted her butt. "We're not. So relax."

"Then what are you doing?"

"You're an anal virgin, and I want you to enjoy it when I finally take your incredibly sexy ass. So, I need to prepare this little hole, loosen it up."

She swallowed and licked her lips. His groin tightened and he clenched his teeth to keep from groaning. "How will you do that?" she asked.

"Very, very pleasurably. Now turn around and be quiet, Mrs. Caldwell."

He waited until she returned to her assigned position before cupping her butt cheeks and jiggling them. His subs had always loved this, especially after a spanking. Rickie giggled, confirming that the same held true for her. Very slowly, he inserted the tip of a well-lubed finger into her, pressing past the tight circle of muscles. When she stiffened, he jiggled her cheek again with his free hand. Carefully, he rubbed his finger in a small circle, softening and stretching the delicate tissues. As she relaxed, his finger slid in deeper.

A small sound of pleasure escaped her lips. "You like this," he said.

She turned her head to meet his gaze, her cheeks flushed with arousal. "Yes," she whispered.

He gently smacked her butt with his free hand. "Yes, what?"

She paused for a beat, then licked her lips. "Yes, Sir."

Good. She was learning. Caressing her bottom once again, he pulled his finger out until only the tip remained inside. He pushed it back in and started to pump it.

In. Out. In. Out.

Her hips rolled into his movements, ensuring a deep penetration. His prim and proper wife was getting her rocks off. *Thank God.* "I'm going to give you two fingers now. Breathe."

She inhaled deeply, her chest expanding. When she exhaled, he inserted two fingers, jiggling her ass to keep her relaxed.

"Again," he ordered her. With his fingers spread, he massaged the narrow opening. The tension drained from her body. He reached between her legs and cupped her. She ground against the heel of his hand, her engorged clit telling him exactly how much she was enjoying the scene. Her juices flowed, wetting his fingers. The scent of her, the feel of her—it was paradise.

She continued to gyrate, pushing his fingers deeper into her pussy and her ass. Her breathing accelerated and her entire body flushed a very pretty pink. She was close. Too close. He pulled his fingers out of her to get ready for the next step.

"Jamie!" she protested.

"Not yet."

"I'll beg... Sir."

"Yes, you most certainly will," he agreed, grinning behind her back. He reached into his pocket and got out the small butt plug he'd selected for her first bout of anal play. He covered it with lube, then very carefully, he pushed the plug into her ass, holding his breath. When it locked in place, she groaned and rocked her hips. *Mission accomplished.* He blew out in relief.

Reaching behind, he plucked a cushion off the couch and tossed it onto the floor at her feet. "Kneel down with your chest on the table. Open your arms and hold onto the edges." With a nod, she obeyed. A surge of pride roared through him. Rickie was so fearless, so trusting, letting him direct their play. It was a side of her he'd never seen before. A side of her he'd love to see more often.

She rested her face on the table and cocked a brow. Okay, maybe she wasn't quite trusting, not yet. He scowled at her. "Don't move."

It was time to let her stew. Going for his bag of toys again, he yanked out a blindfold and covered her eyes. Then he pocketed the remote control for the butt plug and walked over to the front door and opened it.

Rickie lifted her head. "Jamie? You're leaving?"

Ignoring her question, he made his voice low and sharp. "Don't. Move."

She swallowed and put her cheek back on the table. That was more like it.

Leaving his wife in a suitably submissive pose, he shut the cottage door behind him and set off to get a beer at the resort bar. The remote had a range of 100 feet, so he could be far enough away for her not to know he was around and still give her a great lesson in who was boss. Who controlled her pleasure.

He palmed the remote and gave it a little zap. When he heard Rickie's surprised yelp, his cock jumped and a broad smile cracked his face. Tonight was going to be so much fucking fun.

ଛ 🎦 ଓ

"Bastard."

Erica clung to the edges of the table and gritted her teeth as she rode through the vibrations from Jamie's little toy. She could picture him grinning like a loon each time he pressed the button, imagining her reaction. Or could he see her? Was he watching even now? She wanted to take the blindfold off, but if he was keeping an eye on her somehow, he'd know she hadn't followed his instructions. And to be honest, she was enjoying the tingles from the object in her butt, as strange and unfamiliar as they were. What was weirder was her sense of anticipation. She'd never been more aroused, more excited. Not even that first night with Jamie.

The last twenty-four hours had been unpredictable and thrilling. Each one of Jamie's revelations about his previous lifestyle had sparked myriad fantasies in her mind. When he'd pulled up her skirt in the parking lot at the restaurant and spanked her, she'd been shocked. But then the sting had dissipated and warmth had rushed to her bottom, to the area between her thighs and she'd wanted more.

His rapid breaths on her neck, his heart beating a frantic rhythm against her shoulder, his erection pressing into her hip had been clear signs that Jamie was approaching the boundaries of his control. Ecstatic and elated that she could do this to him, she'd egged him on, pushed him further. Energy had flowed through her and she'd felt that rush of adrenaline that Jamie often described. Her orgasm, when it had hit, had stunned her in its intensity.

She was so messed up. That certainly wasn't the type of thing she should enjoy—was it? A small part of her insisted it wasn't normal for a grown independent woman to want a man to tell her what to do—to spank her, for heaven's sake! What had happened to the feminist inside her? Oh, she was still swinging her bra into the bonfire. But the other part of her knew with certainly that *this* was exactly what she'd been craving. Knew *this* was the reason she'd been drawn to Jamie from that first night. He wanted to dominate her, and she needed to submit to him.

They were meant for each other, and maybe now that they were starting to work out their issues in the bedroom, the rest would follow. Maybe—

A zap interrupted her thoughts. Unlike the previous tickles, this one was powerful. Her hips jerked against the table as the vibrations ignited the nerve endings in that most private of places. Abruptly, they ended. She groaned. Why so short? Her husband was a cruel, cruel man.

Panting, she struggled to regain her breath, and insecurity took hold. What if a maid or some maintenance guy let himself into the cottage? Blindfolded, on her knees, half-lying on the table with her butt in the air, a plug sticking out, this was a disaster in the making.

Why had she let him talk her into this? Maybe she should just get up and end this right now. Making up her mind, she let go of the table and sat back on her heels. Zap! Her butt cheeks clenched around the plug, and a moan escaped her lips. Oh God. He really was watching her. Or had it merely been a coincidence? Pushing to her feet, she stood and raised the blindfold. She held her breath as her eyes adjusted to the candlelight, expecting another warning zap. When none came, she exhaled in a rush. He wasn't watching her like some peeping Tom after all.

She didn't have to stay in that embarrassing position if she didn't want to. Jamie would never know if she had obeyed him the entire time or not. But if she didn't, if she pretended to obey, wasn't that defeating the whole purpose? He was trusting her; she needed to trust him. She claimed she wanted him to be in charge; now was the time to prove it.

Kneeling, she returned to the position he'd left her in and gripped the edges of the table. If there was a chance this experience could save their marriage, she'd take whatever he had to give.

As though he'd heard her thoughts, the vibrations restarted, strong and escalating. *He could control the intensity and pattern too?* The vibrations slowed and sped up, over and over, growing in strength and shortening in duration.

Her hips began to pump, driven by the punishing assault. Never before had she thought she could derive such sensual pleasure from her butt. Would it feel as good to have Jamie take her this way? He wanted to. He'd made that clear in their talk about must-haves. A pang of fear made her belly clench. Jamie was a lot bigger than the little toy inside her.

The vibrations began pulsing on and off, rippling up her spine. She shivered and goose bumps broke out all over her body in a wave. Her hips jerked and she bumped against the table over and over again, the coolness of the wood making her heated clitoris throb. *Oh, my!* She could sense the slickness between her thighs, could smell her arousal, overpowering the scent of the candles Jamie had lit. Unbelievably, she was on the verge of coming.

As she prepared to let herself go, to plunge into the abyss of sensation, Jamie's admonishment echoed in her mind: *Self-pleasuring is not permitted. Unless I order it.* She stilled. He hadn't ordered her to come, but he *was* the one controlling the vibrations. If she orgasmed this way, would she be disobeying him? She hadn't touched herself, technically. But she hadn't exactly followed his "Don't move" order either.

The vibrations stopped and she sank against the table to regroup. She knew they'd start up again. Jamie wasn't finished having fun with her. A minute later, they returned, a mild tingling. Behind the blindfold, she screwed her eyes shut and concentrated on staying as still as possible, on absorbing the exquisite torturous shocks. Her entire world narrowed down to one area, one sense. Everything magnified, heightened.

Her eyes almost rolled back in her head as the vibrations sped up, turning the lower half of her body into the Devil's playground, Jamie's playground. She had to resist the mounting pressure, the spiraling need. Sheep. That was it. She'd count sheep.

One sheep. Two sheep.

She imagined them jumping over a low white picket fence.

Three sheep. Four sheep.

"Ahhh!" she groaned over the music as the vibrations reached a crescendo. She was on the tipping point when the vibrator turned off. Shaken and exhausted from her efforts, she sprawled onto the table. If Jamie tried to put her through another round, she'd lose the battle against her impending climax for sure.

Out of nowhere, hands clasped her hips. The maintenance man! Her heart raced and a scream tore from her throat.

"Shh… It's me," he murmured next to her ear.

"Oh, thank God," she said, pressing her forehead against the cool wood as adrenaline flowed out of her. She was safe. With Jamie. And now that she knew some random resort employee wasn't holding her naked butt, the thrill of having Jamie's hands on her again renewed her waning energy.

"Had fun?" he asked.

The beer on his breath and the amusement in his voice set the tone for her response. "Not nearly enough," she said. He'd brought her to the brink, then stopped. Had that been his goal? What had he called it? Orgasm denial. Bastard. Then again, he hadn't come either.

"Are you ready for more… fun?"

Pride be damned. She needed him. Licking her lips, she laid everything on the line. "I'm ready for you, Jamie. So very ready." It seemed like forever since she'd been in his arms, felt that incredible rasp of hard flesh.

"Soon, Mrs. Caldwell." He stepped back and trailed his hand across her sensitized bottom. The heat of his fingers seared her. She sucked in a breath and prayed he wouldn't make her wait too much longer.

Five sheep. Six sheep.

Hearing the rustling of Jamie's bag of toys, her nerves rioted. What other surprise had he planned for her?

Suddenly, he was behind her, removing the blindfold. He took her hands and drew her up so she sat on her heels. Then placing small sweet kisses on her skin, he massaged the prickles out of her arms. When he arrived at her shoulders, he continued nibbling his way up her neck, her ears, her chin before finally—finally!—landing on her lips. He nipped the bottom one, then sealed their mouths together in a heated kiss. She hooked her still tingling arms around his neck and reveled in his desire for her. Too soon, he released her lips and stared into her eyes, his own burning pools of blue. With a muttered curse, he swung her into his arms and carried her across the room to the bed.

He set her down on her back. "Keep your knees up," he said, hopping down to the living area. He snagged the bag of toys off the couch and moments later crawled onto the bed. Her brain raced, trying to keep up with him. Before she knew it, he was kissing her again, his tongue plundering her mouth, consuming her. He was like a starving man, and she rejoiced. This was the Jamie she'd wanted.

"I'm going to restrain you." His low, throaty voice and his chest rising and falling with his rapid breaths made her tremble, evidence of his barely contained desire. She wasn't certain how she'd like being tied up, but the spark of excitement in his eyes told her she'd enjoy his reaction to it. He waited while she debated with herself. When she nodded, his hands snaked behind her back and her bra was undone and removed before she could do more than gape. He plunged his hand into his magician's bag of tricks and withdrew two long silk scarves. Did he have a bunny in there too? She pressed her lips together to trap the giggle that threatened to escape. A mood killer for sure.

His brow furrowed in concentration, Jamie tied a slipknot around her wrist, then tied the other end to the bedpost. Once he'd done the same to her other arm, he sat back and stared at her. Red marked his cheekbones and his eyes darkened like a stormy sky. She wanted to laugh at his strained expression. Her rescue team lieutenant might need a rescue of his own tonight.

As though on fire, he leapt off the bed, startling her. He made quick work of removing his shirt and pants, dropping them to the floor, but he kept his tight black boxers on. She didn't know whether to pout or take a picture. Even at thirty-three, with his broad shoulders and rippling abs, her husband could easily grace the cover of any firefighter calendar.

She tried to beckon him to her, but stopped when the bindings at her wrists dug into her skin. "Ow!" she said, wincing.

"Stay still." Frowning, he ran a finger around the edge of the scarf, as though testing its tightness. "We wouldn't want this to leave a mark."

Although his tone was mild, the heat flickering in his gaze belied his words. Her stomach clenched with panic. Did she really believe that he wouldn't hurt her?

As she continued to watch him in silence, he leaned over her and touched his lips to hers. "Trust me," he whispered, turning her inside out, upside-down. This was exactly what she'd asked for—begged for, in fact—wasn't it?

When she tilted her head in assent, he smiled and began tracing a path of kisses along her neck. He grazed her collarbone with his teeth and nipped at her shoulder. Shivers raced up and down her body. She struggled to keep as still and as quiet as possible, but she lost that battle when he turned his head and brushed her upper chest and breasts with his soft hair. *He knew what that did to her.* She moaned loudly and arched her back, writhing beneath him, wanting to clasp his head and rub his hair over her aching nipples again and again. But she couldn't. Her helplessness was excruciating and exquisite.

Jamie lay an arm across her hips, pinning her to the mattress, before latching on to her right breast. His tongue lashed the taut peak and his teeth raked the puckered areola. When he sucked her nipple deep inside his hot mouth, an arrow of pure bliss shot to her core. As though sensing it, he reached between her legs and slid his fingers into her folds. "You're so wet for me," he whispered.

His voice, rough and pleased, left her throbbing and needy. Before she could form a response, his lips closed over her breast, the suction so intense she screamed. At the same time, he plunged two fingers inside her, making slow circles against her ready walls. He twisted his fingers, pressing down toward the bed... toward the vibrator. How could she have forgotten it was there?

"How do you feel?" he murmured.

"Full. Oh my God. So full... Sir."

"Good girl." Pulling his fingers out, he whipped off his boxers and knelt between her legs, moving so fast she didn't even have a chance to complain. He gripped her thighs and lifted her up so the backs of her legs rested on his lap. The movement stretched her arms and pushed her breasts forward in a silent offering.

His arms supporting her back, he entered her with one powerful thrust. He froze when she cried out, his gaze shooting to her face. The worry in his eyes melted her heart. She tilted her hips so he'd sink in even more deeply. Understanding her unspoken message, he pumped into her, slowly at first, then with increasing speed.

Her lower belly was a mass of twirling, whirling mini tornadoes, each spinning higher and higher with every push of his hips. She could barely breathe with the enormity of what she was feeling. So full, so aroused, so ecstatic—so in love. By showing her how to submit, Jamie had given her this.

The click, barely audible over Jamie's rock music, was followed by an intense buzzing in her butt. *The vibrator.* Her gaze flew to his face and her breath locked in her chest. Eyes dark, jaw clenched, he gripped her hips and pistoned into her. Her belly contracted at the raw lust in his features, the smoldering passion in his eyes.

Assailed by Jamie on all fronts, she detonated. The orgasm rocked through her, scorching everything in its path. Jamie slipped the plug out and she screamed, her body bowing, as the movement catapulted her into another wave of erotic spasms.

Fingers digging into her thighs, Jamie slammed into her, shouting her name as he joined her in ecstasy.

A few moments later, still breathing heavily, he reached past her and yanked on the slip knots, releasing her wrists from the restraints. Collapsing onto the bed beside her, he dragged her into his arms and rolled onto his back.

Sated, drained of her previous turmoil, she lay sprawled across his chest. Beneath her ear, his heart beat a dance club rhythm. He speared his fingers into her hair and brought her head up. Meeting her halfway, he captured her mouth in a slow, languorous kiss. His tongue lazily stroked her lips. Without moving, he ended the kiss and stared into her eyes. "Thank you for giving me back this part of myself. I love you, Rickie."

She smiled, her heart full. She had her husband back. Both of them free at last from the veil of deception they'd wrapped their marriage in. Second only to the birth of their daughter, this day had been the best of her life. Jamie had given her more joy, more peace, more fulfillment than she'd ever thought possible. She tightened her arms around him, knowing the night would end. But praying that the feelings never would.

CHAPTER 7

Hours after the most cathartic sex of his life, Jamie awoke to the insistent beeping of his watch. He threw out his hand and grabbed it off the nightstand. Three AM. That gave him just enough time to shower and pack up their gear before heading out.

Rickie sighed in her sleep and plastered herself against his side. He grinned and ran his fingers over her smooth shoulder, remembering last night. His cock rose to full mast as he pictured her tied to the bed posts, knees splayed wide. He'd wanted to eat her so bad, but once he'd slipped his fingers into her hot pussy and she'd started grinding on his hand, every thought of control had fled. He'd had to be inside her then, had to take her hard and fast. The way they'd both needed.

Exhausted from all the sexual activity, Rickie had been asleep in minutes. He on the other hand, had lain awake reliving every precious moment. Time and again, he'd returned to her expression when he'd said he loved her. For the first time in years, he'd seen acceptance in her big brown eyes. They'd won a battle today, in the war to save their marriage. With her smile, she'd shown her belief in him. And with her submission, she'd proven her trust. But she hadn't yet surrendered... She would though. They were communicating better and finally starting to enjoy each other. And it was all thanks to Rickie, to her willingness to explore, to step away from her rules. To face her fears.

A born organizer and negotiator, she'd always brought her

arguments to the table, but because he'd thought it would make her happy, he'd always let her win. In that respect, he'd failed her, failed their family. Not anymore. Now they were both at the table. Both talking and sharing. Both willing to compromise. They'd only begun to scratch the surface of their problems, but building this trust between them was the key to solving them all.

Yes, eventually he'd have her surrender. But not today. Today he had other plans. Speaking of which, he needed to move his butt or it would be too late. Quietly, he slipped away from Rickie's warmth and into the frigid shower.

When he returned to the room, a towel knotted at his waist, Rickie was still asleep. He turned on the bedside lamp and took in the sight of her. One he hadn't seen in a long time. She seemed so innocent stretched out flat on her stomach with her face buried in the pillow. He eased the sheet back, baring her perfect ass. Seeing it, his palm itched. Should he? The round globes looked so succulent, so bitable. He resisted. Barely. Maybe just once… What the hell. Life was too short to keep second-guessing himself. Standing next to the bed, he landed one resounding smack on the cheek he'd spared yesterday.

With a speed he hadn't known her capable of, she twisted away from him, stopping on all fours to glare at him. Damn. She was so fucking hot with her sex-rumpled hair and piercing eyes. Good thing he didn't want a true sub. She looked more like a Domme than anything else right now. A really pissed-off Domme. When he grinned, she frowned and lowered her eyes to the bulge beneath his towel. "Again?"

She sounded so disgruntled, he threw his head back and burst into laughter. Pulling the sheet to her chest, she sat back and watched him, her eyes wary, her mouth pouting. "What's so funny?" she asked after a while.

He sobered and sat beside her, smoothing a wayward strand of her blonde hair. "Nothing. I'm just really happy."

Her pout turned into a smile and she hooked her arm around his nape. "Me too."

The moment too perfect to pass up, he pulled her against his chest and kissed her. Their tongues met in a gentle dance. No rush, no pressure. Just an unhurried exchange of emotion and affection.

Not wanting the kiss to turn into more, he released her lips and rested his forehead against hers, his hands cradling her face. "Now, get dressed. We've got a big day ahead."

She glanced at the radio-alarm on the nightstand and her brow furrowed in confusion. "It's the middle of the night."

He chuckled and pushed her toward the bathroom. "You'll enjoy this. Go."

When she was out of his reach, she turned back to him, her hands on her waist, glorious in her nakedness. "What exactly is *this*?"

"We're going to see the sunrise."

Her eyes grew round as clamshells. "You're not thinking of hiking up the Haiku Hidden Stairs are you? Because you know how I feel about that."

Jamie shook his head. Rickie kept herself in shape, but she was more a walk along the beach girl than a mountain hike girl. "I promised no extreme sports, and I'm a man of my word."

After a moment, she opened the dresser and got out a pair of short pants and a t-shirt. She yawned and threw a longing glance at the bed. Shit. The last thing he wanted to do today was force her to do anything. "If you'd rather go back to sleep, we can see the sunrise another day." When he could spank that cute butt into following his orders. "I just thought it would be fun."

She crossed over to him and smiled. "I can sleep some other time."

He kissed the bridge of her nose. "The place we're going is an hour away, so you can rest some more in the car. We'll have breakfast there."

After a quick peck on his mouth, she sauntered into the bathroom, swaying her hips in a most inviting manner. Did the woman have no idea what she did to him, all naked and pink like that?

When the shower turned on, he flopped onto his back on the bed and grinned. He was going to throw Rickie for another loop today. As much fun as yesterday had been, he wanted to show her—*prove* to her—that he was still Jamie, only better. He had no desire to control her outside their bedroom activities. And even then, not every sexual encounter had to be a scene. Spontaneity turned him on just as much as it did any other red-blooded man.

Most of all, he wanted her to know how much he valued her thoughts and opinions. He'd missed talking to her, whether it was shooting the shit after a difficult shift, or late-night philosophical discussions. Strong and independent, she was so much more to him than a sub: she was his wife, his partner. The love of his life.

Unlike many Doms, he was a sucker for romance. And this new twist in their relationship wouldn't keep him from sharing romantic moments with her. Starting with the world's most beautiful sunrise.

An hour and a half later, Jamie turned off Kalanianaole Highway into the almost empty parking lot of Makapu'u Lookout. He shut off the engine and in the glow of the interior light, Rickie's sleep-heavy lids lifted and she smiled drowsily.

"Good morning," he said, brushing his lips against hers.

"Are we there?"

"Yep." He checked his watch. They had enough time to hike up to the lighthouse before the sun rose. "Let's go." After securing the roof and doors of the Mustang, he shouldered the backpack full of water and supplies, then switched on his flashlight and took Rickie's hand. "Ready?"

"Since I have no idea where we are or where we're going, all I can say is: 'Lay on, MacDuff, and damned be him who first cries "Hold! Enough!"'" She bent into a curtsey and with a wide sweep of her arm, indicated the general direction where lights bobbed up the mountain.

Joy bubbling in his chest, he gathered her into his arms and spun her in a circle. He loved seeing her this way, so carefree, without her day planner and rigid schedule in hand. Maybe she was finally learning she didn't have to control everything to be safe. Setting her on her feet, he kissed her soundly. "Christ, I've missed you, Rickie."

"I've missed you too, Jamie." She kissed him lightly and laced her fingers through his. "Let's go see this sunrise you've been telling me about."

Hand in hand, he guided her through the darkness to a paved walkway where only a few other early morning enthusiasts were slowly making their way up the mountain. Not even two miles long, the trail led to the Makapu'u Point Lighthouse at the southern edge of the ridge.

The sun was just beginning to breach the horizon when they reached the end of the trail. Standing on the edge of the ridge, they seemed to hang over the vast Pacific Ocean. A narrow band of golden light was sandwiched between mile upon mile of jet-black water and dark puffy clouds. As the sun rose, the ocean and the sky above the clouds turned a steely gray while the band of light grew, revealing the sun, a golden ball of fire bathed in a riot of pinks, oranges, and yellows. Other people who'd gathered along the ridge beside them cheered its arrival.

Jamie placed Rickie in front of him and wrapped his arms around her waist as they watched, lost in the wonder. "It's so beautiful," Rickie said, her voice barely a whisper. "At times like this, I wish I were an artist."

He glanced down at his wife's face, resplendent in the sun's first rays, and agreed wholeheartedly. His arms tightened around her and he laid his cheek on her head, enjoying the feel of her in her arms. Right here, right now, she was his.

Another cheer rose from the crowd when someone spotted a huge white bird soaring in the early morning light. They watched as it spiraled down to one of the islands below. Jamie used the opportunity to share with her some of what he'd learned when researching this spot. He pointed out the islands of Moloka'i and Lana'i across the Kaiwi Channel. A few minutes, later, she indicated a mass rising out of the sea. "What's that one? It looks odd."

"That's Manana, also known as Rabbit Island."

She cocked her head, as though studying it from a different angle would help. "Well, I suppose it resembles a rabbit head." She turned in his arms and hugged him hard. "I'm so glad we got to see the sunrise together. I'll never forget this, Jamie."

Neither would he. The sun reflected in the water, creating a rose lane, like a red carpet laid out for a queen, ending right at Rickie's feet. If this wasn't a sign, he didn't know what was. On impulse, he dropped to one knee in front of her. Five years ago, his proposal had been far less than romantic. But maybe he could make up for that now.

Taking her hand, he kissed her wrist and looked up into her astonished eyes. "Rickie, I know our marriage has had more ups and downs than it should have. You were right to want a divorce. I wasn't behaving like the man you'd married. But I've grown up since then, and right here, right now, I pledge myself to you. I promise to love you above all others, to honor your needs and desires above my own, and to cherish our life together, every single day. I'll be honest with you at all times and in all things. You're an angel for giving me this second chance to make you happy."

As he spoke, tears welled in her eyes and spilled onto her cheeks. She knelt with him and clutched their joined hands against her heart. "Jamie, no. I wasn't right. I shut you off, shut you out. How could you know what I wanted when I didn't even know it myself?" Her voice broke. Blinking away her tears, she turned toward the ocean and inhaled deeply. Her lips curved up and when she faced him again, joy danced in her brown gaze. "I pledge to be the wife you deserve. To love you above all others and to honor your needs and... desires."

At her salacious grin, his belly tightened. "Minx," he said on a groan. "I promise to cherish our time together and to stop worrying about things that might never be." New tears trailed down her face as she continued to smile. His heart ached, knowing exactly how difficult that last promise had been for her to make. She was still terrified of something happening to him because of his job. And her fears were real. He risked his life every day.

Hauling her against his chest, he buried his face in her soft hair. "I can't ask for anything more," he whispered.

Slowly, he became aware of clapping and whistling. He helped Rickie to her feet, grinning at the crowd that had formed a half-circle around them. His wife's cheeks were as pink as the sky. She squeezed his hand. "Say something!"

Laughing, he beamed at her and very loudly told the group, "She said 'yes.'"

She swatted his arm and glared at him playfully. A man in the group called out, "You sure about this, dude? She looks like a handful."

Jamie tucked Rickie under his arm and palmed one luscious ass cheek. "That she is, my man." A handful and so much more.

෨ 🚂 ෬

As Jamie led her back down the paved pathway to the car, Erica's mind was still reeling from the miraculous sunrise, and Jamie's very unexpected reaffirmation of their wedding vows. After yesterday, seeing him so confident in Dom-mode, she'd never in a million years have expected him to go down on one knee and proclaim his love for her like that. He was such a multi-faceted diamond. One she still barely knew after five years of marriage. From today, she'd make it her mission to change that. She had so much to learn about him, and she hoped that their newfound intimacy would help keep the lines of communication open.

A short way down the path, Jamie veered to the side and stopped at a large plaque that indicated where whales could be seen in the wintertime. "Too bad we'll miss that," she said.

"Yeah, but we can see whales pretty much any time at home." He set the backpack on the ground and yanked out a bottle of water, drinking deeply before handing it to her.

Grateful Jamie had thought to bring water, she took a long sip, letting the water hydrate her throat. It was barely past sunrise and already their clothes were sticking to their bodies. "God, that feels good."

He plopped a baseball cap on her head and grinned. Seeing him so happy, her belly warmed. She couldn't wait to find out what else he had planned for their day. Handing her a bottle of sunscreen, he took the water back. "Before we head out, put this on."

"Head out where?" she asked as she applied the lotion.

"We're taking that trail." He pointed to a small foot-beaten path behind the plaque.

She ventured forward a few steps to investigate the trail, squinting to see the twists and turns. "Where does it go?"

"Down the mountain to the coast."

She glanced at her running shoes. Not the best footwear for hiking. "Is it steep?"

"You'll be fine." He held out his hand and she took it. When she gripped him a little tighter than necessary, he didn't even grimace.

Within moments, the trail went from packed-dirt to exposed rock. She kept Jamie's hand firmly clutched in hers, stepping where he indicated. A strange mixture of embarrassment and relief made her belly flip when she noticed how he used his body as a bulwark in case she slipped.

"Easy," he said when her feet skidded on some loose stones.

By the time they reached the coastline, her insides were quaking. She relaxed her death grip on Jamie's fingers and had to laugh as she held up her shaking hands for him to see. "You'd think I'd just gone down Mount Everest."

Humor shining in his eyes, Jamie cupped her face and gave her a loud smacking kiss on the mouth. "You did great." He grabbed her hand. "Come on. You're going to love this."

Jamie's eyes sparkled like those of a small boy exploring a pile of toy cars. His eagerness was contagious. Thrilled to see him so happy, she followed. They stopped in front of a series of tide pools framed by glistening rock ledges. The depths glowed a gorgeous cerulean blue, while the shallows reflected the moss below, giving them an emerald sheen.

A large wave rolled in, crashing against the rocks, adding its white foam to the array of colors. The spray from the waves showered over them, cool and invigorating. She squealed with delight. "I wish I had my camera. Chloe would love photos of this."

With a wink, Jamie set the backpack on the ground and reached into one of the many pockets. He yanked out what appeared to be a waterproof camera. "Will this do?"

"My, my. Aren't you the Boy Scout," she teased. When his gaze locked on hers, the desire burning in his eyes made her breath hitch. He shouldered the backpack and raised a brow. "I'm always prepared. For anything. Are you?"

Oh boy! What else did he have in that backpack? "Did you want to..." Her voice faltered and she trailed off. What was wrong with her? Why was it so hard for her to say that little word? It was only three letters for heaven's sake. She filled her lungs with ocean air and tried again. "Did you want to have *sex* here? Because"—she pointed to the people playing in the tide pools around them—"we aren't exactly alone." Her voice had lowered to a whisper when she'd said the word, but at least she'd managed to spit it out.

Jamie stepped in close, towering over her. His eyes reflected his amusement. "Oh, we're going to have"—he lowered his voice to a whisper, imitating her—"sex. But not here."

Her stomach grumbled loudly and her cheeks flushed. He laughed and heads turned at the joyous sound. "But not until I've fed your hungry belly. I wouldn't be much of a husband if I didn't keep you well-fed as well as well-fucked, now would I?"

"You're so bad, Jamie Caldwell," she said, loving his playfulness.

Pointing to a boulder a few yards away, he said, "Let's have our breakfast there." He waited while she removed her shoes, then with a hand on her butt, he boosted her up onto a flat spot. She scrambled a bit, but managed to settle in without falling on her face. Jamie on the other hand, easily hefted himself onto the sun-warmed rock despite the weight of the backpack. He set the pack on his lap and opened it. Even though she could barely stand the suspense, she waited without saying a word. Jamie was enjoying teasing her, and she didn't want to ruin it for him.

Finally, he pulled out a thermos and handed it to her. "Coffee?" she asked, her voice high and hopeful.

"There's cream and sugar too. Well, cream substitute."

With desperate fingers, she clawed open the thermos and poured coffee into the attached cup. After adding some creamer and sugar, she inhaled deeply. "This smells divine, Jamie." She took a sip and enjoyed the savory warmth taste of it.

"Eat up." He plunked a foil-wrapped package on her lap and waggled his eyebrows. "You're going to need your strength."

"Hmm… that sounds… promising."

"And you know I always keep my promises."

Yes, he did. Which was exactly why he'd never promised he'd come home safe and sound at the end of every shift. He couldn't. Well, she'd made promises too, ones she planned to keep. Pushing the negativity aside, she passed Jamie the coffee and unwrapped her breakfast surprise. The spicy sent of Portuguese sausage filled her nose. She took a bite of the still-warm sausage and egg sandwich. Delicious.

Water shot out of a fissure in the rocks, the plume reaching a good thirty feet, startling her. The sausage went down the wrong way and she choked. Coughing and gasping for air, she dropped the sandwich and smacked her chest. His work-face on, Jamie raised her hands into the air. "Keep coughing," he said, handing her a napkin. His cool tone calmed her and she quickly disengaged the bite caught in her throat.

As she regained her breath, Jamie took her hand and pressed it to his lips, a sheepish expression on his face. "I thought it would be fun to see your reaction when the water came through the blowhole. It wasn't. And I'm sorry. I should have warned you."

Before answering, she took a sip from the bottle of water he offered her. The liquid soothed her throat. "You couldn't have predicted what would happen. Does the blowhole have a name? I want to know what to call the thing that almost killed me." She chuckled, trying to lighten Jamie's mood.

"The Dragon's Nostrils."

Another plume of water shot up, making her snort. "I can see why."

When she finished her sandwich, Jamie reached into his backpack and got out a couple containers and handed one to her. She opened it, and now it was her turn to feel like a kid with a favorite toy. "Oh, Jamie!" The container was filled with pineapple spears, slices of mango, pieces of watermelon and cantaloupe, and a few other fruits she couldn't name. Grinning widely, she took the fork he handed her. "You remembered."

"Hard to forget. Before meeting you, I wouldn't have been able to name half of what's in these containers."

When they finished eating, Jamie packed up and gave her the camera. "Let's get some photos for Chloe."

Coming down from the boulder, she yelped when her feet touched the burning rocks.

"Too hot for your lily-white Seattle feet?" he asked, his grin teasing.

"I guess I don't have your heat tolerance, Mr. Firefighter."

Enjoying the banter between them, she laughed and put on her shoes. They spent a half hour exploring the tide pools and taking pictures of the fish, corals, and sea urchins. On a sandy part of the beach, she found a colored glass ball and held it up for Jamie to see. "I wonder what this is."

"It's a Japanese fishing float. Fishermen used to use them on their nets."

"Oh, Chloe will love this. Can we bring it to her?"

This was one of the things he loved best about Rickie; her first thought was always for Chloe. He held the backpack while she rolled the ball in an extra T-shirt he'd brought and secured it among their other supplies.

"Ready to see more?" he asked, when she was done.

"There's more?"

"Oh, yeah. The best is yet to come."

Her belly tingled as she anticipated what else he had in store for her. "You know, for someone who insisted the vacation be unscripted, you seem to have done a lot of planning."

He grinned. "When you do it, it's OCD. When I do it, it's research." He winked, and she went wet between her legs. His smile really should be illegal. It was one of the many things she loved about him. It was also one of the things that attracted the fire bunnies. Her smile fell.

"Hey," he said, touching her face. "What's wrong?"

"I'm so happy we've finally found each other again. I just—" She clamped her mouth shut. How could she admit to being jealous, especially after this morning?

"Erica." His use of her full name let her know how serious he was. "What I said up there by the lighthouse, that wasn't bullshit. I meant every word. Every syllable. You're mine. And I'm yours. You're it for me." The corners of his lips kicked up. "Especially now."

After everything he'd done during the last few days, she needed to shake off her worries and simply enjoy being here with him. "I meant every word too. And I'll try to be less insecure."

Jamie gripped her hand. "Let's go." Anxious to know what he'd planned for them, she followed him away from the people and the tide pools, away from the lighthouse. Where were they going? They took a little path and after a minute of walking, it narrowed dangerously. Fear gripped her belly and she dug her heels in. "Ah, Jamie…" Her eyes gravitated to the edge of the trail, then to the water and the waves that crashed onto the rocks. She swallowed. "I don't think I can do this."

"Rickie, you're one of the bravest women I know. You can do it. But if it makes you feel better, I'll put a harness on you. I'll go first and anchor the rope on the other side, then you can cross. Sound good?"

"You brought your climbing gear?"

"Like I said, I'm always prepared." He made quick work of strapping her in, a small smile playing on his lips.

"You're enjoying this, aren't you?"

His eyes twinkled. "Damn right. I love seeing you all trussed up." He dropped a kiss on her lips, then crossed the narrow section of the path with sure-footed ease. "Your turn."

Sweat dripping down her spine in an unnerving trickle, she inched forward, cautiously placing one foot in front of the other. Although she tried to focus on Jamie, her gaze was drawn to the edge. All she could hear, all she could see was the water crashing on the rocks below. Her heart started to pound against her ribs and her chest felt tight.

"Erica. Eyes on me." Jamie's commanding tone pulled her back. "You can do this, honey. Even charging into an unstable mountain of debris didn't faze you." He tugged on the line attached to her harness. "I've got you."

She nodded. He was right. This was nothing compared to the horror they'd gone through the night of the earthquake. Straightening her spine, she kept her eyes locked on Jamie's and stepped cautiously toward him. When she reached him, she fell into his arms, panting. "Please don't tell me we have to go back that way." She'd overcome her fear, but once was more than enough.

He touched her nose and pushed a bottle of water in her hand. "We don't. Now drink. I don't want you to get heatstroke."

After having her fill, she gave him back the bottle and made sure he drank too. He was always seeing to her needs and forgetting about his own. That was going to stop. He helped her out of the harness, then tucked it and the rope into the pack. Wanting to carry her share of the load, she tried to swing it onto her back. The unexpected weight made her stumble. Laughing, Jamie took the bag from her and easily settled it on his shoulders. "I think I'd better carry this."

"How have you been handling it this whole time? It weighs a ton."

"This isn't even half the weight of the two SCBAs you dragged through all that crap at the courthouse."

She shrugged and bit her lip. "Maybe. I barely noticed." Adrenaline and the fear of losing Chloe had carried her through the ordeal. She'd marched into the debris, her mind empty of all thought except reaching Chloe and Dani. Her eyes welled as she remembered once again the soul-wrenching terror she'd felt when she'd thought she'd lost Jamie. His incredible strength and skill had saved them all.

"That's because you're incredibly brave." Tucking a strand of hair under her cap, he brushed her mouth with his. "Come. Let me show you what you worked so hard for."

They entered a cave, about thirty feet deep. It was large and impressive and had a great view of the ocean. But it was also dark, with who knew what crawling along its walls. She angled her head toward the back of the cave. "There?"

"From the look on your face, it's clear that cave sex is out."

She peered inside again and shuddered. "It might even be a hard limit."

He laughed. "I have a much better place in mind."

They walked on the rocks, along the water, pausing every now and then to let a big wave retreat. Soon, they arrived at another series of tide pools. But this time, they were alone. She turned to check if anyone could observe them from above. They couldn't.

Behind, she heard a splash. She whipped around and stood gaping at Jamie, who'd launched himself into the clear turquoise water. Stark-naked.

When he surfaced, drops of water gleamed in his dark hair. He looked like a veritable water god, and she felt like his virgin offering.

Okay, she wasn't a virgin, but the rest of the imagery held. "Join me." His husky voice made her nipples harden and her belly quiver with desire.

She tugged off her shirt, capris, and shoes. Wearing only her bra and panties, she approached the edge and dipped her toe into the surprisingly warm water.

"Uh-uh. All of it," Jamie said.

"But—"

"No one can see us, Rickie."

After undressing faster than she ever had in her life, she tossed her underthings on top of her clothes and jumped into the tide pool. It would be harder for anyone watching to make out her nakedness in the water.

When she surfaced, Jamie was sputtering and wiping water from his face, an evil glint in his eyes. "Jamie. I didn't mean—" She stopped talking when he began stalking toward her, the water god transformed into a water dragon. *Oh no!* Was he in Dom-mode? Was he about to punish her? Her eyes stinging from the saltwater, she folded her arms over her breasts and stared down at her reflection. "Mr. Caldwell, I'm sorry. I shouldn't have splashed you. Please. I won't do it again."

"Rickie." Jamie's expression held a confusing mix of concern and exasperation. "Babe, I was just teasing you." He stroked the back of his fingers along her cheek. "Relax."

She caught his shoulders and used the buoyancy of the water to hoist herself up and wrap her legs around his waist. Clasping him to her chest, she nuzzled his neck. The warmth of his body and the saltiness of his skin comforted her. "I love you so much, Jamie. I want to make you happy, but I don't always know how."

"You do, babe. You do make me happy. I don't want you worrying about this D/s thing. We do it when we want to. When it feels right. Besides, I'd never punish you for something you did when we weren't in a scene. I don't expect—or want—you to be submissive outside of those times."

All the fear and anxiety about the future she'd kept bottled up inside her evaporated in the heat of his gaze. Jamie was giving her everything she'd ever wanted in a man, everything she'd ever wanted in a husband. "I need you, Jamie," she whispered against his lips. Making her intent clear, she shifted over his erection and lowered herself onto it. Inch by inch she sank down. The sensations of being filled, of being stroked deep inside where she needed it most, were so exquisite, tears filled her eyes.

Jamie groaned. The sound rumbled in his chest and she felt it against her heart. With his hands cupping her butt, he lifted her up and down in a slow teasing rhythm. When she moaned in pleasure, his mouth closed over hers, swallowing the sounds. He sucked her tongue into his mouth, uniting them in a never-ending circle.

Leaning her backward so she floated on the water, he flicked his tongue over a distended nipple. The gentle lashing sent shivers coursing through her body. As though she had the attention of a hundred lovers, the warm sun caressed her face, the gentle waves lapped at her body, and the light breeze kissed her wet skin. Making love had never felt so foreign and exotic, and she was loving it.

When Jamie closed his lips over one nipple, grazing it with his teeth and sucking hard, she arched her back and almost earned a mouthful of water for her efforts. Laughing, Jamie supported her while she caught her breath. "You up for a little experiment?" he asked with a twinkle in his eye.

Her insides clenched and she felt a new slickness where they were joined. Jamie could induce an orgasm with that sexy smile. She bit back a moan. "As long as it doesn't involve swallowing copious amounts of water."

"No worries. Hold onto my hand and leave your legs loose on either side of my hips."

Where was he going with this? Frowning, she did as he asked. He supported her with a strong grip on her hip and clasped both her hands in one of his. "Keep your head up," he said as he began to rock her back and forth. With each swing, he impaled her deeper and deeper until he was embedded to the hilt. As he increased the speed of the movements, he pulled her harder against him while he flexed his hips to heighten the impact and depth of penetration. He stretched her, filled her completely, bumping against her needy clitoris with each thrust.

"This is… my variation… on suspension sex," he gasped between pants. "Like it?"

She *loved* it. She'd never experienced anything so liberating in her entire life. With his grip on her hands, he kept her elevated so the water skimmed her lower back in a sexy, thrilling massage. The rapid movement kept her breasts bouncing and swaying, never letting her forget their aching, puckered peaks. She was so on fire, she could almost hear the sizzle as drops of cool water splashed on her hot skin. Every sensation, every touch, every sound built up the delicious pressure until she could take it no more.

Shivering and shuddering, she threw her head back and screamed Jamie's name. Her orgasm hit in wave after wave of blissful contractions. In the recesses of her mind, she heard Jamie call her name as he pumped into her one last time, his fingers tightening on her as he achieved his own climax.

After a moment, he lifted her out of the water, holding her tightly against his chest. With heavy arms, she hung onto his neck and slumped against him, replete and happy. "Jamie, that was so…" At a loss for a word to encompass it all, she let the sentence hang.

"Incredible?" His warm breath made goose bumps ripple over her skin, and she trembled with small aftershocks. Still inside her, Jamie groaned and kissed her throat.

She tugged on his ears until he lifted his head. Letting herself fall into his warm loving eyes, she said, "You're what made it incredible, Jamie. You make every time incredible."

"Does that mean you want to go back to having only vanilla sex now?" he asked, arching a dark arrogant brow.

"God, no. This was magical and perfect. But I want to taste all thirty-one flavors."

He grinned and cupped her face. "Rocky road coming right up, ma'am." Laughing, they sank into the water, wrapped around each other.

CHAPTER 8

After spending the remainder of the day visiting Honolulu and Pearl Harbor, Jamie and Rickie headed back to Turtle Beach. Jamie chose to drive up the western side of the island so they could catch the sunset over the ocean.

Rickie patted his thigh. "You've been quiet since we visited the Arizona Memorial."

He shot her a small smile and covered her hand with one of his own. He didn't want to put a damper on their day, but their sightseeing had affected him more than he'd have thought it would. "I was just thinking about my grandfather's brother, Great Uncle Joe, and his wife Charlie. Did I ever tell you she was here, at Hickam Field, when the Japanese bombed Pearl Harbor?"

Her expression somber, Rickie shook her head. "No. Your father told me Joe lost his eye in the Doolittle Raid, but I didn't realize that Joe's wife had been military too."

"She wasn't. Not exactly. She was a flight instructor, and her first husband an officer on the Arizona. She was in the air when the attack began."

"Oh my God."

"It wasn't until it was all over that she found out her husband wasn't one of the survivors." At Rickie's harsh inhale, he shot her a reassuring glance and squeezed her hand.

"Charlie must have been devastated," she said, emotion thickening her voice.

"She was, but a year later, she met Joe in Texas where she was working with the Women's Auxiliary Ferrying Squadron." He shrugged. "Life goes on, you know?"

Rickie's only response was to turn away and stare out the window. *Smooth move, asshole.* Jamie wanted to kick himself. Of course, she'd feel a kinship with Charlie. She was probably seeing herself in Charlie's shoes right now—a young widow, trying to move on and make a life for herself. Shit. Just the thought of Rickie loving another man, of his daughter calling that man "Daddy" made him want to puke.

They drove in silence up Veterans Memorial Freeway until they reached Kamehameha Highway. They hit the coast as the sky was beginning to darken. Needing to salvage the day, Jamie pulled the Mustang off the road and parked.

"What are we doing here?" Rickie asked.

"Let's go watch the sunset on the beach."

A smile played on her lips. "End the day like we began it?"

"Seems fitting." He grabbed a blanket from the backseat and stepped out of the car, waiting for her to join him. They dashed across the two-lane highway and the deserted beach to the water's edge, laughing like children. Jamie took a moment to lay the blanket out in a dry area, shielded from the road by an outcropping of rocks. Chasing each other, they ran in the wet sand, jumping the waves as they rolled in. Rickie squealed when a bigger wave bore down on her.

Jamie lifted her against his chest and carried her up the beach. Kissing her, he twirled them around until they grew dizzy and tumbled onto the blanket in a giggling, squirming heap.

Tugging the blanket, he rolled Rickie underneath him, wrapping them in a cozy cocoon. As he stared into his wife's eyes, a deep yearning took root in his heart. He'd do anything to keep her, to keep from losing her again. She was everything to him. He just hoped she'd learn to accept that being a firefighter wasn't a job to him, it was who he was. If she asked him to quit, he'd do it. It might kill him, but for her, he'd do it.

Love shone in her eyes as she traced the line of his jaw. She bobbed her head up and clamped his bottom lip between her own, sucking gently. His cock hardened and he groaned, nudging against her thigh.

Nipping at his chin, she snaked her hand between their bodies and undid his shorts. He dropped his head down to her neck and suckled the slender column. "You're playing with fire, Rickie."

"Good thing I found this long hose, then," she quipped. Her fingers wrapped around his engorged cock, sliding from the base to the tip, around, and back down. He shuddered and closed his eyes as the world around him blurred. Her hands felt like heaven on him.

Rising up on his elbows, he brushed strands of wind-blown hair off her face. "I love you, Rickie. I'd do anything for you. I hope you know that."

"I love you too, Jamie."

Their mouths met in a tangle of lips, teeth and heat-seeking tongues. Jamie poured all his wants, needs, and desires into the kiss, wishing he could make her understand how completely she'd captured him. How completely she owned him. He played the dominant, but she held all the power. She literally had him by the balls.

"Take your pants off," he whispered, almost feral with his soul-deep need to possess her.

Her wiggling as she struggled to get out of her pants cranked up his appetite. Using her toes, she shoved his shorts and boxers to his ankles, and he kicked them off impatiently. Together they removed her shirt then his. He wanted to feel her against him, skin to skin. With nothing, not even air between them.

Before he could get his arms around her, she set her hands on his chest and closed her teeth over one of his nipples, increasing the pressure until he groaned and arched into her mouth. With her fingers, she traced patterns over his chest, his ribs, his abs. She moved quickly as though she wanted to touch him everywhere at once. Then, in a move worthy of Jackie Chan, she flipped him onto his back and rose above him, intense determination on her face. "My turn," she said, moving down his body. Her nails trailed fire as she disappeared under the blanket.

Her lips closed over his cock, wet heat enveloping him as she sucked. When the head hit the back of her throat, he went rigid. She'd never taken him this deep before. He burned with the impulse to thrust his hips and fuck her perfect mouth.

Her tongue swirled around the head of his cock, rimming the sensitive underside before dipping into his slit. Losing the tight rein he'd had on his control, he groaned and flexed his hips.

She stopped moving.

Shit. Had he hurt her? Reaching under the blanket, he gripped her shoulders and pulled her up. When her head popped out, she licked her swollen lips and frowned. "Why'd you stop me?"

"You're making me crazy and I don't want to hurt you. Ever."

She tapped his chin. "I was just giving you time to enjoy the moment."

Pulling her up so she straddled him, he pushed on her ass, impaling her with one powerful swing of his hips. "I'll enjoy this moment instead," he said, groaning when her muscles tightened around him.

The pink and orange glow from the setting sun burnished her skin as she moved above him, meeting each push with one of her own. But it wasn't enough. "Ride me, Rickie. Drive me wild."

"Yee-haw," she said, sitting up and setting an increasingly frenzied pace. Hips pumping, breasts swaying, she was more beautiful than ever. She came with her eyes closed, her breasts pushed out and her mouth open on a gasp. The sight of her lost in the ecstasy they'd found together sent him over the edge. With a final hard thrust, he filled her, giving her all that he had.

The world spun by him in a chaotic swirl of colors, sounds, and smells until he stilled, emptied of everything but his love for her.

They lay panting on the beach as the sun sank into the endless ocean. Jamie ran his hand down Rickie's back and over the curve of her ass, enjoying the way she shivered under his touch. "We should get going," he said, finally, reluctant to let her go. But with the sun gone, the wind off the water felt cool, and he didn't want her catching a cold.

After getting dressed and folding the blanket, Rickie grabbed the front of his shirt and yanked him to her. Laughing, he went willingly. She hugged him tightly, surprising him. "Hey. Everything okay?" he asked.

"You've made me the happiest woman in the world. This is the best honeymoon I could have ever asked for."

"Worth waiting five years?"

"Oh yes." She gave him a quick heated kiss. "We weren't ready for this five years ago. But we're ready now. I can be the wife you always hoped I'd be."

He shook his head. "You already are, sweetheart."

Taking her hand, he led her back to the highway.

The air filled with the screech of tires and the terrified squeals of animals. A sickening thud and deadly silence followed. A cold, empty silence that sent adrenaline coursing through his body. Scenting smoke, he stopped under the lone street lamp and handed Rickie his phone. "Call 911. Ask for the fire department."

Shock on her face, Rickie took his phone and nodded. Knowing she'd follow his orders, he took off in the direction of the accident. In the dark, he couldn't see it yet, but he could smell it. A few yards away, the odor intensified and he knew he was close. The road turned a little and just around the bend on the eastern side, he saw the red glow of fire. Jogging across the highway, he recognized the remains of two wild pigs. The driver had probably swerved to avoid them but was too late, and the car had rolled on impact. Hitting the two large animals, weighing around two to three hundred pounds each, would have been like hitting a barrier.

He approached the old overturned sedan, assessing the situation. Two passengers. Male driver. Child in the back. At least the boy was in a car seat. Jamie opened the driver's door. "Hello."

The man's eyes opened and stared at him blankly. "Sir," Jamie said, filling his voice with authority.

The man blinked and understanding flashed in his eyes. "My son. Please help my son."

Looking up, Jamie noted the man's legs were trapped between the dashboard and the seat. Smoke was filling the interior of the car and he could smell gasoline. He didn't have much time. He unbuckled the belt holding the car seat. If the kid had any injuries, he'd be better off remaining in it.

With the car seat clasped against his chest, Jamie jogged back to where he'd left Rickie. Her eyes grew round as she spotted the bundle in his arms. "Is he—"

"He's alive. I don't know what his injuries are, so leave him strapped in. I have to go back for the father."

When he turned to leave, she grabbed his arm. "The fire department said they'd be here in ten minutes."

"Fuck." He blew out a breath. "I can't wait that long. The car's about to explode."

She gasped and her fingernails dug into his arm. Tears filled her eyes and her bottom lip trembled. "No! Jamie, it's too dangerous."

Cupping her face, he swiped his thumb through the wetness on her cheeks. "Sweetheart, if it were me trapped in the car, you'd want someone to help me, wouldn't you?"

"Yes, but—"

"It's who I am, Rickie." The child, who couldn't have been more than a year old, let out a loud wail. "I'll be fine. But right now, that boy needs you." After drying her face with her hands, she crouched down beside the car seat and stroked the boy's hair, murmuring in that soothing way she'd had when Chloe was little.

He ran back to the car. Flames licked out from under the hood and the smoke inside the vehicle had thickened. He had to get the man out now. To his advantage, the car was an old model with manual seat controls instead of electric ones. He braced his feet on the doorframe and engaged the lever with one hand while using his shoulder to push the seat back. It took all his strength to move it a few inches, but it was enough to free the man's legs. The victim screamed as gravity dragged them down.

"I'll have you out in a minute, sir." Eyes stinging, Jamie wiped the sweat from his forehead and maneuvered himself under the upside-down driver, wrapping his arm around the man's legs. A roar ripped the air as fire burst through the dashboard, melting it. Heat seared his arm. *Shit.* He had to remember he wasn't wearing bunker gear.

Ignoring the pain, he released the seatbelt and, with a grunt, caught the heavy man across his shoulders in a fireman's hold. Even though he was hurting the man, Jamie had no choice. Agonized cries blasting his ears, Jamie stumbled away, moving as fast as he could. The screams finally stopped and the man's body went lax. Thank Christ he'd passed out.

The heat from the fire built, and even from across the road, it seemed to burn his back. He had only seconds to get himself and the man to safety. Spotting a road barrier a short distance ahead, he hurried over and lowered the man behind it. The car exploded, and Jamie dropped to his knees, covering the injured man's head and chest with his body. A fireball filled the sky, the roar so thunderous it made his ears ring.

Parts of the vehicle crashed to the ground next to him. With a growing sense of unease, Jamie realized how close he was to Rickie and the boy. Had the debris reached the beach where he'd left her?

Surging to his feet, he tossed the still unconscious man over his shoulders and ran. Fear constricted his chest, making him breathless. The acrid smoke of burning tires and metal scorched his eyes and throat. Nothing mattered more than finding Rickie. He'd almost lost her in the earthquake barely two weeks ago. He couldn't handle this again. Not so soon. Not ever.

His pulse thundering in his ears and his heart pounding against his ribs, he shouted for the one woman who'd ever meant anything to him. The one woman he'd give up his life for. The one woman he couldn't live without. "Rickie!"

ಐ 🚂 ೧ಜ

As the night sky filled with fire, Erica continued to stroke the boy's hair, tears streamed down her cheeks. *Jamie's okay.* He has to be okay. Panic rolled over her like a weighted blanket, compressing her chest and making it impossible to breathe.

Stop it! Stop it now!

He couldn't be dead. Not like this. Her hands dropped to the ground and she pressed her forehead to the cold sand. She'd thought she'd come to terms with his job after the earthquake. She really had. But it had been different that night. She'd been involved in the rescue, not left alone and waiting, desperate to know what was happening.

If he were dead, she'd feel it deep in her heart, wouldn't she? Jamie was her soul mate, she understood that now. Finally. Pushing to her feet, she checked the boy to make sure he was secure, then headed for the fire. If Jamie were injured or trapped, she'd find him and help.

A shadow rose out of the dark, massive and oddly shaped.

"Jamie?" she asked, a tremble in her voice.

"R-rickie?" He coughed and started again. "You okay?"

"Yes! I thought you were hurt or trapped or—" She pressed her lips together to keep from admitting what she'd really thought.

Jamie carried what she now realized was the driver over to the lit area and lay him on the ground beside the boy.

"Da?" the child asked, reaching to touch the man's shoulder.

"Shh," Jamie murmured. "Your daddy's going to be fine. You're going to be fine."

When he moved away and turned back to her, she launched herself into his arms. Tears poured down her cheeks uncontrollably. Her need to hold him, to hear his heartbeat, and to feel his warmth was basic. Almost primal. She couldn't get close enough to him, couldn't hold him tightly enough.

After a moment, Jamie loosened his embrace and raised his head. "You thought I was dead." The sound of his voice, raw with emotion, tore something inside her, and she realized not all the tears were her own. His eyes were bright glittery pools as his gaze pierced hers. His breath caught and he crushed her against his chest and buried his face in her neck. "When I saw how far the debris was falling, I-I..." He trailed off, his breath hot on her skin as he gripped her even more tightly. "I'm never letting you go."

Erica's heart skipped a beat, echoing painfully in her chest. Jamie had thought she'd been injured. Or dead. Both their minds had immediately jumped to the worst possible scenario. Yet, he'd kept his head and managed to rescue the boy's father. A sob shuddered through her, and she breathed deeply to keep from breaking down.

A strong odor stung her nose. She pulled back with a grimace. "What's that awful smell? It's like roasting flesh."

Jamie dropped his arms from her waist and shrugged. "The car hit a couple wild pigs. That's what made the driver spin off the road. The fire must have reached their carcasses."

She pressed a hand to her stomach, sickened at the thought of the poor animals cooking in the car fire. Jamie lifted a hand to wipe the sweat and soot that was dripping into his eyes.

Her eyes zeroed in on his arm. The sleeve of his shirt was charred and his skin was a black bloody mess. Blisters swelled through the layer of soot. *The smell of burning flesh was coming from him.* All the blood drained from her head as a scream built in her throat and clawed its way out. "Jamie, you're injured!"

Catching her around the waist, Jamie said, "Rickie, I'm fine. I told you I'd be fine and I am."

Unable to speak, she simply held onto him and stared numbly at his burned arm until the squawk of sirens signaled the arrival of the police and fire department. The firefighters quickly put out the smoking vehicle while a police officer took Jamie's and Erica's statements. All the while, Jamie kept his good arm around her waist. Even injured, his first concern was for her. The thought made her heart ache.

The paramedics bundled the driver and his son into the ambulance. "Sir, you need to have that burn treated," one of them said to Jamie when he went to unlock the Mustang.

Jamie shook his head. "I'm fine."

"Let a doctor assess it." Erica took the keys from him. "I'll drive."

She followed the ambulance and squad car, retracing their earlier path along Kamehameha Highway to Wahiawa General Hospital. Erica was beginning to wonder if this day would ever end. At the same time, she didn't want it to, because she had no idea what would happen once they returned to the cottage.

An hour later, she paced outside the emergency room doors while the doctors treated Jamie, as well as the driver and his son. Earlier, a nurse had offered her some tea, but Erica's stomach was such a knotted mess, she wasn't sure she could keep anything down.

Would she feel this way every time Jamie was injured? Every time he went to work?

Like a garrote, panic choked her, leaving her gasping for air. If she didn't calm down, she'd have a full-blown attack. Her throat ached with the need to scream. Her fingers strained with the need to hit. She wanted to throw herself on the ground kicking and crying like Chloe used to do sometimes. Instead, she inhaled deeply, filling her lungs, holding, then expelling her breath until the emotions receded, until she regained control. She had to be strong, for her husband and for her daughter. She didn't even know how serious Jamie's injuries were. Silently, she prayed that they were minor, that they wouldn't keep him from the job he loved. But in that secret place in her heart, she admitted, if only to herself, that maybe it wouldn't be so bad if he had to find a different job. One that was safer. One where she didn't have to worry every day.

No!

Jamie would hate her if he knew she'd even thought such a horrible thing.

The emergency room doors opened and out sauntered her husband, a crisp white bandage on one arm and a pretty young nurse on the other. The nurse's eyes sparkled and her face flushed with admiration and... desire. Erica had seen it happen over and over. And she couldn't blame the woman. Jamie had that effect on everyone with two X-chromosomes, as well as on some without. People reacted to heroes, and Jamie was one tonight. He'd saved two lives and spared another from widowhood. The little boy's mother had hugged her son and husband tonight. And she'd been able to do that because of Jamie's bravery.

Spotting her, Jamie said something to the nurse, then walked over. He stopped in front of her and his smile faded. "What's wrong?" he asked, his voice and eyes filled with concern.

Gah! Why was she so weak? She pressed her lips together and skimmed her fingers over the bandage. Following her gaze, Jamie sighed. "It's just a second-degree burn."

Her stomach turned as she remembered. "Don't minimize this. It smelled horrible, like your flesh was charred."

"That was the hair, honey. It's just like a super bad sunburn."

"Can we go now? I'm sure you're ready for a shower, some clean clothes, and a beer."

He grinned. "Fucking A. And not necessarily in that order."

After some discussion, he agreed to let her drive. Since Jamie was always a little nervous when she was at the wheel, the miles passed in silence. She concentrated on keeping her emotions in check. She'd be a regular Florence Nightingale and take care of her husband for a change. She needed to get him cleaned up and fed. With any luck, Jamie had some pain relievers in that backpack he'd lugged around all day. He'd need some before the adrenaline left his system and the pain from the burn set in.

Back at the resort, she found a plastic bag and covered the bandage. Then she washed the soot and sand from his warrior's body while he relaxed in the tub. She couldn't recall Jamie ever letting her do this. They'd taken some exciting showers together, but this was different. She ran her soapy hands over his broad shoulders, his ridged abs, and his powerful quads. Jamie's entire body was laid out for her touching pleasure. He seemed to be enjoying it too, if his growing erection was any indication.

He waggled his brows and pointed at his groin. "Want to hop on?"

Laughing, she tickled his side. "Don't you need any recovery time?"

"Not with you, babe."

"I guess I'll have to be the adult tonight. You need to get in bed."

"Now you're talking."

"You are the worst patient, Jamie."

The water splashed as he rose and climbed out of the bath. She dried him with a fluffy hotel towel, enjoying the fact that his erection never wavered. They'd have to do this again when he was healed. When she could join him in the tub and soap them both up.

After helping him into a pair of boxers and a T-shirt, she handed him three tablets of ibuprofen and a glass of water. Much to her relief, he swallowed them without argument. When she removed the bag from his wrist, Jamie picked his shorts up and pulled a tube out of his pocket. "The doc gave me this ointment to put on it. I'll be good as new by the time we get back home."

Home. The word hit her like a plank. In a few days, they'd be going back to Seattle, back to the real world, back to nonstop pressures and distractions. Jamie would return to the station where he'd face potentially life-threatening situations on a daily basis. And she'd go back to worrying about him every minute that he was on the job.

Could she go through that again?

The ache in her chest made her gasp. She wobbled and Jamie caught her, sitting her on the bed. "Rickie? Tell me what's going on." He held her in his arms, rubbing slow circles on her back. Sobs burst through her clenched teeth, and she surrendered to a tidal wave of mixed emotions.

"Just hold me, please. Hold me for a little while."

They stretched out on the bed and Jamie pressed his chest against her back, his thighs tucked against her bottom, solid and reassuring. His arm around her waist held her in place and with his lips on her ear, he whispered, "I'm right here, babe. It's okay. I'm right here."

She squeezed her lids closed, desperate to stop the fresh wave of tears brought on by his words. Her husband was a true hero. But was she cut out to be a hero's wife?

CHAPTER 9

The first light of dawn pouring in through the window above the bed roused Erica from a fitful sleep. Her eyes popped open and her heart raced until she got her bearings. Hawaii. The cottage. Jamie spooning her. She warmed, feeling his arm still pressing her against his chest. As he'd promised her when she'd cried: he was there. He was always there for her.

She shifted to move her arm that had gone numb during the night. The movement brought her bottom into firm contact with his groin. It twitched against her and began to swell. Should she slip under the covers and give her husband a good morning treat? He deserved it after coddling her all night.

As she began to shimmy down, her gaze landed on his bandaged arm and memories of the explosion came crashing back to her in a paralyzing cascade. She must have made a distressed sound because Jamie's arm tightened around her. When he woke up, he'd want to talk about what had happened and why she was so upset. But what could she say? If she lied and pretended that everything was okay, she'd ruin all the trust they'd so painstakingly built up between them this week. If she told him the truth, they'd be at a stalemate, unable to move forward with their relationship.

Behind her, Jamie shifted and his arm grew heavier on her hip as he relaxed into a deeper sleep. Careful not to disturb him, she slipped out of the bed, grabbed her phone, and walked out onto the lanai.

Although the temperature was already high, the breeze from the ocean was cool. The sky was a kaleidoscope of pinks, oranges, and reds as the sun climbed out of the water. Oahu had to be one of the most beautiful places on earth. But after yesterday's sunrise vow renewal, every sunrise would pale in comparison, unless Jamie was by her side. She had little hope of that unless she fixed the mess they were in.

Stretching out on one of the chairs, she considered her options again. Neither one appealed to her. Maybe she needed a second opinion. And she knew just who to ask. Before she could chicken out, she dialed Dani's number and, with her heart in her mouth, waited for the woman to answer. It didn't take long. "Erica? Is everything okay?"

"Yes. Why wouldn't it be?"

"Hon, it's six in the morning in Oahu. People on their honeymoon are supposed to be so exhausted from their… uh… nocturnal exertions that they sleep half the day. At least that's what I've heard."

Erica chuckled, but it wasn't a pleasant sound. "Last night was tiring all right. But not for the reason you think. Jamie was injured."

"What? Is he in the hospital? Do you need me to fly out there?"

"No. He's fine." Erica mentally kicked herself. She should have anticipated Dani's reaction to the news and broken it to her more smoothly. Dani's loyalty to Jamie was legendary. Erica spoke with a lightness she didn't feel. "You know what a hero he is. He pulled a man and a young child out of an overturned car seconds before it exploded. His arm was burned during the rescue."

"Fuck. Is it bad? Will he need surgery?"

"No, nothing like that. The doctor gave him some ointment to put on it and said he'd be better in a few days."

"That's good." She let out a long breath. "So if everything's hunky-dory, why do you sound like you just lost your best friend?"

"Because I think I might have."

"Erica, what's going on?"

A lump formed in her throat and the backs of her eyes burned. Squeezing her lids shut, she breathed deeply several times. She was *not* going to cry again. After a moment, she felt steady enough to get to the real reason she'd called Dani. "When the car exploded, I thought…" The lump became a boulder, preventing her from speaking.

"You thought Jamie was dead."

"For a moment, I wanted to die too. I wanted to curl up into a ball and disappear."

"You were scared, hon. It's normal."

"It was more than that. I got a glimpse of how my mother must have felt when my father was killed." She straightened her shoulders and stared at the waves rolling onto the surf. "I wanted to die, and I barely had a thought for my daughter, for what would happen to her if she lost both her parents. What kind of mother does that?"

"A terrified one. Listen, Erica. You're not like that. I bet you shook it off, then charged over to the fire to help Jamie."

Erica shifted in her seat and ordered herself to voice to the ugly truth festering in her chest. "I told Jamie I could accept the risks of him being a firefighter. But after last night and the way it made me feel, I don't know that I can go through the agony of not knowing day after day without becoming… less." More like her mother with each passing week.

A heavy silence hung between them.

Dani finally broke it. "Do you want him to quit the service?"

Erica's breath caught in her throat. God help her, some small selfish part of her did want that. "I don't know. Do you think he would?"

"He'd do anything for you. But Erica, that knife has a double-edge."

"What do you mean?"

"Answer this. How have things been going between you two since you got to the island?"

Erica stared through the glass doors at Jamie's sleeping form. "I followed your advice about being honest with him. It was hard, but I told him how I felt, what I wanted. And he did the same. We've connected on a level I didn't know existed." Her heart constricted painfully. She loved him so much.

"Yet you're debating asking him to deny a part of who he is, a crucial part. If you do that, you'll drive him to keep things from you, to hide an essential piece of himself. Like he was before when you were so miserable."

It's who I am, Rickie.

Jamie's words, stated so baldly when she'd tried to stop him from going back for the driver, slid through her heart like a knife. A double-edged one. The tears she'd been fighting spilled over and dripped down her cheeks and off her chin. "I can't do that to him.

"Dani, what am I going to do? I want him whole. Just the way he is."

"Then tell him that. *Show him*. He'll love you all the more because you aren't forcing him to be half a man."

With the edge of her T-shirt, Erica wiped her cheeks. Dani was right. She had to prove to Jamie—and herself—that she was prepared to love him and everything that came with him—the total package. That brave, fearless, selfless side of him had attracted her as much as his man-in-charge side. For them to be happy, for their marriage to survive, she had to accept both sides of her husband.

After a few more minutes of chatting, she thanked Dani and hung up. Jamie and Chloe were her life. If she wanted a secure loving family, she had to get a grip on her fears. Had to accept the risks of Jamie's job and know that if the worst did come to pass, she'd survive. She'd raise their daughter to be a successful confident woman. She was not her mother.

But one question remained: how could she tell Jamie all this in a way he'd understand? After her meltdown last night, he'd have serious doubts about anything she said, and she really couldn't blame him. An about-face would set off his alarms. Words would not be enough. Something Dani had said came to her then. Show him.

Good advice. But how?

Tiptoeing back inside the cottage, she found the book she'd snuck in her suitcase. An erotic novel about what she now understood was a D/s relationship. Maybe it would give her some ideas. If she gave him what he wanted, showed him that she accepted his Dom side completely—surrendered to it—perhaps he'd also believe that she'd finally accepted that his being a firefighter was one of the many reasons she loved him.

On the way back to the lanai, she caught sight of Jamie's little bag of toys. Hmmm... There might be something in it that she could use. Snatching up the bag, she brought it outside. Total submission wouldn't be easy for her, given her controlling nature—yes, she knew she was a control-freak—but Jamie was well worth the effort.

ಸಃ🚒ಜ

Jamie threw the pillow off his face and glared at the sunlight piercing his skull. The dull throbbing in his head matched the one in his arm. The burn wasn't bad, but it stung. He loved fire, but it could be a bitch of a mistress.

He stretched out, wanting to pull Rickie to him, needing to

reassure himself that she hadn't left him again. But his hand met only cold sheets. He jackknifed in the bed and scanned the room. Empty. His heart raced until he spotted her purse on the dresser. Relieved, he flopped back onto the bed. Like most women he knew, Rickie had her life in that purse, and she'd never wander far without it. When she returned, they'd have a chat about last night. He'd really hoped she'd come to accept his career, but her reaction proved she was still struggling with it. He didn't know how to help her, except...

The thought was too depressing to complete. Shoving off the bed, he collected the supplies he'd need to take a shower and change his bandage. The shower would help clear his mind and calm him down. How he handled the next few hours would affect the rest of his life in a major way.

After the shower, he examined his burn. The blisters were almost gone and the angry purple had faded to a bright pink. A little like Rickie's ass after the spanking he'd given it the other day. His groin tightened and he raked a hand through his damp hair. There'd be no more of *that* until he figured out what was going on inside his wife's head. And her heart.

He changed the bandage, then wrapped a towel around his waist and stepped out of the bathroom. His gaze zeroed in on the one object out of place.

His wife.

Rickie sat on her heels by the door, naked. Her knees were spread and her hands rested on her thighs. She kept her eyes fixed on the floor in front of her. Christ. She was *presenting*. Where the fuck had she learned to do that?

His instinct was to charge across the room, yank her to her feet, and demand to know what the hell she was up to. Instead, he rocked back on his heels. If this twist in their relationship was something she truly wanted, he owed it to her to hear her out. But could he deal with controlling another person to this extent again, even for her?

She still hadn't looked up. Knowing what she was waiting for, he crossed his arms and snapped, "Erica."

Her gaze lifted and she smiled brightly. "Good morning, Sir."

Did she just want to play a little? He really couldn't tell.

"Good morning. Come here."

"Yes, Sir." When she shifted to all fours and began crawling to him, his stomach dropped to his knees. She stopped in front of him and kissed his bare feet before looking up, her expression expectant.

Seeing her prostrate herself before him, his stomach revolted. He swallowed the stream of curses that wanted out of his throat and schooled his features. "Good girl," he said, patting her on the head. When her eyes lit up, his gut clenched. If she really meant this, he was in some serious trouble. He had to know. "Is there something you wish to say?"

She nodded. "I have a gift for you, Sir. May I give it to you?"

"You may." Still on her knees, she crawled over to the dresser. Turning away from her, he sat on the bed and worked on appearing calm. She returned and knelt at his feet, her hands curled around whatever she was holding. "Speak," he ordered when she remained silent.

"I offer myself to you, as your obedient s-slave, Sir."

Jamie clenched his teeth to keep from hissing. He'd had slaves before and that was not something he wanted for Rickie. He motioned for her to continue.

Casting her gaze downward, she opened her hands, revealing a collar she'd made by snapping together two ankle restraints she must have found in his toy bag. "I hope you will agree to be my Master."

"You want me to collar you."

Her cheeks colored. "Yes, Sir. I want to belong to you." Her voice sounded shrill. Was she excited or nervous?

"Rickie, what the *fuck* is going on?"

She dropped the collar onto the floor. The clank of the snaps hitting the wood resounded in the quiet room. Shifting onto her butt, she hugged her legs to her chest and rested her forehead on her knees. Hiding from him. Shit.

"I thought this was what you wanted." Her voice broke.

He slid off the bed and sat beside her on the floor. "I don't want to own you, babe. Why would you even think that?"

"You keep saying stuff like, 'You're mine.' How else am I supposed to take that?"

Threading his fingers through her hair, he tugged her head up. "Honey, it just means you're the love of my life and I want to keep you with me always. Not that you're my property." When she closed her eyes, he had a sinking feeling. They needed to clear this up right now. "You don't want to be, do you?"

"Be what?"

"My slave or my pet."

She arched one of her perfect blonde brows. "What if I did?"

He leaned against the bed and let his head loll back. "I've tried that before. Some submissives experience a deep sense of satisfaction from having someone control their every move. They enjoy serving their Masters and being treated like a possession. I have to be honest with you: it's not my thing." Lifting his head, he pinned her with his gaze. "If you're serious, though, I'll do this for you. You have to know, I'd do anything for you."

Heaving a sigh, she shot to her feet and grabbed her robe off the chair. "After the way I acted last night, I wanted to show you that I'm not changing my mind. I'm in this with you one hundred percent." She threw the robe on and gave him her back.

"Rickie, don't turn away. Don't ever be embarrassed about anything you feel."

Throwing her hands up, she faced him. "How can I not be embarrassed? I thought if I let you collar me, you'd understand what I was offering. That I was giving myself to you completely."

His chest ached with love for her, for how much she wanted him and their marriage. Going to her, he cupped her cheeks with his hands. "I got the message loud and clear, Rickie, and I'm honored that you thought to give yourself to me in that way. But I don't want to own you, or anyone else. I want to be your partner, your equal."

"Even during sex?"

"Well, no. If we're in a scene, I need you to be submissive and obedient. Not because you must, but because you trust me enough to submit to my will of your own volition."

She stared at him, her brow furrowed. He could only guess at the analysis going on behind those gorgeous brown eyes. "So, if we're partners in real life, does that mean"—she paused and licked her lips—"you're mine?"

Chuckling, he dropped his hands to her ass and pulled her to him so they were chest-to-chest and hip to hip. "More than you'll ever know." He bent to scrape his teeth along her neck and enjoyed the goose bumps that sprouted under his lips. "Without you, I'm barely living."

"That's how I feel too." She hooked her arms around his shoulders, sinking her fingers into his muscles. "I missed you so much while we were separated, but I asked you to leave, because I didn't know how we could go on the way we were. Since we've been here, I feel so close to you. I'm just so afraid of—" She clamped her jaws together and buried her face against his chest.

He sighed and held her close. "If you haven't been able to come to terms with the risks of firefighting in the five years we've been together, Rickie, I don't think you ever will." Inside him, an axe dropped, cleaving his heart. He knew what he had to do for her, for Chloe, for their marriage. "I'll quit if that's what you want."

Her head jerked up and she dug her nails into his arms. "No! No, Jamie. You can't do that."

The horror in her voice caught him off-guard. "Babe, my job is the reason we split up in the first place. It's always been the source of our problems."

"I was wrong. I didn't really understand that you're the man you are *because* you're a firefighter. I love how courageous and selfless you are. How you're willing to put your life on the line to help a stranger. How you get up every day knowing you'll make a difference in someone's life. You're a warrior and a hero, and I never want that to change."

The pain in his heart eased as warmth flooded his chest. She was giving him everything he'd always wanted. But were her words for real? He peered deep into her eyes, trying to read her, to gauge her commitment to what she was saying. All he could see was truth. Still, he had to be certain. "How do I know you're not just telling me what I want to hear?"

"You don't trust me?"

"Let's just say, my faith is a little shaky."

"Why? I haven't lied to you."

He stepped away from her and put his hands on his hips. "Is that so? Tell me, that first scene we did, when I left you on the table with the butt plug in your pretty ass, did you follow my orders?"

"Yes." She blinked then averted her gaze.

He chuckled. She was such a bad liar. "Trust begins with the truth."

"Okay, okay." She rolled her eyes. "I did get up. In fact, I almost stopped the whole thing."

"You didn't. Why?"

"Because I realized I needed to trust you. I should have realized that a long time ago." Closing the space between them, she tugged at his chest hair. "What can *I* do to earn *your* trust?"

"It's simple. Be honest with me. You should have told me you'd struggled with the test and why."

Her brows rose, taking over her forehead. "That was a *test?*"

He shrugged. "We can't engage in any serious play unless I'm absolutely sure I can trust you to tell me the truth and use the safewords if you need to. Even the best Doms can make mistakes and misread their subs' reactions."

"So you won't trust me until I use a safeword?"

He laughed and tapped the tip of her nose. "No. I hope you'll never have to use them. Not because there's anything wrong with that, but because I hope there will never be a need. If we have open and free communication, if you let me know when you're scared or hurting or confused, we'll always be in sync."

"And I haven't been communicating openly and freely."

"Not even close."

"Well I'd like to change that. Please give me another chance. Sir."

"Tonight, after the luau, we'll have a scene. A little bit of edge play to introduce you to something very special to me." The idea of Rickie laid out on the table submitting to his favorite play made him go rock hard. He wasn't sure he'd survive the thrill of seeing his wife with waves of blue heat racing over her body.

Her eyes glittered as she yanked the towel from his hips and caught him in her fist. "I can hardly wait."

CHAPTER 10

As the luau began to wind down, Jamie placed a bottle of water on the table in front of Rickie. "Drink up, babe. I'm heading back to the cottage to get things ready for you."

She glanced around, nervously licking her lips. "We're going to do it? Do the scene I mean?"

"Join me in ten minutes." The cottage was only a short distance from the open-air restaurant, and the path was well-lit. She'd be safe alone.

When Rickie nodded, he jogged back, pumped and excited about the upcoming scene. Fire play. He'd taken to it when he was still a novice in the lifestyle, but it had quickly become his specialty. For years he'd dreamed of sharing his love of fire with Rickie, but it wasn't until this week, until today, that he'd ever considered making the dream a reality.

In the sitting area, he pushed the furniture against the wall to make space for the massage table he'd borrowed from the spa. He placed a cushion from one of the lanai loungers on top of the table, making a nice comfortable space for Rickie.

He dragged an end table and set it at the head of the massage table. Next, he laid out the equipment he'd need. Since all of his was at home in a well-hidden box, he'd have to make do with what he'd scavenged from the grocery store, the pharmacy, and the lumber store: a dozen torches made with chopsticks and two-inch gauze, a stainless steel pitcher he'd filled with rubbing alcohol, dry gauze for swabbing, gauze soaking in alcohol, a survival candle in a sturdy holder, and several packets of instant ice from the first aid kit. Under the table, he stashed the fire extinguisher from the closet.

Almost ready. Picking up the remote, he found an easy-listening station that Rickie would like, then he lit the candles he'd used the night they had their first scene. The room needed to be dim, not dark. He caught sight of himself in the mirror and grimaced. The khaki shorts and Hawaiian shirt didn't fit the Fire Master image. Unfortunately, his leather pants were at home in the box with his equipment. Would Rickie like them? Maybe he'd find out some other time. But only if tonight went well. For now, he'd have to settle for jeans and a tight black T-shirt. Only natural fibers would do. Anything else could melt, or worse, ignite.

He'd just finished changing when a knock at the door made him jump. He checked his watch. Ten minutes exactly. Rickie was nothing if not punctual. He hit the lights and wiped his palms on his thighs, then took several deep breaths to center himself before opening the door.

Rickie clutched her purse, and he could almost hear her knees knocking. Smiling, he held out his hand and slipped into his Dom role. "Welcome, Mrs. Caldwell."

She swallowed and placed her hand in his, letting him draw her into the cottage. Her eyes widened as she took in the candlelight and music before zeroing in on the massage table. He could see her confusion as her brow furrowed, and he had to bite back a grin. She'd probably been expecting whips and chains. Not that he had anything against those. If things went well, he'd introduce her to those toys, but not tonight.

"Get undressed and I'll explain what I have planned."

"Everything?"

"Yes."

She walked over to the bed and reached behind to unzip her dress. Her fingers shook and she couldn't grasp the zipper tab. Jamie went to her and gently brushed her hands aside. Might as well start the warm-up right now.

Inch-by-inch, he lowered the zipper, exposing creamy flesh that glowed gold in the candlelight. His lips followed the descent with butterfly kisses along her spine. She moaned and her head fell back. Putting his hands on her shoulders, he slid the wide straps of her dress down her arms and over her hands. The dress puddled on the floor. Kneeling, he hooked his fingers into the waistband of her tiny panties and stripped them off her legs. Unable to resist the temptation of her fabulous ass, he pressed his lips to each round cheek, kissing and nibbling. He was careful not to leave any marks that could collect the alcohol and burn her.

Spinning her around, he found himself at eye-level with her pussy. Her beautiful bare pussy. He almost swallowed his tongue seeing all that exposed pink flesh. Placing a small kiss on her mound, he promised himself to return for a taste if the scene went well. He stood and took her hands. "You're so goddamn gorgeous, Mrs. Caldwell."

A blush blooming on her cheeks, she slipped off her shoes and followed him over to the massage table. "So why couldn't I wear any perfume or use any lotion? And why did I need to shave my p-pussy?"

"Hop up here and I'll explain."

With his help, she climbed onto the table. And squeezed her legs together.

"Uh-uh." He pushed her knees apart. "Remember, never hide yourself from me."

"Okay."

He crossed his arms and frowned. "Do you need another lesson on how to address me, Mrs. Caldwell?" This scene could be dangerous, and it was critical that she accept her role as sub and his as Dom. There was no room for leniency or error.

"No. No, Sir."

"Very good." He lit the survival candle then picked up a torch from the end table and dipped it into the jug of rubbing alcohol, pressing it against the side to squeeze out any excess liquid. Drips led to unexpected results and he didn't want anything unexpected to happen tonight. He could feel Rickie's eyes on him as he went through the preparations, feel her tension and worry. He passed the torch over the open flame, and it ignited with a burst of light and heat.

She gasped and leaned far back on the table. "W-what are you going to do with that? Sir?" she asked, barely managing to tack on that last word. Knowing she was frightened, he let it slide.

Away from her face and the equipment on the end table, he waved the torch around, making shapes in the dark. "Tonight, my sweet sub, you and I are playing with fire."

"But you're a fireman!" Her hands flew to her mouth. "Sir."

The outrage on her face made him laugh. "Haven't you ever wondered what drew me to firefighting? I'm not from one of those families where half the men are in the fire service."

She set her hands on her thighs and kept her gaze downcast. Did she know she was presenting again? This time though, it didn't bother him. He loved seeing the glint of her juices in the light of the flames.

"Fire is magical. It gives life, and it takes life away. Some fear it, others worship it. I have a healthy respect for fire, and because of that, it gives me great pleasure. A pleasure I can share with others. A pleasure I want to share with you."

Lifting her head, she offered him a tremulous smile.

Time for a demonstration. He stretched his uninjured arm out and ran the torch along the inside of his forearm. The fire followed his lead before quickly extinguishing itself. He brushed his arm on his thigh to complete the pattern.

"Oh!" She grabbed his arm and touched her fingers to the area where the flame had been. "Did it hurt, Sir?"

"Not at all." To him, flames on his flesh were like a lover's tongue. Sometimes it was a long broad lick, other times, a short sharp lash. Either way it turned him way the hell on. Just that small taste had made him hard. He couldn't wait to get on with it. But this wasn't about him, it was about Rickie.

"Aren't you afraid to get burned again, Sir?" Her eyes went to the damaged skin on his other arm. "Fire hurts."

"It's all about the fuel. The fire last night was gasoline-based, which burns very hot. I'm going to use 70% rubbing alcohol. Since it burns just above normal body temperature, it will feel warm, but not hot. Now, if I used 90% rubbing alcohol, it *would* burn you."

"So you want to do that on my body?" She made a face that had him smiling. "Now I get why you wanted me to shave, Sir."

"That and because the thought of your naked pussy turns me on." When she squirmed, he grinned. He was so loving this. "If the fire starts to feel too warm or if things get too intense for you, you will use your safewords. Tell me what they are."

"Yellow for slow down. Red for stop."

"Perfect. You're handling this very well." He trailed his fingers down her arm in a calming gesture. He wasn't going to explain about subspace; no need to alarm her. In this kind of play, it was the Dom's responsibility to see to the sub's well-being; his responsibility to check her skin for color changes and hot spots; his responsibility to push only as far as the sub could handle. And with Rickie, those were responsibilities he cherished. "If you have any questions, ask me now."

"Not a question, but I do have a request, if that's permitted, Sir."

"Go ahead."

"Can you walk me through this, Sir? It will help me relax if I know what you're doing. I really don't want to mess this up for you."

He blew out the torch and set it on the steel platter he'd left on the end table for that purpose. Caressing her cheek, he smiled. "I have every intention of walking you through it, step-by-step until you're comfortable with the technique. There shouldn't be any pain. At least not more than you find enjoyable. Fire play is sexy and sensual. It feels good, like the best high imaginable. I want you to have that."

"What if something goes wrong?"

"You remember I told you I was in the lifestyle before we met. I was a Fire Master. I did shows and taught workshops on fire play. I won't lie to you; in unskilled hands, even the basic techniques I'm going to do tonight can be very dangerous. Lucky for us, I have a lot of experience, and if something does go wrong"—he pointed to his chest and grinned—"I *am* a firefighter and an EMT. Relax. You're in good hands."

Judging by the angle of her brows, she still wasn't convinced. "Aren't you out of practice though, Sir?" she asked.

"I've kept it up. I do demos when we get prospective members for the technical rescue team."

"You're teaching them about fire play and sex?" Her eyes bulged.

"No! I test them to be sure they aren't trying to get onto the rescue team because they've developed a fear of fire. One member who panics in a fire situation puts the whole team at risk."

She massaged her forehead. "How did I not know about all this? I'm your wife. A wife should know when her husband has a strong passion for something."

Placing his hands on either side of her hips, he leaned forward until his face was inches from hers. "Fire play was part of my BDSM life, so I kept it from you. I'm sorry about that. But we've made promises to each other now—no more secrets." He closed his eyes for a second. "There's so much I want to share with you about me and about this life. I hope you'll let me."

She kissed him, her lips soft and pliant. "Of course, I will. I'm dying to know all of you."

People said he was brave, but compared to Rickie, he really wasn't. He always went into situations with both eyes open, knowing exactly what he had to do, and he remained in control the entire time. Rickie, on the other hand, had no idea what he was going to do and where that was going to take her. She was placing herself in his hands.

Her courage in the face of incredible vulnerability humbled him. He would go to any lengths to see this through and do her proud. "Then lie down on your stomach, Mrs. Caldwell, and give yourself over to the experience of a lifetime."

∞ 🜚 ∞

Erica quelled the almost overwhelming instinct to leap off the table and run screaming into the dark night. Jamie wanted to set her on fire and he actually believed she'd enjoy it. Was he crazy or was she? Definitely her. She was crazy in love with her husband. That was the only possible explanation for her willingness to humor him. She had to trust that Jamie really knew what he was doing.

Swallowing her fear, she stretched out on the table, and Jamie tightened the bun she'd made with her hair.

"I want you to close your eyes and breathe deeply." His hands began massaging her back, kneading the tense spots below her shoulder blades. He moved down her body, tapping his fingers on either side of her spine. "In. Hold. Out," he instructed her, his voice low and soothing. He made wide sweeping motions over her bottom, her legs, and her feet, before returning to her back. The friction from his hands rubbing her skin made her moan.

"One of the key ways to ensure you don't feel any pain is to release endorphins into your system." His hand smacked her bottom in a series of short, sharp slaps.

The shock had her gasping and clenching her fists. Just when it was starting to sting, he stopped and rubbed her cheeks, his touch whisper light. "The side benefit of endorphins is that they allow you to experience greater pleasure."

As though demonstrating, he spanked her again. Though the smacks were harder, they didn't hurt. All she felt was a burning heat that seeped between her legs. Had he turned her into a pain slut, or had she always been one and just hadn't known? She flushed and buried her face in her arms.

"Don't be embarrassed if this turns you on. It's kind of the point." He caressed her bottom again, his fingers dipping down to her folds. "If you're a good girl, I might even let you come."

Hearing his amused tone, she shivered and remembered the night he'd tied her to the bed. She'd had to count sheep to keep from climaxing until he gave her permission. Would he really be able to bring her to that point with this fire play?

Without removing his hand from her bottom, he stepped closer to the end table and picked up the torch he'd used on himself. She stiffened, knowing her play date with fire was about to start.

"At first, I'll use my hand to let you know where I'm going to lay the fire." He dipped the torch in the alcohol then brought it to the candle. It lit with a flash. "Ready?"

She shut her eyes tightly. "Yes, Sir," she lied. Goose bumps pebbled all over her body and her toes curled. She was so *not* ready.

Jamie stilled. "Erica." She looked at him over her shoulder, meeting his gaze narrowed. "You must be honest with me. If you can't do that, we stop right now."

Upsetting Jamie, risking their newfound connection, scared her far worse than the fire. Steeling her spine, she lifted her chin. "I'm sorry, Sir. I can do this. I'm just a little scared."

His hand brushed her back and his features softened. "That's normal. It's your first time and you have no idea how the fire will feel. I'm going to do a little test on your butt. If you don't like it, we won't go any further."

A test would help. She pressed her lips together and nodded.

"Trust me," he said, lifting the torch over her.

When it touched her skin, she felt a moment of warmth, then Jamie's hand passing over the spot. That was it?

"How did that feel?" he asked.

"A little warm."

"Hot?"

"No, nice. Does it get worse than that?"

"It will get a little hotter, a little more intense, but in a good way. Before we begin, tell me the safewords again." She rolled her eyes, then closed them, glad her head was buried in her arms. Laughing, he smacked her butt. "I know you rolled your eyes, naughty sub. Obey my order."

"Yellow to slow things down, red to stop."

"Very good. You'll feel a series of continuous movements over your body. I'll stop every now and then to change the torches and give you a little break."

"Thank you, Sir." Jamie seemed to understand how much she needed to know what was happening. She'd never have consented to try this with anyone else.

His hands moved over her skin. Wherever he touched her, a lick of heat followed, then a swipe of his hand completed the dance. He repeated the short confident strokes on her bottom, her back, her legs, even her feet. Every nerve in her body was on high alert, hypersensitive. She tried to anticipate where he would go next, but she couldn't identify a pattern.

Every few minutes, he changed torches, barely missing a beat. She felt like a musical instrument and he the virtuoso. The heat and the stroking were oddly comforting. She felt herself drifting, on the verge of falling asleep, like when she had a massage or got her hair done.

As though sensing her lack of alertness, Jamie smacked her bottom. "On your back, Mrs. Caldwell." He helped her turn over on the narrow table and placed a neck roll under her head. "You're going to want to watch this."

She tensed. "Why?" Even though she'd enjoyed the fire on her back, she wasn't at all sure she'd enjoy having her breasts set on fire. When he frowned at her, she continued, stumbling to cover her mistake. "Are you going to do something different, Sir?"

Like a little boy who had the full attention of his parents, he grinned. "I've got a few tricks up my sleeve."

Light as a rose petal, he ran his palm between her breasts, over her stomach, down one leg, and up the other before cupping between her thighs. "Open."

"Are you going to put fire on my p—" Her throat constricted and she had to breathe in and out before she could spread her legs. She indicated her crotch with her hand. "Are you, Sir?"

He chuckled and dipped his finger in her folds. The gentle glide had desire pooling in her belly, a pool where fire danced on the surface. "You still have trouble saying it."

Frustrated with him for teasing her and with herself for responding so wantonly to this fire pleasure, she curled her hands into the towel beneath her. "I said it earlier. It's probably because you're standing there staring at it that I can't say it now."

He circled her clitoris, never touching it. "I love your pussy and the fire loves it too. But you're not ready for such intense play tonight."

A noise rose from her throat, startling them both. Could she actually be *disappointed*?

Jamie arched a dark brow, a smirk on his handsome face. "Don't worry, Mrs. Caldwell. Even though the fire won't, the heat *will* kiss your pussy later. But only if you ask nicely."

The desire to glare at him was so strong, she snapped her lids closed and took a deep breath. Wetting her lips in what she thought was a seductive move, she arched her neck. "Please, Sir. When you think I'm ready, please let the heat kiss my... p-pussy." There'd she'd done it.

He slipped his finger inside her. "Not good enough. Say it again."

Her eyes shot open. She locked her gaze on his. "Please let the heat kiss my pussy, Sir."

Bending, he sucked one of her pussy lips in his mouth and tugged. She hissed and arched her back at the delicious stretch. It left her feeling open and exposed. Vulnerable and extremely aroused. Why had he never done this before? Then she remembered: she'd never been completely bare before. He did it again and she moaned. Oh God. If he promised to do that again, she'd get waxed or even undergo laser hair removal. Her back bowed as desire ripped through her.

A wide grin on his face, Jamie released her. His lips gleamed with her juices. She'd never seen anything sexier in her life.

"We'll get to that, but first, let's have a little fun." He picked up a piece of gauze from the table and dipped it in the alcohol, then he did the same with a fresh torch.

Using the gauze, he swabbed a trail across her stomach. When he lit the alcohol with the torch, blue light streaked across the line he'd drawn. Her hips twisted and she gasped, shocked by the beauty of it. Jamie's hand quickly swiped over the area. His eyes met hers, his expression blank. "Like it?"

"Jamie." Small spasms continued to shake her body. She swallowed and started again. "Mr. Caldwell, Sir. That was amazing."

"Not too hot?" he asked.

When she shook her head, the blankness on his face changed to relief, revealing how worried he'd been that she'd reject his fire, his passion. It only made her love him more.

He rubbed the gauze from just above her belly button, up the middle of her body, to the line made by her nipples. "Keep your head back," he warned before touching the torch to the bottom of the path. Fire raced up her stomach to her chest. Her body undulated as the heat followed the flames—straight to her face. Despite knowing better, she squealed.

Jamie's hand followed, extinguishing the flames, and rested in the valley between her breasts. Her heart beat wildly under his touch. "Shh, relax," he murmured. "Breathe."

She repeated the exercise he'd shown her. When her heart rate settled, he smiled. "Okay, now?"

"Much. The flames near my face frightened me, Sir."

"I won't let them get past here." With his finger, he drew a line just north of her breasts. Was he really going to make a bonfire out of them? Moving his hand down her body, he swabbed the length of one thigh, set fire to it, and put out the flames with a brush of his hand.

After doing her other thigh, he switched the gauze for one he picked up from a bowl on the table beside her. "I'm going to try something new." He squeezed the gauze in his hand. "This is going to be fun for both of us. Remember to tell me how you're feeling. Safeword if you need to."

She took in the flush on his cheeks, the sharpness of his features and the hunger blazing in his eyes. The last time she'd seen him like this was after he and the team had worked all day to rescue people trapped in a subway tunnel. Jamie was riding high on adrenaline and excitement.

Thrilled to share this rush with him, she nodded for him to continue. He ran his alcohol-drenched palm over her stomach, lit the trail and blew out the flames. The multiple sensations had her moaning and writhing. His hand stroked between her breasts. Heat followed, then coolness. Over, under, around each breast, circling closer and closer to her nipples, but never touching.

Each time he lit the wetness, blue flames ran over his hand and her body until his breath extinguished both fires. For that small moment in time, they were joined in the flames. Desire grew inside her, soaking her pussy. Her chest heaved as her breath came in short pants.

When Jamie stopped, she raised her head to see why. He picked up a washcloth from a bowl and wiped her breasts and stomach with it. The coldness of the wet cloth had her shivering. "Did you enjoy that?" he asked.

"Yes, Sir. Why did you stop?"

"To keep the fire from burning you, I have to keep moving it around. When I use my hand as a torch, the fire is always on me in the same spot."

"Oh! Are you hurt, Sir?" She tried to sit up, but he stopped her with a heavy hand on her shoulder.

"I'm an expert at this. I know exactly how much I can take." He held his hand out where she could see it. His skin wasn't even pink.

She dropped her head back and sighed. "What you were doing, Sir. It felt so good."

"You were close to coming."

Embarrassed that he'd seen through her, she bit her lip. "How did you know, Sir?"

"I know you." A big sexy grin on his face, he picked up several cotton balls and placed them in a zigzag pattern that moved up her torso. "This is flash cotton. The balls burn very quickly and feel hotter than what you've experienced so far. Don't be scared. I won't let you get hurt."

"Why do you want to use these, Sir?"

"Remember those endorphins I mentioned? The sudden heat from these will cause an endorphin release. If you relax, this will feel fantastic."

She lifted her brows, playing the coquette. "And then you'll let me come, Sir?"

"Yes." He coughed and shifted his stance. "When I light the balls, breathe out. Let the heat flow through you."

When she inhaled and held her breath, Jamie lit the first ball in the zigzag pattern. At first, she felt nothing. Mild warmth started and quickly turned into an intense heat. Followed by nothing. He lit the next ball, then another. The sparks zipped all the way up her torso. Her mind spun, incapable of putting into words what she was experiencing. Like a wave, her body rolled as the flashes of heat shocked her, one after the other. Finally, there were no more. She lay drifting, dazed, and uncomprehending. There'd been no real pain, only heightened awareness. Her pleasure magnified as Jamie's hands skimmed over her belly and breasts, his light touch grounding her.

His breath on her cheek made her sigh. She wanted to turn her face and kiss him, but she was too comfortable. "How are you holding up?" he asked, his voice barely a whisper.

"Fine." Relaxed almost to the point of lethargy, the word "Sir" never left her lips although she'd thought it.

He pressed his mouth to hers, his kiss tender and sweet. "You're doing great, babe. Do you want to continue?"

She smiled. "More." He smiled back. Euphoria swept over her at the love in his eyes. In this moment, she loved him more than she'd ever thought possible. Her kinky fireman hero husband. God, if he only knew what she was thinking...

When she giggled, his grin grew. "I think it's time to let the heat kiss your sexy pussy."

Her mouth opened and the words "Oh, yes!" flitted through her mind. She didn't say them, but Jamie apparently heard them anyway. He picked up a swab and lit a torch. Her lids drooped and she let them close, sinking further down against the neck roll.

Jamie's hand passed over her stomach, her sides, her breasts in a soothing pattern of caress, fire, and stroke, the motions fluid and even. Hypnotizing. Soon, that pattern was the only thing in her mind, the only thing she knew as she floated on a cloud of well-being. Never before had she felt so free, so serene.

Caress, fire, stroke. Jamie moved down her body to her legs. He nudged her knees farther apart. "Mrs. Caldwell, are you ready to be kissed?"

Incapable of forming words, she moaned her encouragement. Jamie's hand cupped her pussy, warming it. Arousal pooled low in her belly and her inner muscles spasmed. Jamie chuckled as he spread her juices between her lips and penetrated her with two fingers. She bucked against his hand, needing to feel him deeper. His fingers gently stroked that special spot inside her only he seemed able to find, and his thumb circled her clitoris.

Heat and cold ebbed and flowed in an intoxicating mélange. She cracked open a lid and peered down her body to see what he was doing. She gasped when he brought the torch close to her before pulling it away.

Jamie's head jerked up. "Trust me." The growled words shot through her, sending her spiraling. She watched, mesmerized, as he once again brought the flames to within a foot of her sensitive folds. Keeping his thumb on her clitoris, he held the torch in place until the heat became almost unbearable, then retreated, before starting over, a little closer each time. After each pass, he blew on her pussy.

As the heat rose, so did the pressure inside her until she thought she'd scream. She ground against Jamie's hand, riding his fingers. He responded by pulling the torch away and inserting a third finger inside her.

"Mrs. Caldwell, I'm going to bring the fire close to your sweet pussy again, very slowly. You're going to hold off as long as you can. When I give you permission, you will let go."

Let go? What did that even mean? Whatever he wanted her to do, she wasn't ready for this to end. Breathing deeply, she concentrated on all the sensations going on between her legs. It was amazing really. How could he be so coordinated? The three fingers pumping inside her probed and stretched, the thumb on her clitoris stroked and circled, and the heat—the heat danced and kissed, caressed and embraced her pussy like a lover. As the temperature climbed, the exquisite pressure in her belly mounted.

Remembering the sheep, she tried counting: *one sheep, two sheep, three ahhh!*

Each added degree pushed the volcano inside her closer to the point of eruption. She clenched her fists, struggling to restrain the climax that threatened to break loose. Nothing could distract her from the excruciating ecstasy. It surrounded her, filled her, consumed her.

"Please, more," she pleaded, barely conscious of doing so.

The intensity of the heat went up a notch. Desperate for release, she clung to sanity by a thread, bunching the towel in her fists.

"Now. Come for me, Mrs. Caldwell." His sharp authoritative command sent her reeling. He lifted his thumb and blew on her burning pussy. The dam burst and she exploded. Like a constellation, she soared weightless through space and time. Her body spasmed, contracting through wave after wave of pleasure as her orgasm seemed to continue for an eternity.

Jamie's hands and the heat left her body and she groaned in protest until something soft and warm settled over her. Sighing, she drifted, her body light as air. Sometime later, she felt Jamie's strong gentle hands massaging something into her skin. It smelled faintly of aloe. Opening her eyes, she watched him, the concentration on his features, the rippling muscles in his arms. She'd never felt more precious or cherished. As soon as he noticed her eyes on him, he brushed her cheek with his knuckles. "How are you?"

Too drowsy and content to speak, she simply smiled.

"Drink this," he said, laying a straw on her bottom lip. She moaned as cool crisp apple juice slid easily down her throat. Her body seemed to soak it up and the fuzziness in her head started to dissipate.

Jamie set the juice aside and undid the bun in her hair, combing his fingers through it as he massaged her scalp. It felt heavenly. "You were magnificent, Rickie. I'm so damn proud of you." The love in his bright eyes mirrored the love swamping her heart.

"You were right." Stopping, she cleared the cobwebs from her throat and wet her lips. "This was one of the most amazing experiences of my life. It was literally out of this world. Is it always like this?"

"You experienced something called subspace. It's a natural high caused by the release of endorphins and some other chemicals in the body." He traced the arch of her eyebrows, the curve of her cheekbones, the edge of her jaw, and shook his head as though amazed. "I didn't tell you about it because few subs reach it the first time and even fewer get into it so deeply."

"I didn't do anything to make it happen."

"Oh but you did. Deep subspace is only possible when a sub gives herself over to the experience and cedes all control to her Dom." He cupped her cheek in his hand and stared into her eyes for a moment. "You communicated with me, expressed your concerns and worries, and we worked them out. You proved that I can trust you."

Before she could comment further, he swung her up into his arms and carried her out to the lanai. Sitting on one of the loungers, he snuggled her on his lap, making sure the warm blanket covered everything below her neck. She rested her head on his shoulder and listened to the beating of his heart, enjoying the glide of his fingers over the blanket along her arms, her back, her legs. As her energy returned, she warmed up. The strange high, as Jamie had called it, was receding, but she didn't feel sad or hungover.

Instead, her heart was bursting with joy. She bent her neck to see Jamie's face and was surprised by his far-too-serious expression. "What is it?"

"Are you okay with what happened here?"

She thought for a moment, then nodded. "Toward the end, I couldn't have used the safewords even if I'd wanted to. But I didn't want to. What happened was amazing. I can't even imagine what more advanced techniques you might know and how they might feel."

"There's so much I can teach you and so much more we can explore together."

A shiver of excitement swept over her body, making her nipples peak and her pussy clench. She slid her hand to the erection that bulged behind his zipper. "It seems to me that I got more out of this evening than you did."

"That's where you're wrong, Rickie. Tonight, you gave me everything—total surrender and absolute submission." His lips kicked up at the corners in a sexy mischievous grin that made him look like sin incarnate. "I'm a very *satisfied* Dom."

CHAPTER 11

Jamie stopped the car in the driveway to his parents' house and let out a long exhale. His mother had called early that morning before they'd left for the airport, asking if they could come straight here after landing. The family wanted to celebrate his and Rickie's reunion. She hadn't seen his family socially since before the separation, and his mother was determined to change that. Judging by the way Rickie was gnawing at her lip, she was more than a little nervous. He took her hand, circling his thumb on her palm. "Ready?"

Smiling, she dropped a kiss on his mouth. "With you by my side, I can handle anything."

He groaned and pressed his lips to hers again, his tongue sliding into her mouth. She tasted sweet and sexy and, despite the fact that they'd made love that morning, he wanted her again. Would they ever get enough of each other? He hoped not. "Be careful what you say, babe. Around you, I'm always locked and loaded."

She laughed and pushed open her door. "Come on. I can't wait to see Chloe."

He grabbed the bag of souvenirs from the back seat. Rickie had insisted on getting something special for each member of his family and Dani. Did she think she needed to get back into their good graces? As far as he was concerned, she'd done them both a favor by forcing the issue. If she hadn't, their marriage would have continued along the same mediocre path, with both of them hiding from each other, both of them unhappy and dissatisfied. What they had now was so much better, strong enough to see them through any future rough patches.

The sounds of a party in the backyard and Chloe's delighted squeals reached them. Jamie threw his arm around Rickie's shoulders and they entered the yard through a side gate. As soon as they came into view of the patio, everyone stopped talking and stared at them, open-mouthed. His grip on Rickie tightened as he considered spinning her around and taking her back to the car. She glanced up at him, her eyes wide with worry. Shit. Had he been wrong? Was his family planning to give Rickie a hard time?

Just as he was about to tell her they were leaving, everyone started talking at once and welcoming them back. His mother rushed forward and pulled Rickie into a huge hug. She whispered something into Rickie's ears that made her blush and hold his mother tightly. When the women broke apart, both had tears in their eyes.

His mother let go of Rickie and launched herself into his arms. "Oh, Jamie. It's so good to have you home. You both look so rested and happy. You *are* happy, aren't you?"

He squeezed her gently. "We are, Mom. Believe it or not, your Yoda advice really helped."

As he let his mother go, his father released Rickie. Tears ran down her face and his father's eyes were suspiciously shiny. Pulling Jamie against his chest, he clapped him on the back. "Erica's a damn fine lady, son. You've done us all proud."

Jamie's chest tightened. He finally understood how much his parents had rooted for the success of his marriage. They'd never bad-talked Rickie and her decisions, as though knowing that with time, he and Rickie would find their way. He was humbled to realize they'd had more faith in his marriage than he'd had.

"My turn, my turn!" Chloe shouted from her perch on Chad's shoulders.

Mindful of her leg, Chad swung her into Jamie's arms. "Welcome back, bro!"

When Chad went to greet Rickie, Chloe wrapped her small arms around Jamie's neck and buried her face against his throat. "I missed you, Daddy."

His heart filled to bursting at the tears in her voice. "I missed you too, sweetheart. So very much." He could barely breathe as she squeezed him. He'd lost a year of her growing up, and he'd do anything to make it up to his little girl.

Chloe lifted her head and, gripping his chin with her pudgy fingers, kissed his cheeks. "You won't go away again, will you?"

It tore him apart that she needed constant reassurance that he was back for good. But he'd repeat it to her every night until she was once again the confident girl she'd been. "Nope, you're stuck with me. And the next time we go on a trip, we're all going together."

As if he'd triggered a thought, she twisted around, searching. "Mommy?"

Rickie stepped closer, hugging them both. "Right here, sweetie."

Chloe's eyes went from Jamie's to Rickie, then to Rickie's arm around his waist. She pursed her lips, her blue eyes cloudy with uncertainty. "So you and Daddy are friends again?"

Jamie smiled and held Rickie's gaze before turning back to his daughter. "Even better. Mommy and I are besties."

Chloe clapped her hands. "Yay! Let's go back to the party now."

Laughing at his daughter's bossy ways, he carried her back to the patio. Erica sat in a chair and he set Chloe on her lap. He left his girls to catch up and got a beer from the cooler.

He'd just managed a sip when Tori jumped into his arms, knocking the bottle out of his hand. "I always knew you had it in you, big brother."

Since starting her master's degree in psychology, she was constantly analyzing everyone and talking in riddles. This time, he was completely stumped. "Had it in me to do what?" he asked, setting her on her feet and picking up the now empty bottle of beer.

"To tame the shrew, of course," she said, her tone teasing.

His blood beginning to simmer, he narrowed his gaze. "Don't talk about my wife that way, Tori. What happened or didn't happen in our marriage is our business, not yours."

Holding her hands up, she backed away "Hey, hey. I'm just kidding. She seems completely transformed. Check out her body language." She jerked her head in Rickie's direction. "She's relaxed and laughing. Chatting with everyone. I can't remember the last time I saw her like that. Whatever went on between the two of you in Hawaii, keep it up."

Dani dropped her hand on his shoulder and gave it a good squeeze. "Looks like Erica followed my advice."

He twisted around and grinned when she exchanged his empty bottle for a fresh one. "*Your* advice? When did you become Dear Abby?"

"Oh, LJ. Didn't you know?" She shook her head, feigning sadness. "Erica and I have become BFFs since the earthquake. We tell each other *everything*."

His face tightened and his belly flipped. How much did Dani know about the BDSM stuff? *Shit*. If anyone found out... Dani punched his shoulder. "Hey. Lose the boy-with-his-hand-in-the-money-jar look or you'll have people even more curious about this sudden transformation."

"The boy-with-his-hand-in-the what?" Drew asked, joining them. "This I've got to hear."

"It's nothing. Dani was just catching me up on what's been happening at the station." He took a long pull on his beer, hoping Drew would drop the subject.

"How would she even know? From what Chloe's told me, Dani's spent most of the past week here."

Expecting a quick comeback, Jamie glanced at Dani and was surprised to see her flaming cheeks. When she scowled at Drew, Jamie arched a brow. She crossed her arms and scrunched her face. "What else was I supposed to do? Huh?"

"About what?" Drew's face reflected Jamie's own confusion.

Dani swallowed and shrugged. "I like playing with Barbie dolls. Sue me."

Jamie laughed. Sure Dani had wanted to help keep Chloe entertained. She genuinely enjoyed spending time with his little girl. But seeing the direction of her stare, he knew something—or should he say someone?—had been the driving factor for her frequent visits.

As though sensing Dani's eyes drilling into him, William turned away from his conversation with Rickie and Chloe. He pushed out of his chair and joined their little circle. "Welcome back, Jamie."

"Thanks for visiting with Chloe while we were gone. She loves seeing her uncles and her aunt." When William's gaze landed pointedly on Dani, Jamie added, "Especially the honorary ones."

William's lip curled up and he focused on Jamie. "Erica looks good. I trust you had a good time?"

"The best."

Dani reached out and yanked on his tie. "You should try it sometime, Will. It might loosen you up a bit."

Jamie and Drew burst out laughing. Dani didn't even flinch when William pinned her with his eyes.

She leaned forward, her hands on her hips. "Look at you," she said. "Who wears a *tie* to a backyard barbeque?" With a last dip of her shoulders that no doubt gave William an eyeful, she spun on her heel and stalked off to join Rickie and Chloe.

Jamie nearly choked on his drink when he saw his brother's beet-red face. "It's okay, William," he said, his voice hitching with laughter. "You can wear whatever you want."

"I may wear too much, but she doesn't wear enough," he said. "If she was mine, I wouldn't let her out of the house like that." His jaw was so tight, Jamie could practically hear his molars grinding together.

William was pissed, that much was clear. But was it because Dani had joked about his clothes or that she'd flashed him? She was an attractive woman. Most men wouldn't have minded. But William wasn't most men. He had an almost Victorian sense of propriety. "She looks fully dressed to me," Jamie said with a smirk.

His brother leaned in close so Drew, who'd watched the exchange with interest, wouldn't hear. "Danielle isn't wearing a... a bra. Do you think she realizes—" He snapped his mouth closed and shoved his hands into the pockets of his pressed slacks.

"That you saw everything?" Jamie clasped his hand around William's nape and squeezed enough to throw him off-balance. "Dani always knows *exactly* what she's doing."

Dinner was announced, saving him from having to deal with his morally shocked brother. What would William think if he knew the truth about Jamie's more exotic sexual tastes? William would probably disown him.

Catching Rickie's eye, Jamie made his way over to her and Chloe. "How's my little princess?" he asked, fluffing her hair.

"I'm not a princess anymore, Daddy."

"You're not?" He handed his beer to Rickie, then lifted Chloe off the chair, careful to support her broken leg, and sat with her on his lap.

"No. I'm the president. I get to tell everyone what to do."

Rickie's eyes sparkled and she caught her bottom lip between her teeth. He'd get no help from her. Minx.

"Even me?" he asked, struggling to keep a straight face.

"Yes. You and Mommy are my subjects."

Turning to his wife, he shook his head and lost himself in her dancing eyes. Tori was right. Rickie had never looked so happy, so at ease. When Chloe cupped his cheeks and brought his attention back to her, he arched a brow. "And what would you have me do, Miss President?"

"Kiss Mommy."

"With pleasure." With his daughter's giggles in his ears, he leaned sideways and pressed his lips to Rickie's in a light teasing touch that left him wanting more. As much as he was enjoying this reunion with his family, he couldn't wait to get home.

Before his lips left Rickie's, he felt Chloe being lifted off his lap. He ended the kiss and spotted his father carrying her to the food table. Tori came over and handed him and Rickie plates filled to overflowing with a hamburger and all the fixings, chips, and vegetables.

They ate quietly, watching their daughter interact with the others. Rickie laid her hand on his thigh, her lips curved gently. "She's got everyone wrapped around her little finger."

He chuckled and rested his hand on hers. "Miss President really isn't too much of a stretch." Seeing that Rickie was done eating, he took her plate and set it with his on an empty chair. He stood and pulled her to her feet. "Let's shake out our legs a bit." They walked to the back of the yard where his father grew some apple trees. Although it was still early in the season, it appeared they'd have quite a harvest.

Slipping his arm around Rickie's waist, he nuzzled her neck. "How are you handling all of this?" The last thing he wanted was for her to be overwhelmed and fall back into old patterns. It mattered to him how she felt and he'd make sure she knew.

"I've never been happier," she said, her voice filled with such truth and honesty he could do nothing other than believe her. "Your family is wonderful and they all love Chloe so much."

"This is your family too."

"Thank you for this, Jamie. For everything." Tilting her head back, she kissed him, sliding the tip of her tongue over his lips. After a moment, she faced the patio and leaned back against his chest. He clasped his hands over her stomach and breathed in the scent of her shampoo. It reminded him of Hawaii. They stood that way, swaying with the music in the dark, content to be together.

Shifting, she looked at him over her shoulder, swallowing and licking her lips as though gearing up to say something important.

He tightened his hold on her. "What is it, Rickie?"

"Okay. Um… How can we continue this… exploration thing we

started, at home?"

Every muscle, every tendon inside him tensed. His throat tasted like he'd swallowed ashes and his heart raced. Shit. Things *had* been going too well. "You don't want to?"

༄ ༅ ༆

Erica spun around and cupped Jamie's face the way Chloe had earlier. "Yes! Yes, I do." His breath left him in a long shuddery exhale. He pressed his forehead against hers seeming locked in a battle for control. Rubbing his back, she murmured, "I'm sorry. I never meant to alarm you."

"It's not your fault. I overreacted. It's just that I like, no, I *love* having you as my submissive. The thought that you might not be as into it as I am… well, it damn near did me in."

"I love having you as my Dom. The things we've done together this week have brought us closer. I'm anxious to go on more adventures with you. But how will we manage it?"

He blew out another long breath, then smiled. "A lot of people just use their bedroom. We can buy dual-purpose furniture. Or we can convert the spare bedroom into an adult playroom. With a locking door, of course."

She stared at the apple trees. The spare bedroom. She'd always hoped they'd have another use for that room. But until today, she'd never felt confident enough in their relationship.

As though sensing her change in mood, he tugged on her chin. "Whatever it is, tell me. If there's a problem, we'll work it out. We're strong enough to do that now."

Pressing a hand to her lower belly, she swallowed, suddenly nervous. Was it too soon?

"Erica." He'd used his Dom voice on her and without even thinking, she'd looked up. *Oh, he was good.*

"Is it strong enough for us to have a baby?"

His eyes grew round and his arms squeezed her. "Are you—?"

"No!" She lowered her eyes to the middle of his chest and toyed with his T-shirt. "I never went off the pill when you left… when I made you leave." Guilt swamped her again. "When and if we have more children, it will be because we both want them." Her fingers walked up his chest, her eyes followed. "Do you want more children, Jamie?"

He rubbed his jaw as he studied her face. What was he searching for? Leaning his head back, he stared up at the sky. She did the same. The sun had set and a few brave stars twinkled. "I always wanted Chloe to have brothers or sisters. I love being part of a big family, and I want that for her, for us."

Gripping his hair, she tugged his head down. "Why didn't you ever say anything?"

"I knew how frightened you were, and let's face it, another child would have put a huge strain on our already shaky relationship."

"And now?"

He shrugged. "You tell me."

She smiled. "I can handle it now. I want it, a big family."

"So you're not afraid of me dying?"

"I'll always be afraid of that. But this week, you showed me the respect you have for fire. And the love. I'm not going to spend the rest of my life worrying about what might be."

Picking her up, he twirled them around. His mouth closed over hers and his delicious warmth flowed through her. He threaded his fingers through her hair, rubbing her scalp. She shivered and arched her neck. Guiding her head, he deepened the kiss. His tongue swirled over hers, stroking and enveloping. Remembering where they were, she pulled away. "Jamie."

"Shit. Sorry," he said, panting.

Lacing her fingers through his, she began tugging him toward the group. He teased her by yanking her bottom against his erection. *Oh my.* She tilted her hips and pushed back. When she added a swiveling motion, Jamie groaned. The low sound vibrated throughout her body. Her nipples tightened into twin peaks.

He'd given her so much in the last week, there had to be something she could do for him. Then she remembered his must-have. Could she do it? More importantly: was she ready? He ground against her and his hard length snuggled between her cheeks, spreading them. Millions of nerve endings exploded with sensation. "Jamie." Her voice sounded rough and throaty even to her.

"Mmm-hmm?"

"I seem to remember something about a certain must-have. You were pretty adamant about it at the beginning of our vacation."

With a light touch, he turned her face. "You mean—?" His wide eyes and a thrust of his pelvis finished the question.

She rocked her hips, smiling when the movement elicited another sexy groan. "Uh-huh."

"Really?"

"Really."

He glanced at his watch then grabbed her wrist and pulled her to the patio, talking as fast as an auctioneer. "Mom, Dad, everyone, thank you. Great party, but it's getting late. We're going home. To bed."

For a moment, no one moved. Everyone stared at them as though dumbstruck. Then in a flurry of activity, all the adults checked their watches. Dani's shriek split the night. "I called it," she shouted, high-fiving Chad. "Everyone, pay up!"

Erica felt a burning heat rise to her face as bills were slapped into Dani's outstretched hand. Her in-laws had bet on when she and Jamie would leave? "Jamie?"

Tugging her under his shoulder, he grinned like the day he'd received his new bunker suit. "They're a very understanding family. You'll get used to it."

When William dropped his payment into Dani's hand, she clamped her fist around his fingers, forcing him to slide his fingers through her hold or stay trapped. With a challenging glare, he freed his hand, while laughter twinkled in Dani's eyes. "Your brother has no idea what he's getting into, does he?"

"Not at all. But I do," he said, smacking her bottom. "Now, get our daughter, Mrs. Caldwell, and let's get the hell home."

Yipping, she skipped into the house to collect Chloe's things. She couldn't wait to get home, to her Caldwell bed, and have another exhilarating scene with her kinky Caldwell hero.

AUTHOR'S NOTE

Fire play can be a sensuous and erotic experience for both Doms and subs, but only when done correctly. Fire is dangerous, and handling it must be learned. In *Under His Command*, Jamie Caldwell is an experienced Fire Master who learned the art of fire play from a knowledgeable mentor.

Should you decide that this is something you'd like to try, please find a skilled mentor, take a class, or attend a series of workshops. No amount of books or videos can ever replace hands-on training when it comes to fire. Please, for your safety and that of others, let your play always be safe, sane, and consensual.

ABOUT THE AUTHOR

I'm fascinated by the mysteries of human psychology--twisted secrets, deep-seated beliefs, out-of-control desires. Add in high-stakes scenarios and real-world villains, and you have a story worth writing, and reading.

The heroes and heroines of my books are pitted against each other by their radically opposing life experiences. By overcoming their differences and finding common ground, they triumph over their enemies and find true happiness in each other's arms.

Today I live in the Pacific Northwest, thriving on the mix of cultures, languages, religions and ideologies. When I'm not writing, I'm people-watching, imagining entire life stories, and inventing all sorts of danger for the unsuspecting heroes and heroines who cross my path.

> Continue reading for a special preview of
> Kristine Cayne's first Deadly Vices novel
>
> # Deadly Obsession

When an Oscar-winning movie star meets a department-store photographer…

Movie star Nic Lamoureux appears to have a playboy's perfect life. But it's a part he plays, an act designed to conceal a dark secret he carries on his shoulders. His empty days and nights are a meaningless blur until he meets the woman who fulfills all his dreams. She and her son are the family he's always wanted—if she can forgive a horrible mistake from his past.

A Hollywood dream…

Lauren James, a widowed single mother, earns barely enough money to support herself and her son. When she wins a photography contest and meets Nic, the man who stars in all her fantasies, her dreams, both professional and personal, are on the verge of becoming real. The attraction between Lauren and Nic is instant—and mutual. Their chemistry burns out of control during a photo shoot that could put Lauren on the fast track to a lucrative career.

Becomes a Hollywood nightmare

But an ill-advised kiss makes front-page news, and the lurid headlines threaten everything Nic and Lauren have hoped for. Before they know what's happening, their relationship is further rocked by an obsessed and cunning stalker who'll stop at nothing—not even murder—to have Nic to herself. When Nic falls for Lauren, the stalker zeroes in on her as the competition.

And the competition must be eliminated.

An excerpt from *Deadly Obsession*

Lauren rolled her eyes. "Fine. Do it."

Nic bent down and brushed his lips against hers. For the first few seconds, she didn't kiss him back, but she didn't push him away, either. Then, on a sigh, she leaned into him and her arms locked around his neck. His tongue darted out to taste her bottom lip. Mmm… cherry—his new favorite flavor. When her mouth opened, he didn't hesitate.

He dove in. And drowned.

He'd meant this to be a quick kiss, only now he just couldn't stop. His lips traced a path to her throat. Cupping her bottom with his hands, he lifted her up, grinding against her. She moaned. It was a beautiful sound, one he definitely wanted to hear again.

A loud noise pierced the fog of his lust. He raised his head from where he'd been nuzzling Lauren's apple-scented neck to tell whoever it was to fuck off, but as the sexual haze cleared, he swallowed the words. The paparazzi had gathered around, applauding and calling out crude encouragements. Some snapped photos while others rolled film. *Shit.* He'd pay for this fuck-up and so would she.

Print and E-book
Available at Amazon, Barnes & Noble, and other retailers

www.kristinecayne.com

Continue reading for a special preview of
Dana Delamar's first Blood and Honor novel

Revenge

A woman on the run

Kate Andretti is married to the Mob—but doesn't know it. When her husband uproots them to Italy, Kate leaves everything she knows behind. Alone in a foreign land, she finds herself locked in a battle for her life against a husband and a family that will "silence" her if she will not do as they wish. When her husband tries to kill her, she accepts the protection offered by a wealthy businessman with Mafia ties. He's not a mobster, he claims. Or is he?

A damaged Mafia don

Enrico Lucchesi never wanted to be a Mafia don, and now he's caught in the middle of a blood feud with the Andretti family. His decision to help Kate brings the feud between the families to a boil. When Enrico is betrayed by someone in his own family, the two of them must sort out enemies from friends—and rely on each other or die alone. The only problem? Enrico cannot reveal his identity to Kate, or she'll bolt from his protection, and he'll be duty-bound to kill her to safeguard his family's secret.

A rival bent on revenge...

Attacks from without and within push them both to the breaking point, and soon Enrico is forced to choose between protecting the only world he knows and saving the woman he loves.

Praise for Dana Delamar

"Here is to a WHOOPING 5 Stars. If I had to describe this book in about four words, it would be action-packed, sexy, romantic, and adrenaline rushing...." —*Bengal Reads* blog, 5 stars

An excerpt from *Revenge*

Enrico raised a hand in greeting to Kate, and she returned his wave and started descending the steps.

She headed straight for him, her auburn hair gleaming in the sun, a few strands of it blowing across her pale cheek and into her green eyes. With a delicate hand, she brushed the hair out of her face. Enrico's fingers twitched with the desire to touch her cheek like that, to feel the slide of her silky hair. A small, almost secretive smile crossed her features, and he swallowed hard. *Dio mio.* He felt that smile down to his toes.

She stopped a couple feet from him. "Signor Lucchesi, it's good to see you, as always."

He bowed his head slightly. "And you, Signora Andretti." He paused, a grin spreading across his face. "Since when did we get so formal, Kate?"

She half-turned and motioned to the doorway behind her. And that was when he noticed it—a bruise on her right cheek. *Merda! Had someone hit her?* Tearing his eyes off the mark, he followed her gesture. A tall, sandy-haired man, well-muscled and handsome, leaned in the doorway, his arms crossed. "My husband, Vincenzo, is here."

Enrico's smile receded. He looked back to Kate. "I'd like to meet him." *And if he did this to her, he's going to pay.*

Print and E-book
Available at Amazon, Barnes & Noble, and other retailers

www.danadelamar.com